The Navigator

A Perilous Passage

Evasion at Sea

Steve Coleman

Printed in the United States of America

ISBN: 978-0-9850065-0-1

LCCN: 2012904553

S B Coleman

4361 Cliff Road S

Birmingham, AL 35222

www.captstevestories.com

steve@captstevestories.com

This novel is dedicated to the wonderful friends with whom I have had the great good fortune to sail.

Many, many thanks to those who have given encouragement and criticism along the way, especially: Bob Athey, Allan Cruse, Bob Kracke, Anne Miller, Paige Ponder Monaghan, M. D. Smith, Doug Todd, Hans Watford, Sheldon Webster, and my dearest wife, Sumter.

Ocean's Judgment

Foolish is the man who seeks to gain,

By sneak or trick or stratagem,

Some worldly profit it may be

Ashore, he seeks success in landlocked piracy.

Oh, but when he totes his sin upon the ocean,

If self-gain is his sole devotion,

It becomes that poor man's futile notion

To have it tried upon the sea.

For when enrobed in black storm cloud at night,

Justice rises on its highest wave,

Speaks harsh pronouncements of the gale,

Sternly judging the moral metal of a male,

Hurling verdicts of wind and rain and hail.

No matter what his mundane mortal crime may be,

Man dare not take it sailing on the sea.

For, aye, then surely will he be

Condemned for all eternity.

© Stephen B. Coleman, Jr

Chapter One

Joe Anderson's conversation with the water-taxi coxswain was interrupted as a sleek black cigarette boat roared by and cut across the bow, raising a mountainous wave. Joe's reaction was instant shock and then rage, believing he had encountered them before. Perched near him at the helm, the obese coxswain scowled, reestablishing his broad rear on the seat.

"A sorry lot, that is. Bloody drug runners, I'll grant you."

Raising a hand to shelter his eyes and squinting in the glare off the bright blue Bahamian water, Joe watched the cigarette boat throwing up a rooster tail of spray, barreling toward Man-O-War Cay ahead. It was not so much the appearance as the sound of the cigarette boat's engine that made Joe's pulse quicken. One night not two months ago at the remote Great Sale Cay, he had heard that guttural roar with a peculiar *throb, throb, throb* that would cost him dearly. Captain and owner of a forty-foot motor yacht, he had

1

brought to the Bahamas a young couple on a weekend charter. Joe had anchored out and taken them ashore in the dinghy for an evening cookout on the beach. Drinking a couple of beers as he tended the fire that night, he had paid little attention to the sound of another boat approaching in the lagoon, assuming its occupants also would anchor out until daylight. But a few minutes later, he heard it start up again. Peering out into the gloom, he was shocked to see that his boat was being towed away by a black-hulled cigarette boat. Shouting, waving his arms, he ran out into the water, trying to see who and what was going on. They were stealing his boat.

He ran to his inflatable dinghy and pushed it into the water, jumping in and starting the outboard. As he sped toward the escaping boats there was a burst from a machine gun. Bullets raked the water in front of him, and he turned away violently. Air rushed out of the inflatable, now punctured and sinking. He turned toward the shore and beached the flooded dinghy. His terrified passengers ran over to him, and the three of them watched helplessly as their sailboat was towed through the pass and out of sight.

They were stranded on the uninhabited island for the night with no way to call for help. It was not until the following afternoon that another cruising sailboat sailed into the little bay and discovered them. Joe reported the piracy to the Bahamian authorities, but it was too late. His boat, his only means of livelihood, later was found sunk in shallow water south of Miami, a total loss. The U. S. Coast Guard speculated that it had been used for a drug run and then burned and abandoned. Uninsured because he couldn't afford the premiums during the recession, Joe was left stranded in the Bahamas with virtually nothing.

So this cigarette boat passing the ferry on the way to Man-O-War had this same throbbing engine sound, and it had a black hull. Joe was as sure as dirt that it was the very boat that had

2

hijacked his yacht, but on that moonless night at Great Sale Cay, he had seen nothing to help him identify it for sure.

"Seen that boat around here before?" he asked.

The ferry coxswain nodded. "Not often. Just every now and then. Hear that damn engine at night sometimes. Ain't nobody but fools or crooks run like that in the Abaco."

They watched the cigarette boat barrel up to the narrow inlet, slow, and disappear around the turn inside.

"You on vacation?" the coxswain asked.

"Got a little job here," Joe replied. "I hope."

In fact, he was desperate for this job. This was what had brought him out today, made him climb out of the half-mildewed bed of the rooming house in the seedy section of Nassau, pack his one seabag, and head to the Abaco to report to a prospective employer docked at Man-O-War. Ever since his boat was stolen, he had been unemployed and stuck in the Bahamas for two months, all during the economic downturn. It had been a downturn, all right, leaving Joe unpaid and without much prospect for a captain's job. Unfortunately, he had chosen to remain in the islands, hoping for a job delivering a boat back to the US. But with the recession going on, there were fewer boats in the Bahamas and little, if any, need for captains. Instead of using his scant savings to buy a plane ticket home, he'd spent too much looking for work here. Now the money was gone and the prospects were slim. If he didn't get this job, he didn't know what he would do.

In his early adult life, he had earned a master's degree in English, served on active duty for four years as a naval officer, enjoyed married life and a successful career teaching. But then there had been the painful divorce followed by the midlife crisis. That was when he bought the boat and became a professional

3

captain. But with few charters in the suffering economy, and the loss of his boat, he had fallen so far. In his younger adulthood, Joe had believed that a man who was intelligent, thoughtful, sensible, educated, and courageous had the ability to shape his future and improve his situation. But at this point, he was feeling more a victim of circumstance than an agent of purpose. With his master's license nearly expired, he desperately needed employment. It was mid-July and hot as hell in the Abaco, so most boats had long since left for Florida. He felt extremely fortunate to find a job to apply for that would take him back to the States.

Reaching Man-O-War Cay a few minutes behind the speedboat, the water taxi entered a narrow little coral-lined pass into the interior lagoon. He stood at the gunwale along with a pair of other passengers peering past some sport fishing boats and a few sailboats anchored in the harbor. Most transients had long since headed north for cooler, less storm-prone areas. Climbing onto the pier, he set out to find *Mission*, and its owner, Alex Smith.

It occurred to Alex as he restored the extra lines and other gear in the bow locker that, if some emergency occurred requiring them to get at this equipment, then the bundles of cash might be discovered. There was no better place on his sailboat, however, to hide something so bulky as two million dollars in hundreds because at sea, the bow locker is almost never opened. His cash would be delivered after midnight from his Bahamian bank, which he intended to put in the locker then and pull the big duffel that held the spinnaker sail over to hide it.

Perspiring in the deck locker under the July sun, he climbed out and closed the hatch. The latch handles were almost too hot to touch. He blew on his hands and looked across the lagoon to see if the water taxi had arrived. It ran between Marsh Harbour and Man-

O-War Cay during the day, and he was irritated that this new boat captain hadn't shown up yet. Accustomed to deferential treatment his business and social position afforded, Alex demanded the same from hired crew. It was not likely, however, that this individual he'd found through an agency, this so-called sailing master that they'd dug up out of the bars in Nassau, could be counted on for any business acumen, let alone promptness. Of course, Alex hadn't wanted anyone too sharp. All he needed was someone who was sailor enough to stand watches on the long trip to Charleston, would do what he was told, and keep his mouth shut.

As CEO of Smith-Southern, a publically traded distribution company in Atlanta, he had secretly skimmed off profits and salted them away offshore in the Bahamas. With the Lehman Brothers debacle and economic downturn that followed, the company suffered some big losses, until he began some under-the-table price-fixing with Barlay & Company, their biggest competitor. Struggling to regain his wealth, he searched for new opportunities until just this spring. As he moved up to chairman of the board, the company began secret talks for a proposed merger with Barlay. The highly profitable deal had been finalized and would be announced publically on July 25th. In order to take maximum advantage of the merger, he would have to buy all the stock he could before that date. And to maximize his gain, he would need to use his offshore savings, which would be taxed if returned to the US. To avoid those taxes, and avoid having to reveal how he got all that money, he had decided to withdraw from the Bahamian bank two million, which, with a little strategic palm greasing, they were able to provide in US dollars. He planned to hide the cash in his boat and sail to the States. Of course, he would need to launder the money once he smuggled it in. Making a few quiet inquiries, he had made a deal with a banker in Charleston, South Carolina who would handle it for a reasonable enough fee. So all Alex had to do was get the cash to Charleston in time to buy stock before the merger was announced. Luckily, he had the boat to take it there.

His dear wife, Frances, would throw a royal tantrum if she found out, he realized, but she knew nothing of business, so it wouldn't be too hard to keep her in the dark. The problem could be the boat captain, and that was why he was fortunate to find this Joe Anderson, who sounded like a real loser. That kind of man Alex had manipulated many times, and this one surely would do for money whatever Alex wanted.

Joe squinted in the afternoon sunlight, looking for *Mission*. A couple of hundred yards down the lagoon, he saw a mast towering above all the others. That just had to be the Smiths' sailboat. Joe had spent many days and nights at sea, having once owned a sailboat himself in younger, more prosperous years. The opportunity to sail a bigger boat would be thrilling.

He gazed at the little village that sprawled along the shore and went up a sloping hillside. Dozens of tiny, brightly painted wooden houses along narrow little streets lay nestled among palm trees and blooming bougainvillea, hibiscus, and oleanders. He spotted a wood-framed barn-type building with a sign, Albury's Boatyard.

Looking down the shoreline, he spotted the moored cigarette boat. Its name, *Blaster*, was scrawled across its stern in ugly red and gold letters—a title well signifying the owner's lack of respect for sea and nature. His anger welled up again as he wondered if this could be the very boat that had hijacked his charter boat. Its deck was cluttered and in need of paint. A man with long stringy black hair stuck his head out of the engine compartment to toss a toolbox on deck. When the man looked up, Joe looked away, not wanting to be noticed. Somehow he was going to find out more about this *Blaster*.

But not now. First of all the job. He walked down the shoreline the hundred yards to Albury's. His heart beat faster, more from anticipation than exertion and oppressive humidity. Jutting out from there was a pier with the large white-hulled sailboat alongside. As expected, the boat moored there was *Mission*—one of the most beautiful and graceful sailboats he had ever seen. Her sixty-foot-long white hull with gold leaf accent lines glistened along the gunwale more than four feet above the shining water. On deck were lacquered teak handrails and gold paint, trimmed with chrome hardware. The sunlit white hull, with its towering mast, was reflected in the still blue water, creating an inverted mirror image, so pristine that it was difficult to tell which boat was real and which was phantom. Once, when his daughter was little, he had seen the Cinderella Castle at Disney World reflected just that way, dreamlike in the sun.

Just perfect, he thought, pausing a moment to just take a look. Someone was at work at the forward locker at the bow, pulling some equipment out and placing it on deck—the owner, Alex Smith, and not some captain who already had been hired, he hoped. Joe took up his duffel again and walked with quickened steps down the pier. Noting that the man was dressed in navy blue Bermuda shorts and a white polo shirt with his yacht club insignia on it, Joe hoped his own unpressed khakis and polo shirt weren't disqualifying. When he introduced himself, the owner gave him an appraising look.

"Captain Anderson," Alex Smith said, giving a welcoming grin. "Come on aboard."

Smiling back, Joe raised his duffel bag over the lifeline, grabbed the stanchions, pulled himself on deck, and went to shake hands.

"Give me a second to finish this," the owner said and turned back to the locker. "I'm just rearranging some stuff."

He climbed down inside and began stowing in the last few items. "Glad to have located you," Alex called over his shoulder.

"Fortunate for me too," Joe replied. He passed down a couple of life jackets and watched Alex try to stick them in.

"I better put these in another spot," Alex said, tossing them back out, leaving what appeared to Joe to be considerable storage space.

Joe offered him a hand up as he climbed out of the locker and closed the top. He noticed that there was a newly installed keyed lock on the hatch—a very unusual kind of fitting.

"Going to sea, you don't want to store anything up here you might need underway," Alex said, sounding more like making an excuse than an explanation. "Well, let's take you below."

He took up the excess equipment taken from the locker and led the way aft. Picking up his bag, Joe followed him, ducking under the mast stays and slipping under the canvas "bimini" that sheltered the cockpit. As he squeezed past the three-foot-diameter wheel, he noted that even the cockpit was outfitted in varnished teak and chrome. Alex was the kind who would have the best of "toys," even a million-dollar boat, and Joe's excitement increased in the realization that he going to get to play with it. Obeying a brass plaque at the hatch that said, "Remove shoes before going below," they both pulled off their leather boating moccasins in the cockpit. Following Alex down the ladder, Joe caught a few words in a woman's voice.

"I'm too angry to see anybody." Her words were muffled, but clear enough, punctuated by the sound of a slamming door. Joe paused, uncertain. Alex shot him a glance, giving a grin and an apologetic shrug.

"Not to worry," he said with emphatic pleasantness. "Come on down."

Joe tried to ignore the curious exchange and descended the ladder. Happy that there was plenty of headroom for his height, he looked around at the salon, which sparkled with afternoon sunlight coming through the windows, reflecting off the teak interior set off with blue cushions. To his left was a sofa and coffee table, to his right an oval dining table with wraparound seating, and the galley behind. Then he realized that the boat was air-conditioned. *Well, of course,* he thought.

Explaining that his wife, Frances, had retired for a "much-needed nap" in the after stateroom, Alex led him forward to the bow cabin. It was roomy enough to have a built-in chest of drawers and chair, just aft of the bunk, which was V-shaped to follow the contour of the bow. There was his own head and shower, as well. Alex pointed out the third little cabin, across from the head, which had double-decker bunks. The upper was covered with a stack of navigation charts.

"I started pulling out the charts for our trip to Charleston," Alex said. "I'm counting on you to take over the navigation duties. I take it you're qualified for all that?"

Joe nodded, reaching into his pocket. "I hold a master's license, Mr. Smith," he said, producing the document, hoping the owner wouldn't notice it was nearly expired.

As the owner looked over the license, Joe recited his experience and qualifications.

"I charge two hundred a day, plus expenses." Joe tried to say it with confidence, but he was afraid his voice betrayed his desperation.

Alex listened, sizing him up, and then smiled. "Done," he said with a dismissive wave. "And call me Alex." He thrust the charts into Joe's hand and led him back into the salon, where he opened a teak liquor cabinet.

Much relieved, it occurred to Joe that getting this job had been pretty easy.

"Grab a couple of glasses from the cabinet behind you," Alex said, and produced a bottle of Chivas Regal, a bottle of club soda from yet another drawer, and then led Joe back to the galley freezer for ice.

Joe watched the glasses being filled, nodded thanks for the one handed him, and wondered if the production of this bottle of Chivas wasn't a little bit of one-upmanship.

"So, here's to our safe arrival," Alex exclaimed, holding his glass up to offer a toast.

Joe settled back on the sofa, offered a toast to their trip, and sipped the scotch. "Mighty fine," he said, realizing it had been months since he'd tasted good whiskey, and beginning to think he actually was going to enjoy this job.

"I'll buy you a whole case of that if we pull this off," Alex said, and then looked away.

"Pull what off?" Joe asked, pretending to concentrate more on the tasty liquor than on the remark.

"Oh, just the trip," Alex said, taking a seat at the dining table across the salon and not elaborating on his answer. Joe noted a shadow of concern passing over the older man's face. "I need to get this boat back to Charleston as soon as possible.

"Oh, really?" Joe asked, taking another big sip of scotch. "Why?"

"Cumberland Island rule," Alex answered. "Damned insurance company says we're not insured during hurricane season if the boat's south of the Florida-Georgia border."

"I see," Joe said. "No insurance for a boat like this is pretty serious." He started to tell about losing his own uninsured boat, but decided to save that story for later.

"You better believe it. And we're already way late getting out of here." He smiled to mask his concern. "Don't worry, we'll enjoy ourselves."

"You can't imagine what a pleasure this is for me," Joe said, reminding himself about how fortunate he was to find this ticket out of the Bahamas, no matter what the circumstances. "It's been a long time since I've had the opportunity to sail a fine boat like this."

Alex nodded. "I imagine it has, ole man."

Joe took a big swig from his glass, realizing that this man was passing judgment on him. He supposed that he looked a little like someone who had been stuck in the islands a bit too long. Well, he didn't want sympathy, and it was a little irritating to read that in Alex's tone. Having worked for other rich boat owners, he knew that this one was the type more likely to be motivated by his own convenience than by any concern for others.

"We'll take you out for some conch chowder," Alex said, getting up and pouring another shot in Joe's glass, "when Frances wakes up. She was just going down for a nap when you arrived." He cast a quick look of concern toward the after cabin, took a swallow from his glass, and leaned closer. "I should make you aware," he whispered, "that Frances is sometimes a little, uh,

11

agitated." Then he smiled. "But I'm sure you'll find her an interesting and engaging person."

Joe shrugged. "We all have our problems."

Alex rubbed his eyes. "Occasionally, she gets her medicine screwed up, and it upsets her more than a little bit. You may see a side of her that's sort of excitable. If it happens...well, she can get a little unpleasant." He gave Joe an intent look. "I hope you'll be understanding."

Joe smiled. He could identify with wifely issues. Maybe a problem wife was not better than no wife at all. "Of course, Alex," he said. "I'm pretty good at rolling with the punches."

"I'm sure you are," Alex said.

As it turned out, Frances did not appear that evening. At one point, she called her husband back to their stateroom, where he closed the door. Enjoying the relaxing buzz of alcohol that was washing away all his anxieties about getting the job, Joe helped himself to the Chivas. Sitting back to relax, he heard a faint and muffled discussion in the after stateroom. In a short while, Alex reappeared, carrying apologies from his wife.

"I convinced her to take another of her 'calming-down pills,' as we call them," Alex said in low tones. "It's best if she's down for the night."

The two men climbed up on deck, slipped on their shoes, and walked down the pier and across the road to a tiny open-air restaurant near the water. A dozen or so young people in scanty bathing suits sat around in the cafe, drinking beer and eating hamburgers or conch fritters. Off in a corner, sat the man he'd seen on the cigarette boat that afternoon, along with another unpleasant-looking character. As he stared at them, the long-haired one noticed, met Joe's gaze for a second, and then looked away. The

12

waitress, a buxom, pretty-but-not-beautiful brunette in her thirties, with a slightly hard-bitten look, smiled at Alex and came over to take their order.

"Bea, I want you to meet Joe, my new captain," Alex introduced, taking her hand as he did so.

She nodded at Joe, but gave her attention to Alex.

"Bea takes care of me well every time I come here," Alex said, giving her hand a squeeze. "Don't you, Bea?"

"You tell me," she said, giving him a sharp look and pulling her hand away. Joe didn't miss the hint of coyness in her eye.

At her endorsement of the night's pot, both ordered a bowl of conch chowder. While waiting to be served, Joe glanced at the two men from *Blaster,* drinking beer and eating pizza. Although he could not hear what they said, it was obvious their conversation was crude and slurred, increasing his dislike of them. Were they the ones who had hijacked his boat? It had been too dark at the time to recognize them. Did they know him somehow? He swore to himself, somewhere, sometime he was going to find out.

When Bea delivered the conch chowder, Joe realized he was very hungry. He enjoyed it so much, he had a second. After being stuck in the Bahamas for two months, it was funny that he would miss conch chowder.

As they ate the chewy conch in a delicious garlic-and-tomato broth, they discussed the voyage. Alex's plan for the next day was to provision the boat and have some last-minute repairs done. They would leave early the following morning and sail north inside the Abaco and then turn west over to Great Sale Cay, and then head northwest and drop off the Bahama Banks into the Gulf Stream, heading straight for Charleston. As Alex described the trip,

Joe noticed that the unkempt men had fallen silent, and he wondered if they could be listening.

"We'll be well offshore when we leave the Bahamas," Alex said.

"Quite a trip," Joe replied, lowering his voice, stifling an urge to tell Smith not to talk loud enough to be overheard. "Most people cross over to Florida and follow the coastline, staying offshore just enough to ride the Gulf Stream."

"I'm anxious to move the boat on north," Alex said, tilting his bowl to retrieve the last bit of chowder. "Not only have we got the insurance problem I told you about, but I also have some business to attend to."

"What made you wait so late in the year? Most folks are gone by now."

Alex gave Joe a quick glance. "Oh, just the business problem," he said. "Nothing of great importance."

"Well, I'm glad of that," he replied, to which Alex grimaced, making Joe realize there truly was something. "Ordinarily, I would be making this kind of trip without the boat owner."

"And miss this trip myself? Wouldn't dream of it," Alex replied. At that, they fell silent, finishing their chowder while Joe pondered his curious defensiveness.

Bea appeared with two generous slices of key lime pie.

"On the house," she said.

Alex grinned. "Everything?" he asked.

"Take what you get and be happy," she replied, giving him another of her sharp but coy glances. She dropped a check on the table and went off. Joe reached for his wallet, but Alex shook his head.

"On me, ole man," he said. "You're with me now."

"Many thanks."

"Meet you out front," Alex said while waiting for his change.

Joe walked on outside, took a deep breath of the humid, warm air, and thought how wonderful it was to be there. In the twilight of the evening, he could see a motor yacht gliding down the lagoon, its red and green running lights reflecting off the mirror-still water. He read its name, *Sea Splendor*, another magnificent craft he had noted at anchor that afternoon. As he watched it moving through the lagoon, the two men from the cigarette boat came out of the restaurant and paused nearby, also watching the yacht pass. "You s'pose it's that one?" one of them asked the other in a raspy, intoxicated voice.

"Hell if I know," the other answered. "It's either got to be that one or the sombitch on the big sailboat."

"Funny hour for a tourist to be coming in if he ain't got somethin' goin' down," the first man said. Joe glanced at them across the gloom and realized they had not noticed his presence.

"I guess we'll have to take 'em both," he thought he heard.

"Shut up," said the other, giving him a nudge, seeing Joe's form in the dark. The two men paused and then sauntered off into the night.

Joe watched the yacht make the turn toward the pier where *Mission* was docked. He then turned his attention to the two men heading on toward the pier where the cigarette boat was moored. It struck him as curious that people like that would choose to be in sleepy little Man-O-War when they could be spending the night in Freeport or somewhere more exciting. They were up to something.

He looked back at the restaurant to see if Alex was coming. Through the glass door, he could see Alex engaging the waitress, Bea, in a quick conversation, giving her hand a squeeze as he did so. She nodded, and Alex smiled and headed toward the front. Joe turned around so that Alex wouldn't notice that he had seen the exchange.

They had a pleasant walk back to the boat. The sun had set, and lights were going on in the tiny houses, providing the main street illumination. A small, aging rust-red Opel came by, causing them to move to the side of the narrow little lane to let it by. The driver stopped, however, waved a burly arm at Alex, and spoke.

"I received yer fan belts," he said. "Came in on the ferry."

"Great!" Alex said. "And what about the water pump?"

"Didn't come."

"What?" Alex exclaimed. "After all this time?"

The driver shrugged. "Way it is round here."

"Damn!" Alex said. "Well, what can we do?"

"Maybe tomorrow."

"I hope so," Alex said. "We need to leave soon as we can."

"Doing my best." With a wave, he revved up the little car and headed on down the narrow lane.

"That's Marvin Mann," Alex explained. "He operates the boatyard. Damn, we need that part."

"Water pump?" Joe asked.

"Yes, the seawater circulating pump for the engine. I ordered it two weeks ago."

"That's the Bahamas," Joe said, giving the sign of resignation with his hands.

Alex shot him an irritated look. "I expect better performance than that," he said and quickened his pace, leaving Joe a step behind.

Joe paused, wondering if that remark was a bit pointed toward himself. Arriving at the pier, they stopped to admire *Sea Splendor*, which was now moored across from *Mission*. Its occupants were visible inside, an older man and a younger woman, having a nightcap before bed. The interior furnishings reflected even more wealth than the prodigious yacht itself.

"*Sea Splendor*'s quite a name, even for that boat," Joe remarked.

"About as ostentatious as you can get," Alex replied. "Fitting enough for that old fart."

"You must know him."

"You might say I've made his acquaintance," Alex muttered with a scowl. "He started out slinging hash and ended up owning about fifty meat-and-two restaurants. Now he thinks he's hot stuff. Come on, let's have ourselves a toddy, too."

Joe followed him aboard *Mission*, thinking that Alex, with his boat, didn't have much room to talk.

Just to be sure this derelict captain was going to sleep well, Alex dug into his liquor cabinet and urged a brandy on him. As expected, this so-called captain finished off his snifter and accepted another. As they talked, Alex kept an eye on the clock and sipped at his own glass. When he held the bottle out to pour another, Joe refused, but Alex splashed another shot in the glass anyway, knowing Joe would think it impolite not to drink it. He estimated that the man had put away at least ten good ounces of booze. Proof of Joe's intoxication occurred when he stood up, reached out for the mast that projected downward through the salon, and knocked over a deep-sea fishing rig resting there. The rod fell, its heavy reel making a large clunk. He apologized, picking it up to see that it was not damaged, and whispered that he hoped he hadn't awakened Frances.

"Not to worry, my friend," Alex said. "When she's had her sleeping pill, a herd of elephants couldn't wake her." He watched Joe stagger into the bow cabin and close the door. The question was, for how long could he manipulate this Joe Anderson character, keep him in the dark about the money, and then how much would it take to pay him off to keep him quiet? He had been surprised to learn that this charter captain was an educated man, a former naval officer with a college degree. That would make him more challenging. Yes, there was a lot to be worked out, but then, there'd be more than a week to devise a plan. When there was an opportunity to make money, Alex Smith could be ruthless.

He made his way to the after cabin where Frances was sleeping, quietly opened the door and peered in. As expected, she was sound asleep. In the early years of their marriage, he had shared his plans and schemes with her. Over the years, however, as her condition grew worse, he found that he no longer could trust her to be on his side, to keep his secrets, and to satisfy his love. He still loved her, but she simply was not enough, not for an adventurer. Closing the door gently, Alex glanced at the clock again. Two things to do before the night was over: receive the cash and stow it, and have one last tryst with that pretty, sexy, if a little bit too plain, Bea.

The V-berth required a little technique to get into. Joe discovered that the best thing was to turn around and sit down, then swing his legs up in the air and down into the center, his head aft and feet forward. Once in, however, he found the bed comfortable, provided one was wary about sitting up and bumping heads with the overhead. The problem of being six-two was fitting in. What he didn't much like was that the dinghy was stowed on deck above the overhead hatch. The only way out of the forward cabin, therefore, was the narrow little passageway that led past the head and the middle stateroom. He would have liked it better if that hatch could be opened all the way in an emergency. Perhaps Alex intended to put the dinghy in the water and tow it astern when underway, but you couldn't do that safely in open ocean. The thought flashed through his mind of being trapped in the cabin, unable to open the hatch, water gushing in the doorway. What? Was he jittery about this trip? After thousands of hours at sea? Yes, something about sailing with Alex was disturbing, and then there was the uncertain threat of the cigarette boat.

"What the hell is that all about?" he said aloud. Then, realizing that the Smiths were just thirty feet away, he hoped they hadn't heard him. Probably not, he guessed, since both his stateroom and theirs had shut doors, and the air-conditioning was still running. In the dark, the slightly dank smell of a boat, despite air-conditioning, was still there. He sat up and opened the hatch a crack, as far as it would open under the dinghy. He listened to the purr of the compressor pump that ran the A/C, the thought occurring to him that this was one fine way to get back home, even though being divorced and his daughter through college and out on her own didn't leave him much of a home to go to.

As he turned on his side to fall asleep, it seemed funny that he could live to be this age and still have so many unanswered questions. It wasn't that he hadn't thought he had the answers before; he had believed once or twice before in his lifetime that he knew it all. But now he realized that it all had resulted from the dogged, blind drudgery of responsible manhood. Caring about things had gained him nothing. So now he wouldn't care. Truth and utopian ideals, after all, Plato to the contrary, were not static but dynamic perceptions, always changing with events, as relative as time and space.

An hour or so later, semi-conscious, he heard movement in the salon and then the sound of steps on the companionway. Deciding he would relieve himself, he got up and went into the head. Someone hopped off the boat onto the dock, and was speaking in muffled tones. Through a small porthole, he saw the silhouette of Alex, still dressed, talking to two shadowy figures who seemed to be carrying packages of some kind. Though they moved out of Joe's line of sight, he could hear them climbing aboard and walking forward. Creeping back into his cabin, he heard their footsteps above him on deck. The hatch up at the bow was being opened and something being placed inside. Then the hatch closed, and the sound of footsteps went back aft. There was a little more whispering in the cockpit area, and then the sound of the men climbing off and going down the pier.

Perhaps it was just the spare parts Marvin Mann had mentioned being delivered. But at such a strange hour? If Alex had expected it, then why hadn't he said anything about it? Or was it

20

drugs or some other kind of contraband to be smuggled into the States? Joe's first thought was that he wanted nothing to do with this. In the morning, he would take his leave and be done with Alex Smith. But then what? Go back ashore here and rot away waiting for another opportunity? And living on what? No, he was too desperate to get home. Whatever this was all about, there'd be no one in the remote Abaco to care, no coast guard, no customs inspections, no boarding. There would be no danger of that until they arrived in Charleston. By that time, he would have figured out some way to deal with the boat owner and his contraband, whatever it was.

Joe started to go across the darkened salon to the ladder to look out. But when he heard Alex speaking in low tones again, he paused in the shadows to listen. Peering up to the hatch, he saw through the gloom that Alex was talking on his cell phone.

"I'll be at your front door in five minutes, okay? I'm just crazy for you, Bea."

While Joe replayed in his head what he had just heard, Alex was climbing off the boat and walking down the pier.

"That Bea," he whispered to himself. He doubted the idea, but the more he thought about it, the more convinced he became. Doubtless, Alex was a ladies' man, even in his sixties. With a somewhat sickly and unpredictable wife, perhaps he had found that his sexual needs outweighed his marital fidelity. No wonder he had made sure Frances had another dose of sleeping pills.

"Scoundrel!" he said to himself. He shrugged then and remembered that, although he himself had remained faithful to his ex, Eileen, even during the estrangement, still he had no room to cast aspersions on anyone. He, too, had had his sins, though infidelity to his wife had never been one of them. If this Bea woman was what Alex needed to maintain his own fictional world, then why was it Joe's business to judge him? Crawling back into bed, he thought about how caring, that afternoon, Alex had seemed toward Frances. That often was one of the traits of a cheating husband, Joe realized. It's very possible to love your wife and yet make room for someone else in your world, too, if the rationalization is built into that illusion one has of his own life.

The play goes on, he thought. And then he realized, as he always did at bedtime, how terribly lonely he was. As he drifted off to sleep again, Joe became conscious of the sound of lapping water, resonating in the boat's hull like the ticking of nature's eternal clock.

Chapter Two

"I'm telling you, Alex, I have to go," Joe heard Frances saying. "It's going to be a long trip. We can't go sailing out of here until I've had my hair done. I don't want to leave here, anyway. You always want to go somewhere else, taking me out to sea and putting us in danger, deprivation, and all manner of inconvenience."

"I thought you liked sailing, Fran, dear." It was Alex's voice. From the stateroom in the bow, Joe listened with fascination. "You know we always have a great time." From the tone of Alex's voice, it sounded as if Frances, and not he, was at the top of the pecking order.

"And here we are, going with this Joe fellow," she raged on. "Who knows whether he's a good sailor."

Joe grimaced, rolling out from under the sheet and throwing his legs up and over to sit up on the end of the bed.

"Of course, he's capable," Alex was saying. "This captain's had a lot of experience, even in the navy. I told you that."

"You also told me he drinks too much."

"He's had some tough breaks," Alex admitted.

"He's some kind of a Jonah, if you ask me," Frances declared. "And I don't know if I want to go sailing with him."

"Well, he's here now," Alex said. "So hush about all this."

"We'll see," Joe heard her say.

Jonah, huh? That was a hell of a way to be greeted. He stood up and tried to open the door that led from his stateroom into the head without being heard, but the door creaked. Shrugging, he pushed it open. There was just no way to move about on a sailboat without everyone hearing. Noting that the conversation in the main cabin had paused, he stepped through the shower into the head (an interesting arrangement of doors), and turned on the water in the sink. In about two seconds, the water pump hummed, blanking out some of his noise.

"Well, I'm going to Marsh Harbour," she continued on, loudly enough to be heard over the pump, "even if I have to go by myself."

"If it means that much to you, dear, then I would go," Alex replied, "but there are a few things on the boat I have to get fixed before we sail."

"Why it is that things just break down while this boat just sits anchored never made any sense to me," she exclaimed. "For a million-plus dollars, this tub ought to keep up better. Our last boat didn't have so many problems."

"Our last boat didn't have all this equipment on it," Alex countered. "This one has the best of everything, and that means more maintenance, that's all."

"Well, I'd like a little of your tender loving care myself," she said, brushing her flowing red hair from her eyes. "You could at least go with me."

Joe smiled, thinking that, indeed, she, like the boat, required high maintenance. He hesitated a moment or two, took a deep breath, and emerged from the head to greet his hosts.

"Well, there he is. Welcome aboard," Frances said, a social chameleon if he'd ever heard one. From her seat at the table, Frances extended her hand with the air of a duchess. She was still dressed in a pink nightgown with a red silk robe, but her fiery red curly hair was immaculately brushed and fixed. Her makeup was thick, even including eye shadow beneath her steel blue eyes. Joe took her hand.

"I'm so happy to be here," he said, pretending he hadn't overheard a word of what she had said. "What a treat this is. And what a magnificent yacht you have."

She shook her head with a little sneer. "Alex's baby," she complained, pushing out her lower lip. "Loves it a lot more than he loves me." She gave her husband a challenging glare.

"Now, Franny, you know that's not so," Alex countered. "I love it only just a *little* bit more." He winked at Joe.

"Oh, pooh on you!" she replied, her ardor defused a bit.

Alex smiled and shrugged. His wife, a good ten years younger than he, could get away with speaking to him in a way that others could not. Or was Alex just extra indulgent because of his late-night tryst?

Frances slid out of the seat, went into the galley, and began loading bread into the toaster. "I need your cell phone to call for an appointment," she instructed. "The number's there on the chart desk, on a little flyer thing."

Alex went over, found the paper, dialed the number, and then carried the phone to her. "Make it as early as you can," he said.

When she began to talk, Alex sat down at the table near Joe and gave his grimace-grin. "Sometimes, I just have to indulge her whims," he whispered. "If she doesn't get her hair fixed, we'll hear about it for days." He paused. "Could I ask you to go over with her to Marsh Harbour? If I could stay here and meet with the boatyard owner, it would help immensely."

"Sure," Joe replied with a shrug, "unless I could stay and meet with the man for you?"

"I'm afraid I need to do that," Alex said. "Help me out, will you?"

Joe nodded with agreeable patience, wondering, however, if Alex had an additional visit with Bea on his mind. Or was his reluctance to go that far away from the boat in any way related to the mysterious boxes in the forward hold? He glanced at Frances, thinking that she was too full of her own concerns to know what her husband was up to. On the cell phone, she was going on about how she wanted her hair done as if she were already there and in the chair.

"Ten o'clock," she announced, switching off the phone.

"You'll have to hurry to catch the boat over," Alex said. "I'm going to stay here to see Marvin, the mechanic, but Joe's going with you."

She gave Joe a quick, not-so-welcoming glance and then glared at her husband. "I knew you'd find some way to get out of going with me," she said. Taking a plate from the cabinet, she retrieved the toast from the toaster while going on about how they could have lunch there, insisting that they both go.

"I just have to stay here," Alex said, giving a glance of appeal to Joe.

"I'm very happy to go with you, Frances," Joe said, thinking that he'd do anything just to get the sailing trip underway. She shot a look at him that said he'd better mean it.

"I've got to go get ready," she said, glancing at the clock. Then she paused and stared at their guest a moment. "At least you haven't brought some little cutie along with you. Alex is always inviting men with sexy little bitches hanging on to them. I hate cutesy little girls, like the one Dan Moss brought last time. All she did was lie around and make eyes at Alex." She cast a look of disapproval at her husband, who managed to look hurt, as if wondering how she could think such a thing, and then she turned on Joe. "You men are all alike!"

Joe just smiled. "Little girls quit chasing after me a long time ago."

"Ha!" Frances said. "I'll bet." She studied him a moment. "We'll just see about that." She threw the plate of now-rather-cold toast on the table, walked back into the after stateroom, and shut the door hard. Alex watched her go, contemplated the closed door a moment, looked at Joe, and shrugged.

"She's on a tear," he said, picking up a piece of the toast and eyeing it. "Thinks I'm stepping out on her or something." He glanced at Joe.

Keeping a noncommittal expression, Joe shrugged back. "I'm sure we'll get along fine," he replied. He wasn't going to get in the middle of that if he could help it.

27

Alex motioned toward the coffeemaker in the galley. Joe made his way down the narrow passageway with the stove and freezer and refrigerator on one side and the sink on the other. He poured himself a cup and sat across from Alex.

"Don't worry about it," Joe said. "It doesn't bother me."

Alex nodded. "Good," he said, "because I expect you'll get to see some more of her temper before we're in Charleston."

Joe considered asking about the men who had brought the boxes during the night. But then it occurred to him that, if he inquired about the boxes, Alex might change his mind about hiring him. And Alex would realize that he also might know about the tryst with Bea. So it would be better just to avoid any involvement in the whole issue. If Alex and Frances had been married for so many years, the issue of Alex's infidelity must have surfaced long ago. Perhaps all these little temper tantrums were devices she used to keep him in check. Who was he to judge anyway? At least Alex had kept his marriage going, while Joe had allowed his own to break up on the rocks. *No,* he told himself, *just let sleeping dogs lie.*

But what about these secret boxes? Would he be abetting some sort of crime? He didn't like being placed in this situation. It compromised his principles. But he was desperate, damn it. Well, maybe there'd be some way to get to the States and then deal with the contraband, if that's what it was.

In half an hour, Joe and Frances were seated side by side aboard the little ferry, headed across the bay to Marsh Harbour. She was offering incessant conversation, prying into his past, asking about his marriage, divorce, and so on.

"She was just not quite right for you. That's my thought. Just a little too…well, I don't know what. Do you have a girlfriend now? Anybody as devilishly good-looking as you are needs a girlfriend. I don't mean one of those little girls that Alex's friends always want to bring on the boat. I mean someone who would be a partner to you. You don't look so happy. Maybe I need to find you someone. Wouldn't that be nice?"

Joe managed a grin. "I guess maybe I'm too old."

"Don't give me that. You're as young as you feel. For a man your age, you look like an adolescent in heat. Quit sounding like a doddering old fool. I see I've got a lot of work to do with you."

Joe laughed. If anyone else had talked to him that way, it might have made him angry. But she was being so outrageous that it was beyond insult. After all, it was just talk, wasn't it?

"I'll take all the help I can get." He chuckled. Of course, that kind of help was the *last* thing he wanted.

She gave him an appraising look. "Yes, we'll see about that."

Having had enough for the moment, Joe got up and walked over near the boat coxswain, who was steering them toward the breakwater at Marsh Harbour.

"Gorgeous weather," he commented.

The young man, his black locks tied up in a red headscarf, looking as much like a pirate as some of his Tory ancestors may have been, glanced at Joe. "Aye, and we're hopin' for it to stay that-a-way," he replied, turning his attention to the jetties ahead.

"Any reason to think it might change?"

The ferryman reached over to shift his radio to a weather frequency, and nodded his head toward the speaker. They listened to the report.

"There has been little change with the tropical wave located about five hundred fifty miles east-southeast of the southern Windward Islands. However, this system still has the potential to become a tropical depression over the next day or so as it moves westward or west-northwestward at around fifteen miles per hour.

"Showers and thunderstorms extend from near the Dominican Republic east-northeastward into the Atlantic for several hundred miles. This activity has become a little more concentrated this morning just north of the northern Leeward Islands. Slow development of this system is possible over the next day or two as it moves westward."

The mention of the Dominican Republic caught Joe's attention because he had been there once in his younger years. He tried to calculate the distance between the Dominican Republic and this Abaco area of the northern Bahamas. Five or six hundred nautical miles, he guessed, an awful long way, anyhow.

As remote and removed as my old life, he thought, and the sad memories of divorce welled up. But now, he realized, watching the water taxi maneuver to the pier on Marsh Harbour, now, after going through all that pain, his wounds were healed, mostly anyhow. Now getting back to the States would mean a chance to start over, if he could just get there with the Smiths, their fine sailboat, and without any problems with whatever it was Alex had hidden in the bow locker.

Stepping off on the big island, Joe and Frances awoke a cabdriver parked nearby in a '77 blue Ford with a cardboard sign in the windshield: TAXI. The driver, a seventy-ish-looking man with a ring of gray hair below his bald head, had half of his right ear missing, and his rotund body sunk way down into his worn, hollowed-out seat. He laughed when Joe asked if he knew Barbara Anne's Salon.

"What you think, mon?" the driver said. "I'm *new* round here?"

Joe smiled.

"Well, let's get on with it," Frances said. "I'm late."

"Oh, yes, ma'am," the taxi man replied in his deep, melodic voice, giving a chuckle and a wink at Joe.

It was a short ride to the salon. Joe said he would come back in an hour, and then asked the driver to give him a tour of the island.

"Don't forget to come get me," Frances commanded.

"He ain't gon' forget *you*, ma'am," the driver answered. "I'm sure o' dat."

"See you in an hour," Joe called after Frances, suppressing his desire to laugh.

"You come vacationing and gonna spend it with that lady?" the driver said, as they started off on the tour of Marsh Harbour.

Joe glanced at the man. "Just sailing with them," he replied.

"You look like you old enough to know better," the driver said, giving Joe a once-over. They exchanged looks in the mirror. "I never been sailing," he went on, "but I used to work de boats." He shifted his weight, sinking down even further into the driver's seat, making the springs creak. "Gather de conchs."

"I see," Joe answered. The driver, whose permit on the sun visor said he was "Hosea Mason," drove on, passing an old provincial building, making no comment about it.

"I just drives now," Hosea said and sped up to maybe twenty, looking at Joe in the rearview mirror, then looking forward to swerve back into his lane. "Where yo' wife?" he demanded.

Joe shrugged. "I'm divorced," he said, enjoying the balmy breeze from the open windows. "How 'bout you?"

Hosea swerved just in time to miss a young black man on a bicycle. He blew the horn and then waved. The man on the bicycle waved back.

"Me, I'm married," Hosea said. "Second time, same woman." He laughed. "She stay to home, and I stay to de cab. It's best that way."

Joe grinned and nodded. "I know what you mean."

"De best way," the old man repeated, shaking his head, still keeping an eye on Joe more than on the road. "You have trouble with de ladies, too."

Joe glanced up to meet his gaze in the mirror, then looked away.

"Too good-lookin', too kind in de heart," the driver speculated, studying Joe's face in the mirror. He swerved again, keeping the car on the road. "But the main thing is…I can see in yo' eyes; you been hurt."

Joe grinned for want of any other way to respond, not expecting such an intimate appraisal from a taxi driver.

32

"You don't miss much, do you?" he replied, his eyes widening as the man made a sharp right turn onto the main road, not stopping to look. A truck shot past them, going the other way.

"Man drives a cab, he see lots of peoples. Some wid dey wives, some widout; some wid dey wives a'wishin' dey warn't." He laughed, throwing his hand up in the air. "Where dey be marryin', dey be dysfunction."

Joe laughed, too, at that—the word *dysfunction*. He recalled the marriage counselor using that word to describe his ex-wife Eileen's refusal to attend any sessions with him. Joe reached forward and gave a pat on Hosea's shoulder.

"I believe you're an expert."

"No doubt about it," the driver said, "no doubt about it." He studied Joe in the mirror again and swerved back in his lane. "So what you goin' do 'bout it?"

"About what?"

"Gettin' a woman?" Another stare was followed by another swerve. Joe shifted uncomfortably.

"Wait for a good one to come along, I guess," he replied.

"And so you gon' wait till the prettiest little thing makes eyes at you, is that right?" Hosea asked.

Joe nodded. Yes, a true beauty would be the one to turn his eye. That fantasy played through his mind, all the way down to the climbing in bed with a gorgeous young thing, who was gazing upon him with such loving and admiring eyes. Then reality returned. No, it was not likely he would come across such a person at this age. So, why get involved at all? In fact, the very idea of getting in some emotional entanglement again would be foolish. He shook his head.

"I've got no need to hurry," he replied.

Hosea gave a little smirk. "Uh-huh," he said. "Uh-huh."

They returned to the salon by eleven o'clock. After fifteen minutes of waiting around, he decided to go in to see what the problem was. After paying Hosea, Joe entered the salon, reminding himself to compliment her new hairdo. There was Frances, sitting in the waiting room, all coiffed and talking to a blonde lady, about Joe's age, dressed in black slacks and a light blue blouse.

"Oh, Joe!" Frances said. "I want you to meet someone. This is Mary Johnston—isn't that what you said your last name was? Johnston?"

The woman nodded and smiled at him, her greenish-blue eyes meeting his, quick and intelligent and appraising. He paused for a second, feeling almost intimidated by her look, then turned on his manners, went over, and offered his hand.

"How do you do?" he said. She took his hand.

"As I told you, Joe is sailing with us to Charleston. He used to be a navy captain, or a seven-star admiral, or something," Frances bubbled. "He's single, just like you are." She glanced at Joe. "See, I find out all about people just as soon as I meet them. Mary's a great actress and star of film and stage!"

"Well, hardly that!" The lady smiled at the exaggeration.

Frances reached out and touched her, a peevish frown on her face.

"Oh, of course you are, dear! Just like Joe's an admiral."
Frances looked back at Joe, daring him to contradict. "She's from
Birmingham and just down here for a vacation. She's going to go
to lunch with us, aren't you, Mary?"

The woman, whom Joe thought was almost pretty enough
to be a star, looked a bit taken aback.

"Uh, well, I suppose I have time before I have to meet my
tour group," the woman stammered, looking at her wrist watch, not
quite prepared for such a foregone invitation from someone she
had met less than an hour ago. Joe was equally surprised and a bit
irritated. He had no desire to be socializing with someone he didn't
know, and besides, his job was to get Frances back to the boat.

"Well, great!" Frances charged on, turning to the
nonplussed lady. "There's a nice hotel restaurant just down the
street. Alex, my husband, and I ate there when we brought the boat
down in the spring and found it quite good. You'll have to meet
Alex. He's back at the boat at Man-O-War. He's just crazy over
that boat. But that's all right, I love him anyway. Well, except
when I think about how long we've been married, and then I think
I'm getting awful tired of it. Oh, well, who knows? Shall we go?"
She waved good-bye to the hairdresser and bustled to the door.

Joe and Mary glanced at one another. Resigned to the
inevitable, Joe forced a smile.

"Shall we?" he said, gesturing toward the door. She smiled
back, shrugging, and acquiesced. They went to the door, and he
held it for the ladies.

"I think we can walk from here, since it's not too hot yet,"
Frances dictated, leading the way. "It's a block or so. Besides, who
knows where you'll find a cab. We had to blow Gabriel's trumpet
at one driver this morning, just to wake him up. Oh, I hope they
have that lovely crab salad. It was wonderful last time I was there."

35

By the time they reached the restaurant, Frances had them all on a first-name basis. They were shown a table by the open window, set with a white linen tablecloth and napkins. A light breeze blew in and was further stirred by a creaking ceiling fan. Frances insisted on ordering each of them a Yellow Bird rum cocktail, but did not touch hers, saying that she took medicine that didn't agree. Joe wondered if she could have taken any medicine to calm her down, and what she would be like if she hadn't. Mary, however, seemed to be enjoying their hostess and had a confident air about her, feigning polite attention to Frances's ramblings. Despite the hint of a few wrinkles of approaching middle age, the fine line of Mary's Nordic nose, the inscrutable straight line of her lips, and her engaging greenish-blue eyes made her rather beautiful in Joe's estimation. Despite her delicate facial features, Mary appeared athletic, with a feminine muscularity that was quite becoming.

She had lost her husband, Earnest, to a heart attack about ten months ago. Frances already had learned all of this in their first few minutes of meeting in the beauty salon and related it all to Joe as if it were information vital to his future. This was her first extended vacation trip since his death, and she admitted to realizing that she couldn't spend the rest of her life being a grieving widow. At Frances's prodding, she told them about her modest career as an actress. At one time, she had been a professional, but gave it up for motherhood. In recent years, she had acted on occasion in local theaters in Birmingham and nearby cities.

"I'll bet you're very dramatic!" Frances said.

Joe thought it would be hard for anyone to emote any better than Frances. And yet, this woman had a kind of physical, athletic grace in her long-muscled Scandinavian frame that seemed to speak in movement as her voice intoned her feelings.

"Oh, I have had my moments," Mary admitted. "I used to be very good at getting into character and learning my lines. But that's not so easy as it used to be."

"What roles do you like to play?" Joe asked, feeling like he ought to enter into the conversation a little bit. She smiled at him.

"Oh, villainous women," she said, giving him a mock evil grin. "Well, dissembling women for the most part. Those who are hiding the truth, or pretending to be something they're not—Lady Macbeth, for example."

"Ordinary women, in other words," Joe quipped, returning her grin.

"Oh, hush about that!" Frances told him. "Pretense is one of the few weapons we women have, isn't that right, Mary?"

"According to Shakespeare, men are also guilty," she replied, raising her hand.

"All the world's a stage,
And all the men and women merely players:
They have their exits and their entrances;
And one man in his time plays many parts..."

As she recited, she had her gaze fixed on Joe, making him feel that she was trying to see behind the mask of politeness he had been wearing. He gave her an inscrutable smile to indicate that she wasn't supposed to see beyond his "mask."

"You must be very intelligent, Mary dear," Frances commented, sounding appreciative.

Even so, Joe glanced at Frances, trying to determine if maybe there was a drop or two of her feminine dissembling, caustic sarcasm in the remark. He had come to realize that she did not like being upstaged. In any case, Frances changed the subject.

"Do you have children?" she asked Mary after the waiter in white jacket took their orders. "I imagine you would have beautiful children."

Mary smiled. "Two," she said. "My daughter, Dorothy. She and Bill live in Birmingham and have two sweet, lovely little daughters. My son, John, is an accountant like his dad was, living in Atlanta."

"And is he married?" Frances asked.

Mary raised her eyebrows and shook her head with resignation. "Oh, no. He's not married." With a shrug she added, "A confirmed bachelor, I guess."

Joe supposed without judgment that she meant the son was gay, but he didn't ask.

Mary turned to Joe, who had said little. "Do you have children?" she asked.

He nodded and glanced down. He always felt the need to reply as if everything was fine, maintaining the mask, withholding the truth.

"Oh, yes," he said, "a daughter just out of college, living in Atlanta." He picked up his water glass and sipped, using it as an excuse not to go on, thereby avoiding the subject. He just didn't want to get into that with a stranger. Mary regarded him for a moment, but he avoided her gaze.

"Well, I have two children, too," Frances said, keeping the conversation flowing. "One son, one daughter, in their thirties, still

38

just babies. I didn't marry Alex until I was thirty. I wanted to be sure I had found a rich husband, you know what I mean?"

At that, they all laughed.

"Just a money machine! That's Alex," she bubbled on. "Taught young Alex to do the same. Money, money, money! That's all he thinks about, just like his father." She laughed. "Thank goodness our daughter married a professor at Emory and doesn't have to play that get-rich game the way her brother does. What good is money anyway? All you can do is spend it. Lord knows, I do my best to spend Alex's, just so he won't feel unappreciated, if you know what I mean."

Mary and Joe laughed again. Then, out of nowhere, there was a little movement on the edge of the table. Joe glanced down and saw a large spider, about three inches across with yellow-and-black legs and reddish body, climbing up atop the table by Frances's right side. He took his cloth napkin and leaned across to swat it, but realized he couldn't quite reach it.

"Oh, look. A spider!" Mary said, staring at it. Frances glanced down, saw it beside her, and shrieked.

"Help! Get that thing away!" She thrust back in her chair, nearly turning it over. "Help! It's a devil creature! Ohh!"

Joe thrust himself forward enough to knock the spider away with his napkin, turning over Frances's water glass in the effort. Water and spider gushed down the side of the table to the floor. Wet but unscathed, it skittered away and disappeared behind a window curtain. Frances was shaking. Mary reached over and patted her hand. By this time, the waiter had arrived with a cloth to wipe up the spill.

"Oh, here, never mind the water; get the monster," Frances commanded, shrinking back away from the window.

"It went behind the curtain," Joe said, pointing.

With just the hint of a grin on his black face, the waiter pulled the curtain up, spotted the spider, grabbed it by the body and held it up. "Bahamas spider," he said. "No harm to peoples." The spindly legs swam in the air.

"Oh, it's so pretty," Mary said.

"I don't care," Frances said, still shrinking back. "Get that devil out of here. Ohhh, I can't stand spiders." She glanced around at everyone in the room, who all were staring her way in shocked silence. "Get away," she commanded, making a sweeping motion with her hand at the waiter.

Joe went over to hold Frances's chair for her. She watched the waiter go out with his captive and give it a gentle toss out the door. She gave Joe a disapproving look, as if he might have produced the spider, and took her seat. As he assisted in pulling her chair up, he glanced at Mary, and they exchanged grins. As he sat down, Frances gave a great sigh and recomposed herself.

"Good thing I didn't have my pistol," she said. After the look she had given him, Joe wondered if she meant to shoot the spider or him.

Regarding Joe's expression, Mary smiled, more charmed with Frances's volatile personality than troubled by it. The waiter was back with a fresh glass of water for Frances, mumbling an additional apology, which got a dismissive nod from her. Still smiling, Mary swept her hand across the back of her less-than-shoulder-length golden hair.

"I like your haircut," Frances observed, back to her charming mode. "You had it shortened, didn't you?"

Mary nodded and put her hand in her lap. "Thank you. Yes, I decided if I were going to be in the Bahamas a while, I might as well wear it short, for the first time in my life."

Joe thought it did look very nice on her. She noted his gaze and smiled.

"Did I hear that you were an admiral?" she asked.

Joe laughed. "I'm afraid Frances was exaggerating a little bit," he said. "No, I served as an officer in the navy for a few years.

"Well, that's impressive enough," she nodded. Joe made a gesture of dismissal.

"He'd better be impressive when we start sailing for Charleston!" Frances said, giving him a quick but critical glance.

"To Charleston? South Carolina?" Mary was awed. "That's a long way, isn't it?"

"Oh yes. Alex loves adventures, and he's going to need all the help he can get. Goodness knows, I'm not such a great sailor anymore. It's getting a little harder for me," she sighed. "But Alex loves it so much. I suppose we'll just sail ourselves into oblivion one day." She gave Joe a severe look. "That's why Joe's coming along, his seven stars and all. I hope he understands that."

Joe smiled, about to reply that she needn't worry about his qualifications, but was interrupted by the waiter serving their lunch. Having followed her recommendation, Joe and Mary both had ordered the crab salad, and both found it to be just as delicious as advertised.

"Acting must be a fun career," he remarked following one of their mutual glances, feeling that he had to say something to break the tension.

Mary smiled at him with a nod. "Being an actress sounds exciting, and in some ways it is," she said. "But like most things, there is a lot of drudgery."

"Huh," Joe said. "That's surprising."

Mary shrugged. "Well, learning lines is hard work. In fact, when you think about it, I've spent so much time in rehearsal and performing… You know, a stage is just a box with one side missing. You get to be someone else, but you don't get to be yourself, if you get what I mean."

"No one does, my dear," Frances interjected. "I suppose I play a part most of the time when I'm at home, going to those dreadful women's social things."

Joe looked at Frances, realizing that she indeed must be something of an actress just to manage her mental states.

"Well, I didn't mean that, so much," Mary said, "though I know what you mean." She shook her head. "But acting as a career has its own kind of…what? Confinement, I suppose." She lifted her glass and sipped. "It's just that… 'There's a real world out there,' I've been telling myself. 'Someday you've just got to go see some of it.' That's why I came to the Bahamas."

"I'm sure a widow's life is a lonely one," Frances said. "My Alex keeps my life exciting."

When Joe heard that, he smiled, realizing that she must keep old Alex on his toes, too.

Mary sighed. "My husband, Earnest, was such a fine man. But he had not just the job but also the mind of an actuary. His hobby was coin collecting—no, it was not just a hobby; it was his passion. Hours went into cataloging his collection. He had a thing about predicting how long it would take to come across some coin, like a buffalo nickel, for example. He calculated how many cash money transactions he would have to make in stores before someone would hand him a buffalo nickel in change. Very often he believed he was pretty close, and that thrilled him."

"My husband, Alex, is more or less retired, though he thinks he works hard when he goes to the office," Frances interjected. Deals in stocks, mainly, some kind of insider trading or something..."

At that, Joe did a double-take. "Insider trading, you said?" he repeated, smiling. "I think you must have your terminology a little confused."

"No, it was something like that. Alex told me not to say anything about that, but you know me; I talk about anything I want." She looked severe. "Remember that if you ever get the idea of telling me any of your secrets."

Joe was much amused.

"Oh, hush, you," Frances said. "I'll bet you got more secrets than a dog has fleas. There's always been something about you, darkness deep down or something. Don't you think so, Mary?"

Joe quit laughing, but kept on his smiling mask. "So have you found any excitement on this vacation?" he asked her in order to change the subject.

"Well, not really," Mary said. "I guess I made a mistake by not inquiring beforehand about the other people going along on the tour. Most of them are older people, retired. In some ways, I think most of them are retired, not just from business, but from life, too—know what I mean? No, I'm just missing out on the adventure I had expected. It's too much sitting on the porch of hotels or riding around in tour buses looking at what other people are doing." She sighed. "Well, I'll know better next time, I guess."

"I hate those dreadful tours," Frances said, cutting her lettuce with the side of her fork against her plate. "Alex took me on one to France in the eighties, and it seemed to me we never got off the bus!"

Mary inquired about the trip to Charleston, how they would go, and so on. In midsentence, Frances, her own mouth full of crab, burst forth with an idea.

"You should go with us!" she announced, and her eyes brightened as the idea grew. "Yes, why of course! You'd love it!"

Mary smiled at the novelty of the idea. Joe glanced at Frances. Surely, she wasn't serious.

"Well, of course, it would be very nice," Mary replied, acting pleased, "but my tour group has reservations on Tuesday afternoon to fly on to Nassau. It's very nice of you to invite me, though."

Joe realized that Frances was looking to him to respond as well. She was a bit impetuous, he decided, inviting this total stranger to sail with them. Nevertheless, he played along for the moment.

"It would be nice," he said. "But it's going to be a pretty salty trip."

Mary gave him a quizzical look. "Salty?"

44

"Just a long sail in the ocean," he explained. "Once you're out there, well, you're just there, that's all. And if you're the type that gets seasick, there's no way out of it."

"Oh, go on with your seasickness!" Frances countered. "We have Dramamine and scopolamine patches and all other sorts of remedies for that!"

Mary nodded. "It's very nice of you to invite me, Frances," she said. "But I don't think—"

"Oh, I know!" Frances interrupted. "Tomorrow we leave Man-O-War and sail up to Green Turtle. That's just a one-day trip. There's an inn there—what's its name? Oh, yes, Bluff House, and it has a very good restaurant. We can put you ashore there, and then you can take the water taxi back here the next day." She put her hand on Mary's. "Yes, you must come for that little day trip. You said you wanted some excitement, so why not? You'll love it!" She glanced at Joe. "Won't she, Captain?"

Joe responded in the full measure expected of him. "It will be a great opportunity for you," he said, relieved that Frances had shortened the invitation to a single day. "I think you would enjoy yourself."

As soon as the words were out of his mouth, he thought about Alex, wondering how he could explain to his host about why he hadn't resisted this fool idea of Frances's. Well, why was keeping Frances on level ground his responsibility anyway? It would be interesting to see how this actress handled a day on the water. Maybe she'd be moved to recite a few lines from *Babes at Sea* or *Ship of Fools* or something.

Frances pushed on and worked out the details, telling Mary how to catch the water taxi to Man-O-War the next morning. Playing along to be polite, Mary found a little notebook and pen in her purse and took notes, including Alex's cell phone number, her excitement showing. Joe thought but did not say that he thought it was pretty adventurous of her to agree to go sailing on a boat she hadn't seen and with people she had just met. But despite being irritated by Frances's manipulative way of "finding a woman" for him, perhaps it wouldn't be so uncomfortable to have another person on board, for that short time at least. For one thing, it would give Frances someone else to target instead of himself. This Mary seemed pleasant, if you could tolerate that over-inquisitiveness.

Out front, they found her a separate taxi outside. Of course, it had to be Hosea's. Greeting his soul-mate from the morning's ride, Joe held the car door for Mary.

"I'll do my best to be there before nine, tomorrow," she promised. "Oh, how should I dress?"

"Oh, to the nines," Frances declared. "We're very formal on our luxurious yacht." Mary climbed into the cab.

Hosea grinned at Joe and tugged at his half-ear. Joe chuckled. Weren't there any other cab drivers on the island?

"Oh, I'll have to bring my suitcase," Mary said, giving Frances a concerned look. "Hopefully, I'll have the appropriate clothes."

Hosea winked at Joe.

"You just bring whatever you need, dear," Frances replied with a wave. Mary took her hand and then his.

Joe nodded and waved good-bye. He expected that she would call and cancel, and they would not be seeing her again.

When Joe and Frances arrived at Man-O-War Cay in the water-taxi that afternoon, Alex had escorted Bea to the dock where she was waiting to take the ride back to Marsh Harbour. When he spotted Frances in the boat, he took a couple of steps away from Bea and waved to his wife. He could see, however, that Frances hadn't missed a thing.

"Bea, dear," Frances called. "Why, I thought you'd be frying up conch fritters at this hour." Frances climbed out onto the dock and took her husband's arm. "I didn't know they let you out of the kitchen this long."

Bea took a step backward and looked guarded. "I always go over on my night off."

"Why of course, dear," Frances went on.

"I go to church on Wednesdays like everyone else," she countered.

"Good thing, too," Frances snapped. "All we women ought to go to church, repent and say we're sorry." She glanced at her husband. "The men, too. Isn't that right, Alex?"

Alex gave her a smooth, soothing smile. Frances frowned and turned on Bea again.

"Now, where's your husband? Oh, that's right, I forgot. He left you a long time ago, didn't he? Haven't you found another yet? We girls aren't girls anymore, are we, dear? Better find someone pretty soon..." Frances didn't get to finish her tirade before Bea had given both her and Alex hateful looks and stormed aboard the water taxi.

"See you next year," Alex called after her, but she didn't look back. He took his wife's hand. "Now, Fran--"

She jerked her hand away. "You're so, so impossible, Alex. I just don't know how you can be so terrible."

He wrapped his arms around her. "Now, Fran, you just jump to conclusions. You know you do," he soothed. "I just like to be nice to people, you know that. She's just a sweet, ignorant little woman. Of course she means nothing to me. You know that."

She pulled away. "I don't know anything," she said. "I just never know."

"I can't imagine what you're talking about, sweetie," he said. "Oh, and doesn't your hair look nice? What a fine coif they gave you."

"Yes, and I'll coif you, if you're not careful." As quick as a flash of lightning, she gave him a grandly vicious smile. "Oh, guess what! We're going to have a guest tomorrow." She glanced back at Joe, who was following at a safe distance behind, and motioned for him to catch up.

"We're leaving tomorrow," Alex said, stopping in his tracks. "First thing."

"Just as soon as Mary arrives," Frances said. "I'm sure she'll be prompt, won't she, Joe?"

Alex cast a frown at Joe. "Who's Mary?"

"Someone Frances met at the beauty parlor," Joe said.

"A gorgeous lady, a famous actress from Birmingham," Frances exclaimed, pulling Alex on down the road. "And she's not for you, Alex. She's a girlfriend for Joe. Just look at him. Lord knows he needs one."

"It's not my idea," Joe said.

Alex shook his head. "We have to get going," he said, trying to maintain his cool. "We don't have time for guests."

"Oh, she's going with us, Alex," Frances went on. "Just to Green Turtle. Then we'll have a nice dinner at Bluff House, and she can get off there. That's a day's run, isn't it? Of course it is. Your fine new captain, Joe here, told me so."

She threw a raised-eyebrow look at Joe, staring until he nodded agreement.

"See, Alex? That's just the way it is." With that, Frances gave a dismissive wave of her hand and walked on toward the boat.

Alex watched her go, shook his head, and walked on. "When she gets on her high horse," he confided, "I never know what to expect. One time, she disappeared for a few hours and then came back in a twenty-thousand-dollar mink coat!" He sighed. "So I suppose that inviting a guest for one day gets me off pretty light."

"I guess so," Joe said. Perhaps Alex's way of playing up to Frances was how he excused his sneaking around with other women behind her back.

"Aw, what the hell," Alex said with a grin. "Let's go back to the boat and have a toddy."

So, Joe realized, this was the couple he was to spend the next week sailing with in the middle of the ocean. He'd just have to make the best of it. And when the time came, he would have to deal with Alex and his contraband in the forward locker, whatever it might be. He still suspected that Mary Johnston would call and cancel her one-day adventure, so he might as well settle in to a pleasant, cozy voyage with the Smiths.

Chapter Three

The next morning Marvin Mann appeared at eight o'clock sharp, ready to install the rebuilt auxiliary pump and replace the belts on the diesel engine. While Frances remained aboard to wash the breakfast dishes, Alex and Joe walked to the tiny grocery store for milk, ice, eggs, and fresh meat. Prices had to be double what they were back home. When they returned aboard, they found Marvin Mann still working.

"Your engine's got a wee click in a valve," Marvin, on his knees in the galley at an access door to the engine, looked up and told Alex. "It ain't bad, but it's there."

Alex glanced at Joe, concerned. "What caused it?" he asked. "That's one of the best diesels you can buy."

Marvin was holding a red rag and wiping grease off his hands. "Sittin' idle for long periods is the bane of all marine engines," he said. "Happens on all these pleasure boats that sit at anchor around here." He held on to the sink and pulled himself up with a little groan. "I'll put in an additive that will help. After you've run a few hours, it might correct itself."

"Anything else you can do?"

"Not without tearing her down," the mechanic replied, "and I can't get to it today or tomorrow."

"Uh-oh, that's not good news," Alex said. "Can't you squeeze it into your schedule?"

"There're other boats in the harbor, Mr. Smith. I've promised out me time to others."

"I could pay overtime," Alex pleaded.

But Marvin shrugged. "I'd have to order parts, besides, and it takes several days for 'em to get here."

"We haven't got several days," Alex said.

"It could be a pretty serious problem," Joe warned. "We could lose the engine while we're out at sea. That's a long way from a boatyard."

Alex frowned. "And I don't suppose you could fix it while we're underway?" he asked. "You are a captain, right?"

Joe bristled. "Without spare parts, nobody could fix it, even in a yard." He tried not to let his words convey his feelings. Just because he'd been down on his luck and idle for several months was no reason for this rich boat owner to throw off on his abilities.

"Of course, ole man," Alex said. "Didn't mean to offend. I'm just worried, that's all."

Joe shrugged it off, wanting to say but not saying that Alex's precious secret cargo wouldn't rot in the next day or so.

"Leave me an extra can or two of that additive you're talking about, Marvin, if you will," Alex said. "We are on a sailboat, after all, and can sail without the engine if need be."

Now in a somber mood, Alex asked Joe to fill the water tanks. But when Alex remembered that the white hose was stowed in the bow locker, he insisted on getting it out himself.

"I know where everything is located," he said, rushing to cut Joe off at the ladder. "Just leave it to me, okay?"

Following him on deck, but remaining near the mast, Joe watched the older man climb down into the locker and extract the hose, appearing to arrange some things before closing the hatch and dogging down the latches. Taking the hose and connecting it to the hydrant on the pier, Joe decided again, however, despite his piqued curiosity, that for the time being, his silence about the whole matter was best. Besides, it seemed crazy to think anyone as wealthy as Alex would bother with something like smuggling, despite his odd behavior.

"Oh, I know what," Joe said to himself. "He's got a girl stowed away up there." And he laughed.

Alex had said they would get underway by ten, just as soon as Marvin finished the repairs and Frances's guest arrived. But then Frances thought of a lady on the island who makes throw pillows, and she had meant to order some made last time they were there but hadn't, and now just could not leave the island until she had gone to see Mrs. Finch and have her make some for the salon. Well, how were they to get them, Alex wanted to know, since we were headed to Charleston? Joe thought he heard Frances say they should wait for them to be made. He bit his tongue and stayed out of it, however, and let Alex tell her that she had lost her sense of time and space and schedules, et cetera. In the end, Alex and Frances left, leaving Joe to assist Marvin if needed and to study the navigation charts to plan their course for the day.

In the after port corner of the salon was the navigation desk, where one could sit in a comfortable built-in seat, spread a chart on the table, and read the instruments. Excusing himself, he stepped over Marvin, who sat cross-legged on the floor, replacing a V-belt. To make conversation, he explained that they intended to make it to Green Turtle Cay and Alex had said that on the way you had to go out to sea around a small, uninhabited island called Whale Cay.

"Aye," Marvin commented, grunting to loosen a bolt. "Too bad your boat draws too much to go inside of the Whale. With the east wind kicking up as it's been in the afternoons, you'll be toying with 'the rage', I'll imagine." He explained that the small island called Whale Cay sits on the edge of the Bahama banks, where there is a steep and sheer drop-off into the Atlantic.

"It poses no problem in calm weather," Marvin said, "but when the wind comes briskly from the east, as it has been off and on for the past week, swells build and crash against the underwater cliff. That drives all the force of the waves upward. Many more than one sailor has been pitchpoled trying to come back in from seaward." He looked up and grinned. "Even this grand boat can take a spill if it's bad enough."

"I've heard of the problems at Whale Cay," Joe said. "I wonder if Alex knows about... "the rage.""

"Oh, yes, indeed. Alex risked it once last time here, and nearly paid dearly for it," the mechanic replied, buttoning up the engine compartment and taking up his toolbox to leave. "But maybe it won't be so bad today," he added, climbing up the ladder and going ashore.

After an hour, the mechanic finished and left. As Joe pulled out the proper charts and laid out a course to Whale Cay, he became conscious of the deep, guttural sound of a large engine idling. Peering across the salon, he noted the black hull of the cigarette boat, gliding slowly by, ten feet away. He started to turn back to the chart work when he noted that the boat was still there, drifting closer. Its very sleek, long black hull, designed for great

54

speed, reminded him of a water moccasin swimming in the water. An obnoxious type of boat, he thought, recalling one that used to run on the lake back home, disturbing everyone with the noise of its big engines. In the cockpit were the two men who had sat across from Alex and him at the restaurant. They were peering over at *Mission*, studying its deck. Joe ducked down and listened.

"And you didn't see which boat they put the stuff on," the one at the helm said.

"It was late, man," the one with long hair said, "I told you I dozed off. What the hell?"

"You dozed off. You're a sorry good-for-nothin, you know that?" the first man said. "Now we may have to take them both."

The long-haired one spotted Joe looking up from the hatch. Their eyes met, and the man's look betrayed a sort of startled but malevolent look. He mumbled something to the driver, and that man put the boat in gear and moved off. When they were clear, he sped up and out of the harbor. Joe watched them go, his pulse racing. These bastards had to be the ones who'd hijacked his boat, but still there was no proof. And what were they looking for now? The boxes that were stowed aboard that first night?

He tried to go back to his course plotting on the navigation chart, but then someone came onto the pier. He heard Mary Johnston's voice calling hello. So she had come after all. He peeked out of the porthole and saw her dragging two large suitcases on wheels. She was dressed to the nines—sateen pants, frilly white blouse, silk scarf around her neck—more like she was going to attend a ritzy-glitzy poolside cocktail party. It was rather amazing that she would have shown up at all. So here was his "date" Frances had provided. With a bit of irritation that he was being put upon, albeit mixed with a twinge of excitement, he frowned and went topside.

"Good morning," he called, trying to smile and be as pleasant as possible. "Come on aboard." He jumped over to the pier and reached over to take the two heavy suitcases. She must have brought all her luggage. Good thing there were two empty bunks in the middle stateroom because the suitcases would take up one of them.

"What a pretty, big boat!" she exclaimed as she climbed aboard and put her hand over her eyes to peer up at the high mast.

He explained that they had to leave their shoes topside because the varnished floor, or sole, below couldn't stand the scuffing. She had worn Italian-looking thin-strapped black sandals with leather soles, and he wondered if she had any rubber-soled tennis shoes or something. She slipped off the sandals, and he led her down below, explaining that the Smiths would be back soon, he hoped, because they needed to get underway soon.

"This is gorgeous," she said as she descended the ladder to the salon. "I had no idea a boat could be so…luxurious."

"Amazing isn't it?" Joe agreed. "And everything is engineered to function perfectly without an inch of wasted space." He gave her a brief tour, but explained that Alex would want to do that, too, so he didn't want to spoil their host's fun.

Mary recognized the problem with her suitcases just as soon as Joe hoisted them up on the top bunk in the little stateroom.

"I'm sorry I had to bring them, but there didn't seem to be any safe place to leave them."

"I'm sure it's okay," Joe said, thinking that they could tolerate them for a day. It felt a bit awkward to him, standing beside the bunk with her in the little passageway, blocking any movement. "Just behind you there is the head, uh, bathroom," he pointed out. She turned around, and he reached past her to open the door.

"Very compact, isn't it?" she said, peering in, her voice a little strained. She was feeling uncomfortable about being in such close, intimate quarters, Joe realized, considering that they had hardly met. Well, what else but a certain amount of intimacy could you expect aboard a sailboat? He noted her expression, seeing that she was beginning to realize just what she was getting into. It was a pretty daring thing to be going sailing for a day with people you barely knew. Then it occurred to him that, since she had just come from a long boat ride from Marsh Harbour, perhaps she needed to use the facilities.

"Maybe I'd better show you how the toilet flushes. This one's pretty simple." He reached his foot past her and stepped on the pedal, making it flush with a roar. "And when you run water in the sink, you have to pull out on this switch to pump the water out," he went on, embarrassed.

"Thanks for showing me," she said, now more or less trapped in the doorway until he backed up. In so doing, he brushed into her.

"Excuse me," he muttered, stepping into the salon and tripping on the Oriental throw rug. She suppressed a smile. Noting it, he was irritated, knowing not what it was about her that bothered him, except that for a man versed in the social graces, he felt gauche. And even worse, she was managing so much better in this situation than he was. He realized that his frown was betraying him.

"I hope I'm not going to be too much of a bother," she said, coming into the salon. "I started not to come. This seems so impetuous. It was just that Frances, well, you know, urged me so..."

"*Impetuous* is the word of the day where Frances is concerned." Noting her expression, he realized that he sounded equally as critical of Mary for having accepted the invitation. She took a seat at the table.

"How about some coffee?" he offered.

"No thanks," she said. "I rarely drink it." He nodded and took a seat at the chart table. She sat back and seemed to relax a bit. "Have you known them long?" she asked.

"Two days," he replied. "I've been hired to sail them home."

"Will you all be going way out at sea?" she asked. "Going to Charleston?"

"It's possible to sail straight across to Florida," he said, "and then hug the coast going north. But it's much farther that way. Our plan is to go to the upper western corner of the Bahamas and head for Charleston from there."

"Do you put the anchor out at night when you're at sea?"

Joe grinned. "It's a little too deep for that," he replied, trying not to sound sarcastic. "No, you just have to keep on sailing."

"You mean you have to drive the boat all night?"

"Oh, yeah," he explained. "Not much else you can do."

She shook her head. "I didn't mean to sound like a faintheart or anything," she laughed. "I just, well, I feel a little new to all this."

He returned her smile, glad to hear from her something less self-assured and a bit more feminine.

"Just going from here to—what is it called, Green Turtle?—is good enough for me," she added.

"It wouldn't do to bite off too much at once," he said. There was a pause.

"What about Frances? Does she like it?"

"I guess so," Joe gave an offhand gesture. "She seems to have done it many times before."

"She's quite a character, isn't she?" Mary prodded.

Joe smiled. "She seems to have a way of getting what she wants," he replied.

Mary looked at him, seemingly dissatisfied with the short answer. Something about her was irritating him; he didn't know what. He looked at the shiny brass ship's clock on the varnished teak bulkhead.

"They should be getting back anytime now," he said.

She gazed at him a moment. "You don't say everything you think, do you?"

"I guess not," he replied. After a moment of silence, he added, "I hope they get back soon. We need to get going."

"If you will excuse me," she said, standing and heading forward, "I'd like to try out that bathroom equipment you were showing me."

Glad to have a reason to escape, Joe climbed the ladder to the cockpit and looked around. The breeze was picking up a bit as the sun climbed higher in the sky. Coming down the hill toward the pier, thankfully, were Alex and Frances. It was close to eleven, and high time they got underway if they were to have a comfortable day passage to Green Turtle. From their expressions, he could see that Alex looked long-suffering, while Frances was ecstatic.

"I've just ordered some special pillows for the boat. You should have seen the beautiful blue material," she called to Joe. "What lovely work that island woman does."

Joe did his best to respond with enthusiasm. He guessed it was difficult for her to be living the yachting life, surrounded more by men than women. He decided he'd humor her at every opportunity just to keep the peace.

They welcomed Mary as soon as they were aboard. Despite his earlier protestations to Frances for inviting her, at his first glimpse of Mary, Alex looked very pleased.

"Frances didn't tell me how pretty you are," he said.

"Never mind, Alex," Frances interrupted. "Come now, Mary dear, I want to show you around." She took Mary by the hand and led her toward the galley. Alex gave Mary one more look, glanced at Joe, and winked. Frances was fawning over the guest, making sure she understood where the Cokes were, and so on.

It took another thirty minutes before they were ready to depart. In the interim, Alex reviewed Joe's chart work and said it was more precise than his own plotting ever was. Finally, it appeared that nothing else could impede their leaving. Marvin himself came out to cast off the lines and wish them well. Joe and Frances acted as deckhands, taking in the mooring lines, while Alex was at the helm. Mary sat in the cockpit and watched Alex at the wheel maneuvering the sixty-foot boat away from the pier. As

Joe stood at the bow coiling the mooring lines, he smiled to himself at Mary's apparent excitement, realizing he felt elated to be going himself. On a devilish whim, he carried a dock line to the bow and bent down to open the forward compartment.

"Joe!" Alex shouted. "Stow the lines aft in the lazaretto, will you?"

Joe nodded and picked up the coils of rope to carry them back, confirming again Smith's angst over the mysterious cargo.

Alex steered through the little harbor lagoon, past the anchored boats, and then past the little outdoor restaurant where Bea worked. Joe noted that Alex looked, but saw no sign of her. *Blaster* was tied up at the nearby pier. As the sailboat motored by about thirty yards away, a man's head appeared at the hatch, watching them. Remembering their remarks that morning as they had motored by *Mission,* Joe stared back, wishing he knew exactly what they were up to.

Of a size large enough to have a kind of stately grace, *Mission* proceeded out of the narrow pass, into the bay. Beyond the jetty, Alex turned, taking up a northerly heading on the course Joe had plotted. The light green shallow water sparkled under bright, sunny skies, rippled by a breeze on the bow.

As instructed, Joe carried the coiled mooring lines to the stern and knelt down and opened the hatch in the deck to the lazaretto, a compartment similar to the one forward that he apparently was forbidden to open. Then he made his way forward over the teak deck, careful not to trip over the sail rigging, ducked under the canvas bimini, and entered the cockpit. While Alex stood behind the wheel, steering, Frances sat just forward on the starboard cockpit seat, recounting to Mary her choice of color and print for the pillows that Mrs. Finch had promised to finish and mail to their home. Alex offered the helm to Joe, and went below. In a few minutes, he climbed back up to the cockpit, smiling.

"No more valve clicking," he said. "The additive must have taken care of it."

"Wonderful," Joe said. That was something of a relief. Still, he thought, Alex must feel a sense of real urgency about getting on to Charleston. Otherwise, he'd have delayed the trip long enough to wait for the additional engine parts. He watched Alex take a seat by Frances, and Joe tried to piece together both his friend's urgency and the mysterious packages stowed in the bow. They continued to motor along at six knots in pleasant silence until they were out of the lee of the island. Joe noted the easterly wind increasing and declared they could sail on a broad reach.

"Now I'll show you the real beauty of this boat," Alex said, turning into the wind.

Asking Joe to ease the main sheet, and then prepare to winch in on the halyard, Alex found the toggle switch on the steering console and electrically unwound the huge mainsail. After raising the sail with the electrically controlled halyard, Joe then tightened the sheet and outhaul until the sail was drawing well. Next, they let out the jib sail, unfurling it and taking in the port sheet. Alex turned left back to course, falling off from the wind. *Mission* heeled about ten degrees and picked up speed. When the meter indicated nine knots, Alex pulled back on the throttle somewhat.

"We'd better motor-sail," he said, "to make up some time."

Giving Joe the helm, Alex went below and came back with a handheld radio and a pistol in a leather holster. Joe was glad to see that they had a weapon aboard, just in case.

"Oh, no, Alex," Frances exclaimed. "You're not going to shoot at sharks again? I hate it when you do that."

"I can't stand those things," he said, shaking his head. "Don't worry. I'll just keep it handy, just in case. He stowed the weapon in the cockpit table drawer and then turned on his handheld radio and tuned in the weather. They listened as the robotic voice gave the current conditions and forecast. The wind was out of the east at five, gusting to ten knots, and expected to gust fifteen to twenty knots in the afternoon.

Joe listened with a look of some concern. "I hope he means *late* afternoon," he remarked, peering east toward the Great Guana Cay that lay between them and the Atlantic Ocean. "We can't stand too much wind from the east." He went on to explain that offshore winds were not favorable for a good passage around Whale Cay.

"This boat likes wind," Alex said. "Isn't that right, Frances?"

"It may like wind, but I don't," she replied.

"Have you ever seen a rage at Whale Cay?" Joe asked.

"Lord, yes," Frances said, giving her husband an exasperated look. "Alex got us in it, and we almost capsized."

"Oh, it wasn't so bad," Alex said. "The boat just surfed on through."

"Ha, so you say," she went on. "There's a picture on the wall at Bluff House of a ship that pitchpoled some years ago in the rage," Frances said. "Nearly everyone on board drowned."

Joe recalled seeing the picture some years ago, which depicted a vessel twice the length of *Mission* being thrown end over end in a huge wave. Despite the possible danger, Frances's sudden passion for pillow covers had delayed their departure by several hours, exposing them to more of the afternoon winds.

"Do you have to go that way?" Mary asked, beginning to understand the concern.

"You can anchor out south of the pass in Baker's Bay and wait it out," Joe answered, pointing on the chart to a small cove at the northwest end of Great Guana. "People have been known to sit there for a day or two or even longer." He glanced at Mary, noting her alarm at the mention of delay.

"Don't worry," Frances said, reaching over and patting her on the leg. "We have lots of good food and drink aboard. And we know a few good stories."

"But then, well, how would I get back to Marsh Harbour?"

"Frances, you're making Mary nervous," Alex broke in. "Don't worry, sweetie, we'll not have any delays."

Mary nodded with a smile, a bit embarrassed by having shown any distress. Joe glanced at the boat instruments, noted a gust of ten knots being indicated, but said nothing.

Frances was giving Mary her full attention. "Here," she said, reaching into the storage bin of the cockpit table. "We're letting you get sunburned."

She pulled out a bottle of Bull Frog, applied some to her hand, and began rubbing it on Mary's face and neck. Mary pulled back in surprise at the unexpected familiarity, but then presented her face with closed eyes. Joe imagined Mary sitting before a lighted mirror being made up, just before curtain call of a major play.

"Oh, you're getting burned already," Frances exclaimed. "Even with the bimini top, the sun still can get to you."

64

After squeezing more lotion on her hand, she rubbed it on Mary's high but soft-lined cheekbones and sculptured nose. Joe watched, fascinated by Frances's quick familiarity with people. Forever a bit shy, he could never have taken such liberties with anyone but a most intimate *amie*.

Frances finished the job and looked admiringly at her work. "Now," she asked, "how's that?"

Mary, looking run over by a freight train, mumbled a gracious thanks. She glanced at Joe, who looked away. He noticed that Frances was watching them.

"Who's hungry?" Frances asked.

Alex, who was stowing some small line and other loose things in the cockpit, looked up. "Me, for one."

Frances asked Mary to join her in the galley to help with lunch. Soon the ladies were passing tuna sandwiches and apple slices with peanut butter on them up from the galley. Alex took a moment to re-trim the main sheet and the jib. Then he sat beside Mary on the port-side cockpit bench and raised the leaf of the teak table that ran fore and aft just forward of the wheel. Alex asked for a beer, and Joe did the same. Alex turned his attention to Mary, asked all the questions about where she lived in Birmingham, learned that she had lost her husband to a heart attack, found out that she was an amateur actress, and caught up on the things that Frances had pumped out of her the day before.

"How did you learn to act?" Alex asked. "Did you study it in school?"

"I was an English major at Hollins, and minored in dramatics. But I had acted in school plays from the sixth grade on."

"I always wanted to study drama," Frances said, "sweeping about the stage, great lines flowing from my lips." She stood up and made an expansive gesture with her arms.

Mary smiled. "I suppose I learned as much from reading novels and plays as I did from any dramatics classes," she said. "And later on, I became interested in psychology, particularly in Karl Jung's ideas of personality archetypes, which helped me get into character for certain roles."

"Uh-oh, a psychologist, too," Alex quipped. "I suppose you're thinking you've found some fertile ground here."

Mary put on a mock appraising look. "Yes," she replied. "I've been taking mental notes all along."

"What have you learned so far?" Alex asked.

"I keep looking around for the cargo," Mary said. "I mean, here you are going on a long trip in this boat, and so it seems to me you should be transporting something. A funny idea, I guess. I don't know exactly..."

At the words "transporting something," Alex shot her a quick glance, which Joe did not miss and decided it was an entrée to probe a bit.

"Well, illicit drugs are always a possibility," he suggested, watching Alex's face. "There seems to be a lot of that going on around the Bahamas."

"Really?" Mary asked. "On boats like this?"

Feigning his easy smile, Alex nodded. "One time, off the coast near Miami, we sailed past some bales of hay, or so we thought, floating in the water. When we got closer, we could see they were not hay, and then we realized it was a huge amount of marijuana baled up like hay that had been dumped there for some reason."

"I wanted to call the coast guard and report it," Frances said, "but Alex wouldn't let me."

"I was afraid they would think we were involved or something," he replied. "Better just to stay out of it entirely. All I wanted was to sail away from there fast, before the people who it belonged to showed up."

If Alex was hiding anything like marijuana in that bow locker, Joe decided, he certainly was cool about it. Could it be that it wasn't anything, just blown up in Joe's own imagination? Perhaps it wasn't marijuana but something more valuable. He recalled Mary's question about cargo. An interesting idea—what was their cargo? It seemed to be a question more about what was the purpose for the trip. Did you have to have a practical and mundane purpose? Or could she be thinking about cargo on a deeper level?

"Emotional baggage," he thought aloud. They all looked at him.

"I see," Mary said. "Is that what you brought?"

Joe grinned. "Maybe."

"What in the world are you two talking about?" Frances asked.

Mary held her gaze on Joe a moment longer and then turned to Frances. "I suppose we're talking about all those things that have happened to each of us in the past that make us who we are," she explained. "It's part of what we bring along, no matter where we go."

"Ha," Alex said. "Who ever heard of such a thing? *Emotional baggage.*"

"It can get to be quite a burden for some people," Mary replied. "All of us carry with us many little victories, defeats, joys, pains, hurts, anxieties—emotionally packed memories, I suppose." She glanced at Joe. "That's what you meant, wasn't it?"

He nodded. "Someone told me once that it's important to remember that each person you encounter has just come from somewhere and from something. He or she has come from a whole series of events and circumstances that we don't know about or understand, but they affect and influence who that person is."

Mary gave him an intense look. "That's true," she said, looking out at the sunlit, gleaming waters. "I was thinking about how my husband, Earnest, would have enjoyed this sail so much. He liked going to the beach. We used to spend a week each summer on the Gulf, around Fort Walton."

"I always preferred Panama City," Alex said. "There was this shack of a place called Hunt's Oyster Bar. Man. We'd eat dozens on the half shell. Remember that, Franny?"

"Now you don't even dare look a raw oyster in the eye," Frances replied. "I just hate the way things are changing, don't you, Mary?"

Mary nodded, but turned her attention back to Joe. "Would you tell me more about where you came from?" she asked.

Joe met her eyes for an instant and then looked away, shaking his head. "Not much to tell" he said, feeling very self-conscious.

"Oh, don't be so coy," Frances exclaimed. "Lighten up. Tell us something good about yourself, and forget all that deep

68

thought, emotional baggage stuff." She stood up and began gathering the lunch plates. Mary still had her gaze fixed on Joe, but jumped up to help Frances.

"Bring him another beer," Alex said. "Sounds like he needs a bit of liquid support." He emptied his own Heineken and passed the can forward. "I'll take another, too."

Joe smiled at Frances. "Sorry," he said. "I'm having a wonderful time."

"Oh, me too," Mary said. "Look, the water is so green and beautiful. I just love sailing."

Frances went down the ladder to the salon and asked Mary to pass the lunch things down. Then she passed up two more beers and came back up to the cockpit. Mary refused the offer of another for herself.

Joe pointed out a navigation mark off to starboard. Alex peered into the distance, spotted it, and made a slight turn toward it. Joe looked up at the telltales and brought the jib sheet in a little. He looked for a place to put the beer can, saw that the teak cup holder closest to him was holding Alex's cell phone, and decided just to drink all the beer.

"Now, you be careful." Frances lectured. "We don't need any drunks on board, do we, Mary?"

Mary avoided the question. Joe made a sigh of satisfaction and squashed the can in his fingers. "I'll be circumspect," he said, standing up and trimming the jib by pushing the electric winch button for a second.

"*Circumspect?*" Frances repeated. "That's a pretty big word for a boat captain."

Joe laughed. From anyone else that would be a rather offensive remark. From Frances… well, from Frances it was just an observation of unbridled truth.

"I wasn't always a boat captain," he said.

"Interesting," Mary said.

"You'll have to tell us more about that sometime," Frances said. "But not now."

Joe smiled, happy to be off the hook.

By one in the afternoon, the wind became a lot more blustery, but under patchy clouds. They approached the southeastern pass, and Alex pointed out Baker's Bay and some abandoned cabanas on the beach.

"The Disney cruise line used to bring their ships in here for a recreation stop," Alex explained. "But on so many occasions their ships would be prevented from transiting the pass because of rough seas, and so they abandoned the site all together."

Joe took a step to the right and peered forward around the dodger, trying to get a look at the pass into the ocean. There were a few whitecaps.

"How's it look?" Frances asked.

Joe lifted a hand in gesture. "Wind's still picking up, but it doesn't look that bad. Not yet, anyway." On cue, a gust listed them to port.

"Not yet, you say?" Frances said, an edge to her voice.

Without further comment, Joe steered toward the centerline between buoys, the turn luffing the jib, causing a heavy flapping sound.

"We might as well take it in," Alex said.

Joe turned another twenty degrees to starboard to enter Loggerhead Channel, headed seaward. Alex observed the turn, nodded agreement, and then took hold of the genoa in-haul line on the electric winch and pressed the button. With a deep whirr of the winch motor, the huge jib furled. Joe turned back to the left on course, and Alex trimmed the main in close, leaving it out for stability.

"What do you think, Alex?" Frances asked.

Joe noticed Alex looking at Mary a moment, obviously remembering her need to get to Bluff House. Alex got up, made his way starboard, and stood on deck, holding a shroud from the mast, looking. Then he nodded and came back in.

"No problem," he said.

Joe scanned the pass ahead and frowned. Frances noted his expression.

"What do you think, Joe?"

He hesitated to disagree with Alex. "It may be okay for heading out," he said, "but if the wind continues to increase while we go around Whale Cay, that could make a difference."

Alex didn't look happy. "It's not far around to the other pass," he said. "Wind couldn't increase that much."

Joe nodded toward the wind speed indicator, which now registered fifteen knots or so. "The alternative is to go into the anchorage behind the island and anchor. The wind will die down overnight and give us a better passage in the morning." He looked at Alex for agreement.

The man's expression showed he was more concerned about who was in charge than what was prudent. "We'll go on," he said.

Joe met his gaze. They stared at one another for a tense moment. Then Joe sighed and looked away.

"Your call," he said. Above all else, Joe needed this job. He had too much at stake here to risk being fired and put off to be stranded in the Bahamas again. Alex clearly wanted to call the shots and not rely on Joe's judgment. So what the hell? A harrowing passage around Whale now might give Joe a chance to see how the Smiths would respond in a stressful situation. There would be more situations encountered at sea, so he might as well test his employer out now.

Alex turned to Frances. "Everything secure below, honey?"

She sighed, shook her head, and climbed down the ladder. Mary was sitting up to see ahead and looked worried. Joe steered into the channel, and soon they began to feel the boat buck and pitch against the waves that rose in from the deeper ocean, up onto the undersea shelf of the Bahamas.

He glanced at Mary, who was still peering forward, holding on to the rail behind the seat and showing some concern. "It's not too rough," he said to calm her.

She looked back at him and nodded, in her eyes an appeal for assurance. Joe spread his feet to gain a better footing and steered on into the ever-increasing waves, the boat pitching more and more as they transitioned from the shallows to the sea. In a few moments, he realized that they, indeed, were at sea, committed now to a passage around Whale Cay. Ahead, plumes of spray popped up over Chubb Rocks, which jutted out of the churning ocean.

Frances returned on deck just as Alex's cell phone rang. Being closest, she picked it up and looked at the caller ID screen.

"Bea," she read aloud, her eyes flaring as she recognized who that was. "Bea Johnson?" she repeated, and stared at Alex. "That hussy waitress? Why is she calling? How does your phone know her name?"

Alex swallowed, trying to maintain nonchalance. "I don't know," he said, feigning surprise.

Frances glared at him, jumping to conclusions, quite correctly in all probability, Joe knew. The phone continued to ring. When Alex put out his hand to take it, Frances drew her arm back and threw the phone as far as she could out into the sea. Everybody gasped as its last ring gurgled and the phone disappeared.

"Frances? What in the world?" Alex cried. "Are you crazy?"

"No, but you are if you think I'm going to allow that bitch to be calling you on your cell phone, you're crazy." she shouted. Then she burst into tears and stumbled down below.

Alex looked dizzy for a moment, in a panic, and then charged after her. When they were gone, Joe looked at Mary, who wore an expression of complete dismay, and he had to laugh.

"What happened?" Mary asked.

"You can never be real sure," he lied, knowing full well what it was all about. "Never a dull moment."

Out of the pass and in deep water, Joe turned to port to parallel the coastline of Whale Cay. It took about forty minutes to pass the island. During that time, the anemometer read higher wind speeds, gusts sometimes reaching eighteen to twenty knots. *Mission* heeled over with each gust, thrilling Joe, but making Mary nervous. He liked her a little better that way, she appearing not so self-assured as before.

Sea heights grew from two to four feet. Off to the west, he heard the dull drone of an engine and looked back. It was that cigarette boat again, barreling along at high speed a couple of miles away, headed up the western side of Whale Cay. Having a very shallow draft, the speedboat could stay inside and cross over the shoals that the sailboat had to avoid. He watched until it disappeared behind the island and then turned back to the helm, steering them back on course. Mary glanced at him.

"I just don't like those obnoxious speedboats," he explained. He didn't say that he thought less of its crew. Why were they coming this way?

Approaching the northern pass between Whale Rock and Channel Rock, Joe called down the hatch to Alex. He came on deck just as they rolled with a large wave.

"Let me have it, ole boy," he said as if nothing had happened between them. "I'm a little more accustomed to the boat. Not that you were doing badly."

"It's your boat," Joe replied, biting his tongue to keep from sounding too sarcastic.

"That's right," Alex mumbled to Joe as he took the wheel.

Joe stepped away from the helm and surveyed the situation. "Looks like we'll have to jibe the mainsail."

Alex nodded. "Go ahead and wind it in to amidships."

Joe took the winch handle for the main sheet and wound it in with some effort due to the pressure of the wind. The boat rolled as Alex turned to port, lining them up with the pass. Just as they steadied on the new course, a wave picked the stern up sharply, throwing them off-balance. The boat wallowed, and Alex fought to put it back on course.

"Shit." Then he glanced at Mary and grinned. "Oops, sorry," he said, tongue in cheek.

The boat pitched again and wallowed back. Joe speculated that white-knuckled Mary hadn't even picked up on Alex's crudity. Frances came climbing up the ladder, hanging on as the boat tossed about.

"You're not trying to go back in, are you?" she demanded. "This is that awful rage if I ever saw it."

Alex grimaced. "Everything's all right," he insisted.

Another large wave hit them from astern, driving the bow deep into the trough. As a great spume of green water came over the bow, the boat lumbered forward. Alex fought to keep it on course. Then another wave hit with the same effect.

"That wasn't so good," Alex admitted.

"That's just the way a pitchpole begins," Joe advised.

"Oh God!" Frances exclaimed. Mary shot a look of fear at her, not understanding what was happening.

"It means having the boat struck from behind by a wave large enough to send it bow-down and end over end," Joe explained to Mary, making sure that Alex heard and understood the danger. He looked ahead at the pass. It was filled with white-capped rollers and even an occasional breaking wave.

After another wave lifted the stern abruptly, Joe spoke up. "If in doubt, turn out, turn out," he quoted, reciting an old adage from his navy days. Alex did not respond. Joe grabbed a handhold as another wave struck from astern. "I think maybe we'd better ride this one out at sea."

Alex acted as if he were ignoring Joe's advice, and Joe realized Alex just wanted it clear that any decision would be his, not anyone else's.

"We'll come about," Alex announced a few moments later.

Joe nodded, as if it had been Alex's idea all along.

"If we come left, we won't have to jibe the main again," Alex said.

Joe looked to port and didn't like the closeness of the rocks off Whale Cay. "I'd rather see you come around to the right and let me manage the jibe," he suggested.

Another wave sent *Mission* careening. When they were upright again, Alex nodded. "Okay," he said. "To the right. Let me know when you're ready."

Joe scrambled to the winch and hauled the main in close. As he wound on the winch crank, he noticed the cigarette boat at idle in the distance, on the other side of the pass, in the safety of the lee behind the island. They were sitting there watching.

"Okay," Alex called, glancing aft, picking his moment. Then when *Mission* rose out of a deep pitch, he spun the wheel to the right. "Coming about."

Joe jibed the sail as they came around. The boat wallowed hard in a deep trough, listed hard over to port as a big wave hit. Not expecting the violence of the roll, Mary tumbled back against the port bench, letting out a little scream in surprise. Something down in the cabin fell with a crash and a clatter. Alex gunned the engine to give a push to the stern, and the boat came around to a forty-five-degree angle to the waves, heading back out to sea. They pitched hard on the waves, but the boat was riding safely now.

Remembering her fearful look, Joe glanced at Mary, giving her a reassuring thumbs-up. She let out a big breath and looked more relieved, but still concerned. Joe recalled that they could have just stayed inside on the south side of Whale Cay, spent the night in the Baker's Bay anchorage, put the dinghy in the water with the outboard motor, and delivered Mary to Green Turtle that way. But all of this was Monday-morning quarterbacking. It was clear that Alex was the type who would do the daring rather than the conservative, and Joe knew he could count on that being the way it would go in the future.

Once they were out away from the shallows of the Bahamas bank, *Mission* pitched more comfortably, heading into four-foot waves. Joe stared across the line of surf along the shore of Green Turtle Cay, with its safe and secure Bluff House sitting high above the raging waters. He glanced at Mary, thinking of how they could have been sitting at a table there, drinking a Bahama Mama, listening to a marimba band, and talking about the pleasant sail from Man-O-War. She noticed he was regarding her and loosened her grip on the railing a bit, but looked a bit green.

"Aren't we going to be able to go in?" she managed to ask.

Alex shook his head. "Not *this* afternoon."

"But I need to get back to..." Mary broke off, trying to take in what had happened. She looked back toward the pass. "Oh, what about that boat?" she asked, pointing. They all looked back to see the cigarette boat inside just beyond the pass. "Could we call them and ask if they'd come take me in?"

"What makes you think they could come out here if we can't go in there?" Alex asked, revealing his irritation with both the situation and the ignorance of her question.

"That sorry thing would capsize in a second, trying to get through the rage," Joe said, focused on the cigarette boat, ominous in its vigil. Even though it was half a mile away, he could tell that its crew was watching them. Were they waiting for a chance to... what, accost them? he wondered. As the sailboat continued its climb and descent over four-foot waves, he saw the speedboat lurch forward, heard its engine gunned as it went into a tight turn, heading off toward Green Turtle Cay.

Joe glanced at Mary and stared at her for a moment, realizing the implications. "Looks like you're going to be sailing with us a bit longer," he said.

Chapter Four

"You mean I can't go to Bluff House?" Mary asked for the third time as they bucked their way back out to sea and then headed north.

"Well, with the seas this high, the only way I see to get you there is by helicopter," Alex replied. "And I doubt that there are any available, not any closer than Freeport." Alex's tone and expression revealed his own unhappiness with the fact that they would be missing out on a wonderful dinner at Bluff House and, even worse, that their guest was still on board.

"When do you think we can get to shore?" she persisted.

"I don't know," Alex said.

"When does your plane leave?" Frances asked.

"Tomorrow afternoon," Mary said. "I've got to get to Marsh Harbour to rejoin the tour group."

"Oh, Mary!" Frances exclaimed and bit her lip. "You know, we've never had such bad luck!" She shot a glance at Joe, which was recriminating, but he didn't know why. And then he recalled her remark about his being a Jonah.

"I'm just the navigator," he said, suppressing the urge to snap back. What he thought was that it had been Frances's fooling around in Man-O-War that had made them get off so late and be subjected to the heavy winds of afternoon.

Alex motioned in a pleading manner for Frances to take the helm, which she did with reluctance, complaining that she didn't like to steer in high seas. He beckoned to Joe to come below to the chart table in order to set a new course. Mary followed them. Alex looked at his empty cell phone charger stand, and then picked up the radio mike. He raised Marvin Mann at Albury's Boatyard on the VHF and asked him to phone a message to the tour guide at the hotel where the group was staying and tell him about the rage and the inability to get Mary ashore. In a few minutes, Marvin called back to say that the man wasn't in, but that he had left him a message.

"Surely there's something you can do," Frances was saying as Joe and Mary followed Alex up to the cockpit. "Why not take her in close to shore and take her in with the dinghy?"

Alex shook his head. "Why, of course. Let's just put the dinghy out in four-to-five-foot waves, which are breaking on reefs and rocks fifty yards offshore. Then *Mission* can just bust open in the surf, and she can swim on in, suitcases and all, I suppose."

"Well, you needn't be so smart about it," she snipped. She reached over and patted Mary's hand. "Poor Mary, now you're trapped on this boat just like I am." She shot a look at her husband, then jumped up, started down the companionway, and announced she was going to take a nap. Joe saw that Mary had tears in her eyes. She met his gaze and then looked away, wiping her tears on her sleeve.

From behind the helm, Alex sighed. "Nothing to do but head on north around the islands," he said, shaking his head and then concentrating on steering into the waves.

80

"Come down below, Mary," Joe said. "Let me show you on the chart." She dabbed at her eyes with a Kleenex and followed him down the ladder. Joe pointed out their location and explained that the way back to Green Turtle, or even to Marsh Harbour, would be via the Whale Cay pass. "It's too dangerous until the wind dies. So all we can do is to head on northwest on the Atlantic side. Maybe in a day or so the winds will calm enough for us to go in." He gazed at Mary. "But by then, we won't be anywhere near a commercial airport, let alone Marsh Harbour." She looked grim.

Noting her distress, Joe felt more sympathetic. "I think the best thing for you to do is just relax," he said, "and accept the fact that you've missed the plane and will have to make other arrangements later."

She closed her eyes a moment, letting that fact soak in. "Do you think I might have to go... all the way to Charleston?"

Joe stifled a smile. *Wouldn't that be a hell of a note?* "I don't know," he replied.

She paused, taking that in. "I know you told me before, but how far is it?"

Joe set about laying a new course on the chart. "Each minute of latitude is a nautical mile," he explained, thinking that a long-winded explanation might break the impact of it a little. "Each degree is sixty miles." He stretched his fingers out the length of one degree and walked them up the chart. "Looks like roughly four hundred fifty miles after we're across to the western side of the Bahamas. If we average seven knots, we'll make about a hundred sixty miles a day, going day and night, but we won't average that kind of speed until we get in the Gulf Stream. If we turn back to the west tomorrow, and sail across the northern part of Abaco, we'll anchor out one night before we leave." He watched Mary doing the math in her head.

"Four or five days?" she calculated.

Joe smiled. "You'd be an old salt by that time," he said. "Maybe we can find a port somewhere to drop you off before then."

She looked a bit pale, either from the realization of her plight, or perhaps from the onset of seasickness. The boat rolled with a large wave that made her lose her balance and plop down on the salon sofa.

"Oh," she murmured, looking more uncomfortable getting queasy.

"It's better to be topside when it's this rough," he said. Yes, he liked her a little better in this situation, he realized, where she seemed more vulnerable, and dependent on him, perhaps.

"Don't worry," he said. "I'll be here…" He didn't quite know how to finish the sentence. Then, finding the moment embarrassing for some reason, he took up the chart and headed topside, leaving his new shipmate to contemplate the circumstances.

In a few minutes, Mary came up the ladder and took a seat on the port bench, looking worse. Exchanging glances with Joe, Alex shook his head, likely thinking that not only was she a liability, but a seasick one.

Joe slid over close to the ailing woman. "Try standing up and looking at the horizon," he suggested. She staggered up and held on to the top of the hatch. "As the boat rolls, sort of gyroscope yourself so that your head stays level," he added.

She did as she was instructed and, in a few minutes, looked a little better. "I think I'll go lie down a while."

Joe nodded. "Just close your eyes and relax, and you'll be okay," he advised.

Paralleling the line of the Abaco Islands, which made up the rim of the archipelago, they sailed on. Frances prepared some instant soup for supper, and the men spelled one another on the wheel while the other went below to eat. The wind had calmed some, but they still rolled a good bit, in spite of the dampening effect of the mainsail. Any passage between Green Turtle and Crab Cay or Manjack or Ambergris, even in calm weather, would be risky. In these conditions, passage was impossible, subjecting them once again to the effects of the rage, or grounding in unknown waters. And so they remained virtual prisoners to the sea.

It was decided that they would stand three-hour watches, paired off as Alex and Frances together and Joe and Mary together. Joe had some doubt as to Mary's ability to stand watch with him, but it was okay if he had to take it alone. Mary appeared in the cockpit, looking more refreshed. Alex went below and came back with a can of Brasso and a rag. He poured a little of the beige liquid on the rag and rubbed a corner of the anchor bell that hung in the cockpit. Mary watched him at work and then moved over and, surprising both of them, asked for the rag.

"I may as well be doing something useful around here."

Alex handed over the Brasso. As he did so, he gave her hand a little squeeze and smiled at her. "There's some more brass fittings around, too," he said. "Just do a few at a time, and then it's not such a big job."

She nodded without any reaction to the hand squeeze. Joe had noted it, but thought of it as just a kindness. Mary went to work on the bell.

Alex glanced at Joe. "You okay?" he asked, gesturing at the helm. Joe nodded, and Alex went below.

While steering, Joe watched as the bell was being polished. If she had experienced any twinge of seasickness before, she appeared to be over it now, or in control of it, anyway. Nothing was worse than having a seasick person with you. It was unpleasant for everyone else on board, too. In a few minutes, it appeared that Mary was kind of getting into it. Making the bell shine became a pleasant chore. When she finished, she looked at Joe for approval.

"Looks good!" he said, smiling.

Pleased, Mary began going around, finding all the brass fittings and plates to polish, pausing to watch the sun set as a big red ball over the nearby, but so unreachable, island.

Alex came topside to take over the helm.

Frances came up the ladder, calling to Mary. "Come see," she said. "I've fixed up the nice little cabin for you." Mary followed her down, with Frances going on about how she had made up the bunk for her and everything.

As he went below and squeezed past the two women standing outside the middle cabin, Joe realized he'd have to be sharing the forward head with Mary, and that they'd be staying in pretty close proximity. Well, that was to be expected on a boat, of course, he realized. He closed the door to the forward cabin and plopped down on the V-berth for a nap.

According to Alex's instructions, Joe and Mary took the watch at midnight. Joe had not expected her to show up on deck, but she did, right on time. As Alex and Frances went below, Joe complimented Mary on the brass shining she had done. She seemed to be getting her sea legs and was calmed down, accepting the idea that she was off on a sailing adventure. After a while of sailing along in silence, Joe coaxed her into taking the helm, which she did with a tentativeness and lack of confidence. In a short time, however, he allowed her to steer, and she seemed to enjoy it.

Bringing over the chart, and turning on the red-lensed flashlight, he showed Mary the islands they were passing in the dark: Powell Cay, Spanish Cay, Ambergris—all were fingers of rock and coral emerging as low-lying blue-black hulks just peering above the turbulent ocean. There were a few lights of houses here and there, twinkling in the darkness.

Although the wind was still strong, the night air was warm and humid. Joe took his turn at the helm, steering into somewhat diminished waves. Mary stretched out on the port-side bench and napped a bit. In loneliness, Joe began to think of his daughter and his ex-wife, stuck with a wave of sadness that they were not his sailing companions. In the best of all worlds, they could be with him now, enjoying the adventure. Instead, it was this stranger, this misplaced widow from Birmingham, who was here. The sleeping figure stirred in the darkness. Joe stared at her in the gloom, and it occurred to him that perhaps some of his earlier antagonistic feelings toward her had more to do with his guilt about his ex-wife than with anything this Mary had done.

"Well, hello there," he greeted when she awoke and sat up, peering out in the gloom. "Did you get a little rest?"

Mary nodded. "What time is it?"

"Oh, about one fifteen," Joe replied. "Think you could take the helm and let me run to the head?"

She stretched, stood up, and made her way over to the wheel. Joe told her the course, watched her steer a moment or two to be sure she had it, and then went below. As quietly as he could so as not to awake his host and hostess, whose cabin door stood open, he rustled around with the coffeepot and got it going. While it perked, he peered up the companionway to check on Mary.

"Oh, I'm so glad you're back up here," she exclaimed. "I was getting nervous."

"I'm sure you're doing fine," Joe said, but peeked at the compass just to be sure she had stayed on course. The woman's silhouette at the wheel was lit by the dull red glow of the compass light. Perhaps she was adapting to her unwanted sailing adventure.

In a few minutes, Joe went below and came up the ladder with hot coffee. He offered a cup to Mary, who said again that she didn't drink it.

"Time you started, if you're gonna be a sailor." He thrust the cup into her hand and took over the helm. Mary took the cup, moved to the lee-side bench, and sipped. "How're you feeling?"

Mary sipped again. "I don't know...kind of confused...misplaced, or something, I guess."

"Life will do that to you," he said. He wondered, given the fact that she had been widowed a short period of time, if her husband's death hadn't also made her feel "misplaced."

"Do you think I'm going to get off the boat tomorrow?"

Joe grinned. "You're going wherever this boat's going," he said. "Alex is the captain of this vessel, and he has a right to decide what's safest for everyone." He paused. "But suppose we did detour to Freeport or somewhere else where there's an airport, would you rejoin your tour group, or would you just go home?"

"I don't know," she said. "Right now, I don't know what to do."

"Well, don't worry about it," Joe reassured her. "Whenever we can dock, wherever it is, we'll figure out something." They

86

motored along in silence, except for the dull drone of the engine below, listening to the sound of the boat slicing through the sea.

"Oh, what's that sparkling in the water?" she asked, peering down at the boat's wake.

"Phosphorescent plankton," he answered. "Neat, isn't it?"

"Wonderful!" she replied, staring at the little speckles of light flashing in the deep, dark water.

Joe watched her for a few moments and smiled. When he first came aboard *Mission*, his sole thought had been to get himself home, and Alex Smith and his secret cargo be damned. Now, with this somewhat naive and vulnerable young lady aboard, things were getting more complicated.

Chapter Five

It was not so much the smell of fresh coffee or the daylight filtering under the dinghy over his hatch, but the urgency of his bladder that awakened him. Joe performed his half-somersault maneuver to swing his legs out of the V-berth bunk, sat up, and noted the hour—5:40, time to relieve the watch. He noted that the sea was calmer as he made his way into the head. He gave himself a quick washing and then allowed himself the luxury of clean underwear, polo shirt, and Bermuda shorts. When he went past the middle stateroom, the door was open, and he saw that Mary was still sleeping, innocent as a baby, Joe thought. Having felt less than charitable toward her before the fiasco at Whale Cay, but now seeing her asleep, his feelings were changing. How vulnerable she looked, here amid people she didn't know well, with no means of escape. It made her more a *femme en péril*, he decided.

Joe started to awaken her for the watch, and then decided to just let her sleep. But as he was about to leave, her eyes opened. She blinked and focused on Joe, her greenish-blue eyes showing momentary uncertainty and disorientation. Then she shook her head and raised up on an elbow.

"Good morning," Joe said. "Our turn on watch…if you feel up to it."

Mary blinked once more and rolled her eyes. "Again?" she mumbled.

Joe smiled at her and then headed aft to the galley to find himself a cup of that great-smelling coffee. He picked up the pot and stepped out on the companionway ladder to offer refills topside.

"Well, greetings!" Alex said from behind the wheel. He reached for his cup in the teak holder mounted to the helm stand. Joe made his way up the ladder to fill it, passing Frances, who was stretched out on the starboard cockpit bench, napping under a navy blue blanket with the inscription, "Don't Tread on Me." Yes, where she was concerned, he was beginning to believe that warning.

"Seems to have calmed a lot," Joe observed, noting that they had furled the mainsail and were motoring. The great thing about *Mission* was that the seventy-foot-high mainsail furled horizontally on the boom by electric power. Peering out to port, Joe could see the low-lying islands about a mile off.

"We're coming up to the north end of Great Abaco Island," Alex said, pointing to the chart book. "Since the sea has calmed, we can turn in here and go across the bank to Great Sale Cay." He sketched it out with his finger. "At Great Sale we can rest up tonight and then head north toward Charleston."

Frances had awakened to the conversation. "Yes," she said with morning hoarseness, sitting up and brushing her hair down with her hand. "And we can stop and have breakfast in that little village. What do they call it?"

"Coopers Town," Alex said. "We can put Mary off there."

"I like that idea!" Joe said, smiling. "The breakfast, I mean." He set about taking a reading of latitude and longitude from the GPS. After going below, he turned on the VHF radio, tuning to a weather channel, and then listened while plotting the GPS position on the chart. The NOAA weather robot predicted improving weather, despite a frontal disturbance to the south and some significant tropical activity near Puerto Rico. After fixing their position and noting the time, he verified it by noting a couple of prominent landmarks on shore and comparing them to points on the chart.

"Got a course for us?" Alex called down.

Joe drew a line from just forward of the position and then moved the parallel rule over to the compass rose. "Looks like three-one-five will put us to the pass toward Coopers Town," he said, as he climbed to the cockpit. Alex made the turn, steadied up, and asked Joe to take it a while.

"Where is Mary?" Frances asked. "Still sleeping, I guess."

"How'd our guest do last night?" Alex asked. "Did she make it through the whole watch? Or did she flake out on you?"

"I got her to take the helm a while," Joe replied. "I think it helped her calm down."

"The sooner we can get her off our hands, the better," Alex said, handing over the wheel to Joe.

"Hush, Alex," Frances told him. "She might hear you."

"She's a liability I'd like to be rid of," he replied in a quieter voice. "It was a bad idea, letting her come."

"I suppose you think it's all my fault," Frances challenged, her short fuse lighting up.

"Well, you invited her, right?" her husband shot back.

"I did," she said. "I thought it was nice for Joe to have a companion. I didn't know we'd have the problem getting around Whale Cay."

"Oh, hello, Mary," Frances said, affecting a sweet tone when Mary appeared. "Did you sleep well?"

"I did, thank you," Mary said. Joe noted she had taken time to put on a little makeup and lipstick—not a bright, but a more subdued red. She had changed into a light blue chic blouse and white slacks which were very becoming. She looked around at the sea and smiled. "At first, I wondered how in the world anyone could sleep with the boat rolling around so. But then, I relaxed and found it very soothing." As she said it, Mary gave a long, catlike stretch, which Joe noticed was more like you would expect from a sixteen-year-old girl. It made her look so much younger, more tender, more vulnerable, he realized, and certainly more sexy.

"Like being rocked to sleep like a baby," Frances agreed.

Alex gave his unwanted guest a look of reappraisal, Joe observed, a somewhat long look. He glanced at Joe for an instant, smiling. Then he caught sight of a small freighter standing out of the channel.

"Well, we've got a vessel coming out of Coopers Town," he remarked. Everyone looked out at the little rusty red-hulled craft off the port bow.

"Looks like an old converted landing craft," Joe mused, "an LCM-8. I rode those things in my younger years, when I was with the US Navy's Amphibious Forces."

"That's the grocery-boat that goes around the islands," Alex observed from his view at the top of the ladder. "They make good freight haulers in the Bahamas because of their shallow draft." He glanced back at Joe. "Port-to-port passage?"

"Port-to-port, aye," Joe responded, confirming his knowledge of the rules of the road. Alex gave a thumbs-up and went down the companionway. Frances gave Mary a pat on the shoulder and a smile as she followed her husband down the ladder.

Mary settled back onto the starboard bench, watching with great interest as the converted landing craft passed on by. Joe gave a wave to the man in the wheelhouse, but he did not respond.

"I guess they don't like pleasure boats," he remarked.

"Why would that be?" Mary asked.

Joe shrugged. "I suppose it's a class thing, or something. Here we are on a beautiful sailboat, and they're trudging around on an old rust bucket."

"Such is life," she sighed. Together they watched it pass on by, noting a seagull circling around its wake, looking for some scrap of food to surface. "Well, I guess I'd better go pack my bags." There was a moment's pause. "I guess this is where I can find a way to Marsh Harbour?"

Joe nodded. "I guess so."

As they entered the channel, they could see Coopers Town to the left. A small community, a grouping of tiny wooden houses, it is a self-contained society with relatively few visitors. As *Mission* crossed over from deep ocean to Bahamian shallows in light wind, the rolling and pitching eased, and then ceased, as the water changed to light green emerald color. Alex came back topside, and Joe pointed out a vacant wooden pier that appeared to be a public landing. Alex took the helm while Joe asked Mary to follow him on deck. They went aft to the lazaretto and broke out the mooring lines.

"Let's rig some fenders, starboard side," Alex called to them. "That dock looks pretty rough. And I'd like to put a forward spring line over first."

Nodding, Joe attached a couple of fenders to the rail. He showed Mary how to bend the line around a cleat and instructed her to be ready to toss him each line after he jumped out on the dock, since no one was around to help. He prepared the spring line amidships and handed her the coiled line. Approaching with the wind on the bow, Alex brought the sailboat to the pier at a thirty-degree angle. Climbing over the lifeline to stand on the gunwale, Joe hopped off and called to Mary to pass the bowline and then to go aft to toss over the stern line, and then the other spring. It was accomplished well despite a little wind setting them on, and they were moored. Joe commented that they might make a sailor of her yet, realizing as he said it that she would be leaving them there.

Alex stepped ashore and looked around, saying that it appeared no one was stirring that early in the morning. "We'd better lock up, in any case," he said, glancing up forward to be sure the padlock on the forward locker was securely in place.

Joe gathered up the charts, binoculars, night-vision scope, and anything else of value in the cockpit, and carried them below and placed them on the chart table. Then the four of them gathered in the cockpit to go ashore in search of breakfast, and Alex locked the hatch. As they started to depart, however, Frances announced that she had to make a visit to the "powder room" one more time, undid the combination lock to the hatch, and went back below.

While Alex waited for her on the pier, Joe and Mary took in their surroundings. The street, the houses, everything seemed almost in miniature. Most of the buildings were wood-framed, painted pale pink or blue, and had lots of oleanders growing beside them and fuchsia hanging from window boxes. Being early morning, there was little, if any, activity.

When Frances and Alex caught up with them, they walked on and soon spotted Amanda's B&B down the street. Being the best possibility for breakfast, they entered the gate and knocked on the door. With a little of Alex's polite but persistent persuasion, Mrs. Amanda James agreed to prepare breakfast. She seated them at a table in the corner of her kitchen, near a large window that looked out across Abaco Sound, and, "never keeping coffee or spirits in the house, please God," offered them hot tea. It was a wonder to Joe that she could run a B&B without offering coffee. Frances complimented her array of little pottery teapots, each shaped as little houses or animals, all brightly glazed and colorful. One replicated a tugboat with a bearded, smiling captain in the wheelhouse that came off when you filled the pot. Mary kept pretty quiet, but seemed agitated—concerned about what to do, Joe guessed. Mrs. James busied herself in the kitchen, and soon had a breakfast of bacon and eggs and scone-like biscuits on the table.

With Frances taking the lead, they engaged the old lady in conversation as she offered more scones and butter. She told them right off that she was widowed by Hurricane Andrew in 1992, in which her husband drowned trying to ride out the storm on his fishing trawler. Alex asked if she had thought about leaving Coopers Town after the tragedy.

"And where is an old woman to go, I'd ask you?" she replied. "No, dearie, me husband had paid off our home mortgage. So I made it into a nice inn for bed and breakfast, and here I'll be."

Joe decided that, while Coopers Town looked like "the dropping-off place," no one needed any more than a little spot to occupy at the end of the earth. Since being divorced, and later having his boat stolen, he hadn't felt that he had even that much claim to any piece of the world.

"Aren't you afraid of more hurricanes?" Frances asked.

The old lady laughed. "No more than death, I grant ye," she replied. "We all live with fear of some devilment or other." She rubbed a sun-withered, rough hand across her eyes. "There's even more trouble now in the islands—the cursed drug trade. It's brought back crime and piracy and I don't know what all. There's a bad element about these days." She shook her head. "Of course, they don't bother an old woman like me."

They all nodded sympathetically. Joe thought that the old lady had chosen the natural disasters of life in Coopers Town over self-made ones that most people endured.

"'Tween that and hurricanes, a few wee tornadoes, and seas and winds a'ragin', we don't get a lot of peace."In fact," she went on, walking back to the kitchen and bringing more scones, "the weatherman says there's the first storm of the season brewing in the Virgin Islands. Its mighty early in the year and bodes for a bad season."

While she talked, Joe thought he heard a faint, deep pulsing sound outside. Its throbbing was a lot like the pulse of that boat that towed his own boat away that night at Great Sale. The sound faded.

Their hostess pulled herself up from the table to fetch the teapot. As she poured another round, they talked further about the weather. Besides the heat of the Bahamian summer, Joe said the approach of tropical storm season was another reason why it was pretty late to be moving a boat north. Alex said there was no need for anyone to worry. As they finished, Frances noted that it was almost nine thirty. Joe realized that Mary had been silent about her need to find transportation and wondered if she had been just that patient, or what?

96

"Is there a fast way to Marsh Harbour?" Alex inquired, now thinking of Mary's needs.

"There's a new service operating through here," Mrs. James said, plopping back down, more or less pouring her dumpy body into her chair. "They have one of those terrible two-hulled monsters that I don't like to ride on."

"Catamaran?" Alex clarified.

She nodded. "Too fast for me!" the old lady said. "Comes in around noon most days."

"My plane will be leaving Marsh Harbour in two hours," Mary spoke up, looking at her watch. "Do you think I've missed the tour group?"

"I imagine you'd have time to get there," Alex said.

Joe doubted it, but didn't say so. "Maybe we could call and see," he suggested.

"I wonder if I could use your phone," Mary asked.

"It's out of service, I fear," Mrs. James said. "I've been trying to get them to come repair it for over a week now." She shook her head. "We don't get very much attention from the phone company here in Coopers Town," she complained. "There is a pay phone near the wharf, though."

"Does this ferry thing come in down there?" Mary asked. "Where could I wait for it?"

Mrs. James said there was an open pavilion where the catamaran comes in, but that Mary could stay in her living room until it was time. They thanked the old lady for her hospitality. Alex paid her for the breakfast, and the four of them set off toward the boat to help Mary with her luggage, Frances hanging on to Alex's arm.

"Do you think you can catch up with your tour group?" Frances asked. "Do you know where they will be staying in Nassau?"

Mary told him she had an itinerary that wasn't very detailed, but that she could find them okay.

"You could just stay with us," Frances said. Alex gave her a sharp glance, but said nothing.

"That's very kind," Mary replied. "But I've overstayed my welcome as it is." As she spoke, she looked at Joe. He was struck and somewhat surprised by it.

"I was hoping I was going to have a shipmate to stand watches with," Joe said, surprising himself. Then he glanced at Alex, hoping he wasn't speaking too much out of turn.

Frances nodded. "You know we have plenty of room," she encouraged, "and food and so on."

Alex didn't look so encouraging. He gave his wife a surreptitious shake of his head. Mary didn't notice, giving her curious attention to Joe's last remark. She met his eyes for a brief instant, but he looked away.

"After your first experience, Mary," Alex said, "you may have decided you've had enough."

"It's not every day one has the opportunity for a sailing trip like this," Frances persisted, in spite of her husband.

Mary managed a smile of gratitude. "Thank you," she said, turning her inquisitive gaze from Joe and shaking her head with resignation. "I do appreciate it, however. You've all been so nice to me."

"But it's quite a trip," Alex warned again. "It's better for you to go on to Nassau."

As they rounded the bend in the road where they could see the dock, Joe was startled by the view of a black-hulled cigarette boat tied close to *Mission*. In a moment, he realized that it indeed was the same boat he had seen at Man-O-War, the one named *Blaster,* with the two men, which had come up alongside. Then he was further startled to see the one with long black hair jump off of *Mission* onto the pier.

"Did you ever know those people?" he asked Alex.

"I don't think so," Alex said. "Did I see somebody on our boat?"

"Looked like it to me," Mary said.

They quickened their pace. A third man came out of a nearby building and went to a gas pump on the pier. The man who had been on the sailboat was untying one of its lines. Alex broke into a trot, and Joe followed.

"What's going on?" Alex called.

The man dropped the line and turned around. Joe now could see it was the same man he had seen at the restaurant at Man-O-War.

"Boat's blockin' the fuel pumps," the black-haired one answered. "We was about to move your boat."

Joe's first thought was that the bastards were about to tow the sailboat away, just as they had taken his. But he glanced to the right and noted that *Mission* was obstructing the fuel pumps on the dock, and thought for a moment that they had a legitimate excuse. If there was just some way to know if they were the same sorry lot.

Alex let them know he didn't appreciate them messing with his boat. They let him know that he didn't own the pier and that he was lucky that they hadn't just cast it off and let it float out with the goddamn tide. With no apologies to the two, Alex supervised the relocation of *Mission* so that the cigarette boat could come alongside the pier near the gas pumps. The two ladies had joined Joe by that time, and they stood watching the black-haired man pass the gas hose down to his partner, who began to fill the tank.

"They've been on our boat," Joe whispered to Mary and Frances. "Maybe you all need to go see if anything's missing."

While the gassing up was in progress, Alex put on a friendly face and went over to talk to the men. Joe followed.

"When is the ferry to Marsh Harbour due?" Alex asked the marina attendant, after passing the time of day.

"Be here in about an hour, if it's running," the man replied, not even bothering to look up.

"Anybody know where the binoculars are?" It was Frances calling from the cockpit. Alex looked back at her and shook his head. Joe glanced at the man with long blond hair, who looked up when he heard Frances, but then looked down and started to board the speedboat.

Joe took a deep breath, swallowed hard, and walked over to the man. "I saw you aboard our boat," he said, placing himself between this smaller man and the cigarette boat, more or less cornering him, keeping him from boarding.

100

"Just lookin'," the man replied in a surly tone, trying to step around Joe.

Joe blocked his way, deciding to confront him. "Like you were looking over my boat at Great Sale Cay two months ago, I suppose."

The man's face jerked in a shocked twitch. "Don't know what you're talking about," he said.

Then Joe noticed a suspicious bulge under the man's jacket. There was no doubt in his mind that the bulge was the missing binoculars, and his temper began to build.

"What's under your jacket, there, friend?" he asked, trying to keep his voice even.

The man's gaze shifted away from Joe, then focused back on him. "Ain't none of your damn business," he said, a slight sneer on his lips.

Joe stared at him. "It looks a lot like binoculars hanging around your neck," he challenged.

The man's sneer deepened. "What if it is?"

"Then you wouldn't mind letting me see them."

"Aw, screw you, asshole."

Joe's rage flared. With a quick thrust, he reached inside the man's jacket, getting his hand on the object, jerking it out, and grabbed the man's wrist with his other hand before the man could pull away. The binoculars hung from the leather strap that was around the man's neck.

"Let go, sombitch!" the man yelled, pulling backward, Joe jerked hard, and the strap broke, making the man stagger backward. He put his hand to his neck, then looked at his fingers to see if there was blood. The man pumping gas stood up, the hose dripping in his hand.

Joe moved back a couple of steps and held the binoculars up to see the markings. "Your glasses? I see. Then tell me the brand name on them," he said, keeping a wary eye on the thief. Long Hair looked around as he backed away, looking for something to use as a weapon. A piece of two-by-four lay close by. He took it up and moved toward Joe. Waiting for the right moment, Joe planned to dodge his first swing of the board and then kick him in the groin.

"No sailboat sombitch is—" His sentence was cut short by the crack of a pistol shot.

"Stop it!" Frances yelled, standing on the bow of *Mission*, waving Alex's pistol about. The man froze. More or less accidentally, she pulled the trigger again, and the bullet splintered a plank of the wooden pier near his feet.

"Frances!" Alex said.

Joe looked at Long Hair, who now was wide-eyed. "If you knew what I know about her, you'd put that board down in a hurry," he advised.

"Dick! Hold it!" the man at the wheel of the cigarette boat yelled, and jumped onto the dock and walked over, making calming gestures with his hands, glancing at Frances and then at Joe. "Here, now, mister, my man here is a little simple-minded. You know what I mean?"

"A thief, anyway," Joe said.

"You rag-sail bastard," Long Hair snarled.

"Get over there and shut up!" the other man ordered, pointing at the cigarette boat and then raising his fist. Long Hair snorted, gave another nasty look at Joe, but did as he was told.

"Don't take offense, mister," the boss said. "He's just not right in the head, you know? I apologize for him. Please, take your binoculars and just forget about him, okay?"

Joe glanced back at Alex, who was standing on deck.

Alex gestured for him to come on. "Let's go quick before some policeman shows up."

Joe turned his attention to Mary, who stood on the pier beside *Mission*, watching, tears in her eyes. He walked back to her and took her hand. As he did, he saw the men jump back aboard the speedboat.

"You'd fuck up everything if I let you," Joe heard him berating Long Hair in low tones.

"Maybe you'd better come on aboard," Joe said to Mary. She paused uncertainly, and then nodded.

"Cast us off, Joe," Alex said, hurrying into the cockpit and starting the engine.

"I thought I was going to take a ferry from here," Mary stammered. She looked to Frances, who still had the gun in her hands. Frances met Mary's gaze, nodded, and then looked down at the pistol as if she hadn't realized it was there. She lowered her hand.

"We can't leave you here, now, dear," she said.

Mary glanced at Alex and then Joe. Joe told her that he didn't think much of the prospect of leaving her on the Coopers Town dock with those characters.

Mary hesitated, looking with frustration at the phone booth so close and yet so far away. Then she looked out at the black boat and its crew. "What do I do now?"

"Just whatever," Alex said. "We're leaving now. Quick."

It was clear to Joe that Alex wasn't thinking about Mary's safety, but was concerned about his stash in the forward locker.

"Better come on," Joe said. She did as she was told, and Joe went to work releasing lines from the pier, throwing them on deck. As he cast off the bowline last and jumped aboard, he kept an eye on *Blaster*, noting that Long Hair was still leering at him. From the look, it was clear that this man wanted trouble if they ever met again. Then he noticed the third man, the man who sold fuel, and had to smile. He was still standing motionless on the dock, the dripping nozzle in his hand and his mouth agape.

"I should have shot those two," Frances said, looking aft as they motored away.

"Well, you nearly got that guy," Alex said. "Did you know that bullet hit the pier about three feet from him? Jesus, Frances! Suppose you'd really shot him."

"If I'd meant to shoot him," she said, wagging her head from side to side, "I wouldn't have missed."

"It was my fault," Joe apologized. "I got mad, and that's always a mistake."

"Well, that was an impressive bit of, uh, re-confiscating you did back there, old man," Alex said. "I don't know that I like your technique, but it was effective, anyway."

"A scary thing!" Mary replied. "You could have been hurt."

"I guess so," he admitted. "I just couldn't stand the idea of that punk stealing from us."

"I was so worried for you," Mary said with a shiver, reaching over and putting her hand on his, then removing it self-consciously.

He made a modest shrug, then shuddered, the full impact of what might have happened beginning to hit him. "Frances was the real hero," he said. You never knew what to expect from her, he realized, and you sure wanted to stay on her good side.

"I just hope they don't bother us anymore," Frances said. "That was a boatload of thugs if I ever saw one."

"Low-life bastards," Alex said. "Drug runners or pirates. Probably both."

All four of them looked aft, watching the speedboat disappearing off to the northwest.

"I suspect that was not my first run-in with that bunch," Joe said. He told them about his own boat being hijacked that night at Great Sale, how he hadn't been able to see well enough to identify the boat or its crew, but how he had recalled the peculiar *throb, throb* engine sound that this cigarette boat was also making.

"We've got to go to the police, Alex," Frances exclaimed. "We need to call the coast guard and the navy and the marines and whoever." She started to go to the radio below.

"Hang on, Frances dear," Alex said. "We can't have any police."

Because you can't risk the police finding out about whatever you've got stashed in that forward locker, Joe thought.

"And why not?" Frances argued. "Why is it you always want us to be in danger and never get any help? I just don't understand you, Alex. You're just always doing something, and we can't have any help."

"Well for one thing, you're not going to find police much here in the Abacos, not in any hurry. Isn't that right, Joe?"

Joe shook his head. "I'm afraid so. Law enforcement is very scarce out here in the islands." *And where we're headed,* he didn't say aloud, *is an area unpopulated, remote and isolated.* If there was to be more trouble, they'd just have to handle it.

"Oh, so you're going to agree with my husband, are you?" Frances snapped. "You men always think you know everything." She raised her eyebrow and regarded Joe. "I don't like men who seek revenge. It just brings more violence."

"It's a wonder you didn't strangle that character when you had him by the throat," Alex chuckled. "If they stole your boat, no doubt you'd want revenge."

Joe nodded. A thousand times since it happened, he had imagined all the ways he could murder the men who had done it. "But that engine sound is no proof, so I can't be sure they're the right ones. In any case, we'd better keep a sharp eye out for them." He glanced at Alex. "Outside the restaurant at Man-O-War, I heard them talking about finding something aboard some boat. Some hidden cargo or something." He let the idea hang in the air, watching Alex's reaction.

Alex put on his casual don't-worry-about-a-thing look. "Well, maybe they'll go bother somebody else then," he said, "somebody that might have this cargo you're talking about."

Joe marveled at Alex's feigned innocence and then turned to Mary. "Well, so far things haven't gone as planned, have they?" he said.

She put her hands up on both sides of her face. "I didn't know what I was supposed to do," she said. "I should have gotten off the boat back there, I guess."

"That was not a good moment to be making decisions," Joe said. "I think you made the right one."

"Just sit tight, kiddo," Alex replied. "We'll work something out."

As they approached the first turn, Joe took up navigating, pointed out a distant marker to the west, and Alex steered for it. When the course was established, they checked the apparent wind and decided it wasn't worth putting out any sail. Joe volunteered to take the watch, allowing Alex and Frances to go below for some rest. Alex took the pistol, which had been returned to its leather holster, and carried it below. Mary stayed on deck, looking back at the dock and the phone booth diminishing to a speck behind them.

"Where do we go next?" she asked.

Joe pointed to their location on the chart. "No more little towns"—he showed her—"unless we go out of the way to get to one." They both stared at the chart for a while, but didn't say anything, enduring a kind of awkward silence. She turned around and peered ahead while Joe steered west.

"You know," she said, "I can't imagine how my husband would have reacted back there. It would have been such an unusual situation from anything we ever experienced."

"Oh, I'm sure he would have done what was expected of him," Joe replied.

"Earnest was such a steady individual, shoulder-to-the-harness type, almost never upset by anything. He worked for Prudential as an insurance actuary, and more or less had the right personality for that work." She sighed. "He didn't beat his own calculations for life span."

"I can see you loved him."

She nodded. "Our careers were so different, he an actuary and I an actress. I don't mean that our life together was perfect, though. I had my career and an active social life. Ernie would attend functions with me, dress well, be polite and convivial, and so on, when he preferred to be home with a book, or playing with the children when they were young." She reached in the pocket of her slacks for a tissue and dabbed her eyes. "It's not over yet, I guess," she apologized. "I sometimes think it is, and then this happens." She dabbed her eyes again and sat more erect, as if to push it all away.

"And this vacation in the Bahamas was supposed to be a get-away from it all," Joe guessed, "just like I'd like to get away from my past, too." She met his gaze, and they both smiled.

As the day wore on, a haze developed to the west, transforming into a towering cumulus, and the wind rose, coming from astern. Alex appeared on deck around eleven. They decided to hoist the mainsail and rig a "preventer" on the boom to ward off a jibe in the shifty quartering wind. While the two men performed the job on deck, Mary remained in the cockpit steering.

108

"She's catching on, I see," Alex whispered to Joe, giving her an appraising stare.

Joe nodded. He had begun to notice something of a change in Alex's attitude toward her. "I expect she'll be signing on the first ship out of Charleston," he joked. "She's like a kid with a new toy."

"Aren't we all," Alex laughed. "The difference between the men and the boys are the cost of the toys." He fetched a block and tackle from the lazaretto, gave Joe one end, and they unwound it. Being taller, Joe took the device to the starboard beam. While Alex slacked the mainsheet and pushed the boom over, Joe hooked the upper block to an eye on the boom. Then he reached down, slipped the lower block to a cleat on deck, and then snugged up the line.

"Mary, turn the bow into the wind," Alex called.

Mary swung the wheel to the right, but realized the mistake and swung back to the left before Alex could correct her.

"Okay, steady on that heading," Alex commanded as he came over to the wheel stand and toggled the switch that let out the main, while Joe wound in the outhaul on a winch. The huge sail flapped in the freshening breeze. "Fall off to starboard." Alex gestured to the right for clarity. Mary turned right and the sail billowed. "Now, come on back to course, you sweet thing."

"Two-eight-five," Joe coached.

"I know," Mary said. The boat listed, coming abeam the wind, but settled back and increased speed as they regained the original heading.

"We'll make a crew member of you yet, Mary darling," Alex remarked, giving her a wink and a smile.

At one in the afternoon, they observed the motor yacht *Sea Splendor* approaching from astern. As it overtook them, the man and woman in the cockpit waved, and Alex returned the greeting.

"King Greasy Spoon, to starboard," Alex quipped, still giving them his fake smile.

"They must have stopped off at Bluff House or somewhere," Joe guessed.

"How did *they* get there," Mary asked, "since we couldn't?"

"Shallow draft," Joe explained. "They were able to go over the shoal inside rather than going around Whale Cay."

"I see," Mary said, staring at the yacht.

Joe wondered if she was thinking how much better it would have been if they had offered her a boat ride on *Sea Splendor*, rather than ending up on *Mission*. Such was fate, he thought.

As they watched the yacht cruise on off ahead of them, Frances brought up sandwich makings of cheese and cold cuts. Joe and Alex each had a Heineken. Frances invited her husband to come take a nap, but he refused, saying it was his turn to take the helm.

"Well, just be that way," she snapped and went below. Alex smiled and shook his head.

Following Joe's navigation track, Alex changed course more to the west to round the northern end of Great Abaco Island. The wind had shifted to a steady breeze abeam to port. They removed the preventer from the main boom, unfurled the jib, and sailed on a broad reach. By four, the wind had come up enough so that Alex cut the engine, and still they made seven to eight knots.

Joe decided he could use forty winks himself, and Mary, who had a book with her, volunteered to keep Alex company on deck

"Great!" Alex said. "Let me go pour us a drink, and we can get better acquainted."

After an hour, Joe reappeared on deck and found Alex engaging Mary in jovial conversation. Alex had put away a couple more beers. He steered southwest around the island and then turned up into Great Sale's U-shaped lagoon. Furling the sails, they motored closer to shore, watching the fathometer. Joe took Mary up on the bow to show her how the anchor windlass worked. They dropped the anchor in water eight feet deep, about forty yards off the beach of this uninhabited island. His anger flaring, Joe recalled that they were almost where he had anchored his boat two months before. There was another boat already at anchor, about a hundred or so yards away. As they made their way back to the cockpit, they spotted a couple of swimmers in the water near its stern. Alex took up the binoculars and scanned the far boat.

"The *Terajay* from West Palm Beach," he read from its stern markings.

"Could we take a swim, do you guess?" Mary asked. Joe looked over the side at the clear water, almost white from the sandy bottom reflecting up.

"Absolutely," Alex said. "It would feel mighty good, wouldn't it?"

With no more ado, the three went below to change. Joe put on his trunks and climbed back up the ladder bare-chested, feeling a little self-conscious about being so scantily clad. He had been blessed with an attractive physique as a young man. But now that he was in his middle age and a bit overweight, he was not so well proportioned, and it made him more uncomfortable under scrutiny.

Alex appeared, coming up the ladder, already a bit tipsy, carrying a scotch and soda.

"Is that sweet thing, Mary, up here yet?" he asked, looking around.

Joe shook his head. "Is Frances coming?" he asked.

"Still sleeping," Alex said. Something about the way he spoke caused Joe to remember that first afternoon aboard when Frances was sleeping, possibly drugged by her husband.

"The medicine again?" Joe asked, trying to sound offhanded.

Alex gave him a quick glance and looked away. "Who knows," he said, just the briefest hint of disgust or frustration or disappointment or even conspiracy in his voice. Clad in a brief kind of swimsuit, Alex was robust for a man in his age, Joe noticed, his profuse dark chest hair covering a few wrinkles.

Joe followed him to the stern, and the two of them worked out the pins that held the ladder in its folded position. Once they got it down, Joe dove in and felt the cool, clear water chill and sting his sunburned face. As he came up, he saw Alex climbing down and easing himself into the water.

"Great, isn't it?" he exclaimed.

"Wonderful!" Joe replied. "I didn't know it would feel so good." He dove under again and looked at the hull of *Mission*, its keel six and one-half feet down, three feet from the white, sandy bottom, just enough distance to keep them off the bottom at low tide. Though it loomed as a dark shadow, looking massive from this point of view, he imagined about how tiny it would seem once they were far out at sea. In fact, the idea was not a little unsettling.

112

On the other hand, being here in the Bahamas on a grand sailboat was like being in heaven. How could anything in life be better?

When he came back to the surface, he saw Mary in a rose-colored two-piece suit, leaning over the side, looking at him. Her pale bare shoulders were so smooth and supple, and the bulge of her breasts flowing into the bra of her suit was striking. It was not that she was so beautiful, Joe thought, but that she was so humanly attractive, having an aura of needing to be touched and adored in a way.

"How is it?" she asked, smiling at him. Joe, treading water and staring upward, took her in a moment more before he realized he needed to reply.

"Fabulous!" he said. "Fabulous!" It was the first time in so long that he had really looked at a woman and felt this way. Not since his wife had told him she wanted a divorce—no, longer back than even that. He had let a lot of time go by.

"Come climb down the ladder," Alex interrupted. He was still back near the stern, motioning to her.

She turned away from Joe and made her way aft. Joe swam back there to watch her climb down. She was still well proportioned, he noted, watching her bare legs and feet and well-contoured rear descending the ladder. Then he realized that Alex, who was close by the ladder, was eying Mary, as well—ogling her, in fact.

"Jump off," Alex coaxed. "Don't worry, I'll catch you."

Mary thrust herself backward off the ladder and splashed down beside Alex. As she bobbed back to the surface, he took her by the hand and held her up. She held on to him a moment and then took her hand away, giving a couple of swim kicks to move off from the boat.

"Watch out for sea urchins on the bottom," he warned in a gentle voice.

"Oh, I've heard of them," Mary said, "but I don't think I've ever seen one."

Alex took her by the hand again. "Swim over here. I think I saw one." He was pulling her toward the shore. "If you step on one, the spines will sting. I wouldn't want anything to happen to those cute toes of yours."

Joe watched as Alex guided her through the water and pointed down to a sea urchin, hanging close to her all the time. He did not see that there was anything wrong with the way the older man was "being friendly" to her, but felt it was a bit too familiar. He saw Alex smile at her in the same way that he had smiled at that Bea woman. Mary seemed to be growing a bit uncomfortable as well, and swam back a few strokes, just enough to keep a little more distance. Joe felt a vague sense of competition. He swam toward them, feeling that he needed to protect her or something. Still about ten yards away, he saw Alex go up behind her and take her shoulders in his hands. As he continued his idle conversation, his hands moved up and over toward her breast.

"Here now," Mary said, pulling away and spinning around in the water to face him.

Alex smiled, winked, and blew her a kiss.

"What are you thinking?" Mary said sharply. Incensed, she began swimming away.

Alex noticed that Joe had observed it all, and Joe frowned. "What did you think you were doing?" he said with reproach.

Alex gave him a dismissive look and watched Mary continue her crawl stroke, moving away. "Mary, dear,

114

please…let's go sit on deck, and I'll fix us a drink," he called, but she continued to swim away without reply.

Joe gave the older man another look of disgust and swam off, as well, to avoid letting his temper get the best of him.

Mary had made a turn and was swimming toward the other sailboat, which was anchored about a hundred yards away. Joe decided to follow her, knowing that, as someone who often swam laps for exercise, he could make any distance and could help her if she discovered she could not. He heard Alex call to her again, hinting a sort of indirect but pleading apology, and following them. Joe increased the rhythm of his own crawl to catch up with Mary when he heard Frances calling from the cockpit.

"Alex, come back here, dear. I don't think you can swim that far."

Joe stopped to look back. Alex had stopped swimming, treading water and watching them swim away. Frances called to him again, and he began to labor back. Joe swam on after Mary, realizing that she was swimming toward the other boat, where he could see the heads of two people in the water near its stern. He turned around once more at the sound of Frances encouraging Alex and saw her toss him one of the life buoys from the stern. He had exhausted himself and needed a bit of assistance. Joe watched him struggle to the stern ladder and start up it, with Frances scolding him for overdoing it. Mary had stopped to observe the scene and noted Joe was following her. She continued on toward the other boat, but at a slower pace, using the breaststroke, allowing him to catch up.

"I thought I'd swim over and see where these other people are headed," she said when he reached her. "Maybe they're going to Florida."

"Uh-huh," Joe replied and moved along beside her. So, Alex's advances had upset her, he realized, as well they should have, and she was looking for an escape. When they were about fifty yards away from the other sailboat, the two swimmers, a young man and woman, saw them coming. Joe raised his hand to wave and followed Mary, who was still swimming easily.

"Well, hello," the man called when they were about twenty yards away. "That's a pretty good swim from over there."

Joe nodded and smiled, noting that Mary didn't appear the least bit fatigued. She told them they had a pretty boat, and they nodded thanks.

"Where're you all headed?" Joe asked as the two of them moved closer and began to tread water.

"West Palm," the man said. "How 'bout you?" He looked to be in his late twenties, with a tan, almost swarthy face. The woman was about the same age, with long black hair and a tan face. In the clear greenish-white water, it seemed that maybe she was swimming topless.

"We're trying to make Charleston," Joe said, trying not to be too obvious about his observation of the girl.

"South Carolina?" she said, just the hint of slurring in her words. "Jeez, that's a long way."

"Heard about the storm down south of here?" the guy asked. "I don't know if I'd try that even in that big yacht you've got."

Joe noticed then that he was sort of slack-jawed, too, and guessed they had been drinking or were high on something.

"I was trying to get to Florida myself," Mary mentioned. Joe gave an encouraging nod.

"You were?" the girl said, shaking her long dark hair out of her face.

"Mary came along for a one-day sail," Joe explained as if telling a joke, "and now she's been sort of Shanghaied by circumstances."

Mary took up the story and suggested again that she needed to go to Florida, looking at Joe as she said it. They exchanged glances. "Maybe you, too?" she added.

Joe raised his eyebrows. It was a thought.

"We'll be glad to give you a lift," the guy said. He looked at his partner for agreement. "Not but a good day-and-a-half sail from here."

"I'd be glad to pay," Mary said. "Share in the expenses… for both of us." She glanced at Joe again for agreement. He was torn.

"No need for that," the guy said. "I'm Jason. This is Theresa."

Joe gave his and Mary's names and offered a hand to Jason. As he swam closer to do so, he noticed that Jason was nude. Then he realized that Theresa was not only topless, but bottomless as well.

"Y'all wanna come aboard and we'll fix you something cool?" Jason said, moving toward their stern ladder. "Or how 'bout you a little pot?"

"Uh, well…" Joe stammered just as Jason pulled himself up a step, his naked rear showing to be just as tan as the rest of his body. He heard Mary gasp.

"Oh," Jason said, lowering himself back in the water. "We're bare-boaters." He laughed. "Just part of the fun, you know." He glanced at Theresa with a grin and climbed up out of the water again. "Let's have that drink," he said, going on up and turning to face them. Theresa motioned to them to climb aboard.

"I think we'd better get back," Mary stammered, looking at Joe. "Don't you think?"

Joe nodded. "The Smiths will be missing us. I think we'd better not stay. Thanks, though." Mary already was more or less treading backward, turning her head toward Theresa and away from Jason, who stood on deck lighting up a reefer, facing them in all his suntanned glory.

"Well, we're leaving first thing in the morning for West Palm," Jason said. "Call us on channel sixteen if you want a ride."

Offering their thanks, Joe and Mary swam back toward *Mission*, stopping to wave back once more. Joe did appreciate the final view of Theresa, hanging off the ladder, waving to them. One had to say, he thought, that if that pair wanted to bare-boat, they did have the physiques for it.

"Do you think he was mocking us or something?" Mary asked after they had swum out of earshot. "Standing up there on deck in full view like that? Showing off because we're older?"

"Just a spoiled rich kid," Joe said, "given everything he ever wanted and having never been disciplined much."

"Like Alex."

118

Joe nodded. "Hard to know which is worse."

"Well, at least Alex doesn't…What did they call it? Bare-boat?" Mary said, and then she laughed.

"And get doped up," Joe laughed with her. The image crossed his mind of Mary and himself aboard *Terajay,* merrily bare-boating along with them and smoking pot all the way to Florida. It wasn't unexciting.

"I thought they must have been on something," she agreed. Then she sighed. "You know, ever since Earnest died, I've been looking for a strong man, a good character, I mean." She paused in her breaststroke and shook her head. "Earnest was strong, well, not physically but in personality, firm in his moral beliefs." She glanced at Joe and then moved on a few strokes. "Not long after he died, his younger brother, Wade, well… came on to me. Sort of the way Alex did today." She made a painful expression. "I just don't understand why men would act that way. Well, in Wade's case, he works for the CIA and is some kind of secret agent, no telling what he…" She stopped again and looked at Joe. "I feel safe around you, you know. Oh, I don't mean that the way it may have sounded. I just mean that you seem trustworthy, I think. I feel like I can count on you. I mean, can't I?"

Joe met her gaze, nodding, and they stared at one another until she turned away and began to swim again. He watched her move away, considering what she'd said.

"A good man is hard to find," he said, following along behind her. "Hadn't Flannery O'Connor taught you that by now?"

Mary paused and looked back for a moment. "You don't know much about yourself, do you?" she said, more a statement than a question.

"Ask my ex-wife," he replied. But the backhanded compliment did register with him, and he felt a bit elated.

"I don't need her opinion," Mary said. "Say, could we swim over to the beach for a few minutes?"

"Sure," Joe answered. They swam diagonally away from *Terajay* toward a point on the sandy beach midway between the two boats. When Mary's feet touched bottom, she turned and looked back at him.

"I suppose I could stand putting up with that Jason and Theresa if it meant getting to Florida," she said. "How about you?"

Joe pondered the question, gazing at *Mission* lolling at anchor, its gold leaf markings brilliant in the sunlight. Who would suspect that the boat had secret cargo aboard, or that there could be anything amiss aboard such a pristine sailboat?

"No, I'm serious," Mary said, calling the question.

"I don't know," he replied. "I've signed on with the Smiths, so to speak."

Mary treaded water, looking at him. "Does Alex have some control over you that I don't know about?" she asked.

Joe glanced at her, a bit startled at the directness of the question. "Well, I signed on with him," he said again, realizing that he had needed the job so badly that he hadn't felt that he had any choice in the matter.

Mary swam toward shore and began wading out. Joe followed, having a good opportunity to see her up close, water droplets shining on her smooth, delicate white skin. The swimming had firmed her muscles just enough, not to mention her breasts, so ample beneath the almost-transparent suit top. Despite the difference in age, she might give that Theresa some real competition in the nude bathing category.

"So you have to do what he says?" she asked. She, too, was regarding him, and he felt very self-conscious, turning to look off at *Mission* again.

"I agreed to help them sail up to Charleston, and I don't know how I can get out of it at this point."

She continued to stare at him with a look that he didn't quite understand, a concern or something. Then she sighed and waded in. Joe followed, and they swam on toward *Mission*.

"Lord, you're a loyal guy," she said when he caught up. He regarded her a moment before following along. She seemed to want him to go to with her, even if it meant going with that Jason and Theresa.

"Well, there's Frances to think about," he explained. "She's kind of trapped in the deal, too. So if I abandon Alex, I'd also be leaving her in the lurch, and I guess I just can't do that—not to either of them." As he said it, he wondered if she was thinking about what her Earnest, in these circumstances, might have done.

"I see," Mary said, and they swam on without another word.

As they climbed up the ladder on the stern, Alex and Frances greeted them from the cockpit.

"Just in time to splice the main brace," Alex said, holding up his umpteenth glass of scotch. "What could I fix you, Mary? I know what that ole boy with you wants."

Mary said a Coke would do, smiling as if nothing had ever been amiss.

"Some of that Dewar's would suit me," Joe said, pulling up the swim ladder and securing it. He and Mary went below to change. Joe waited for her to clear out of the head before he went in and took a quick shower. Afterward, he put on fresh Bermudas and polo shirt and went topside.

"Quite a pair you met, I suppose," Alex said, grinning. "Bare-boaters, I observed." He waved his hand at the binoculars, and Joe realized that he must have been watching them. Well, Alex must have realized that he had a real concern after the way he had acted with Mary.

"I was afraid you might have jumped ship," he added, suggesting a question while offering an apology.

"Might have," Joe said. Then he picked up the glass of scotch and soda, with real ice, that Alex had fixed him. "Here's to sailing," he toasted and drained half the glass.

Mary soon came out of her cabin and joined Frances in the galley. They emerged with a tray of cheese and crackers, coming to sit with the men. The conversation could not have been more cordial and polite, the afternoon's events swept away by everyone's desire to just move on.

Mary and Frances made their way out on deck and went forward of the mast to see the sunset. From Mary's conversation and her intimate demeanor toward her hostess, it must have been clear to Frances, Joe decided, that Mary was innocent of any wrongdoing with Alex.

"Pretty cute, aren't they?" Alex commented to Joe, appearing at his side with two fresh scotch and sodas, motioning with his head toward the two ladies sitting together on the deck, watching the sun.

Joe sighed, holding in his renewed irritation with his host. "I suppose so."

Alex thrust one of the glasses in Joe's hand and held his own glass up in toast. "To the ladies," he slurred. "We can't do with them, and we can't do without them."

As if there were no cares in the world, they sipped on their drinks while watching the powder blue haze-lit sky, striped by ribbons of white cloud, the lagoon's waters more light green than the newest leaves of spring, all set off by the reddest, reddest blood-red sun slipping into the green sea to the west. When the last crimson rim dipped below the horizon, Alex stood up, found the switch for the anchor light atop the mast. then invited Joe to go get yet another refill on the scotch.

When the ladies returned, the four of them sat in the cockpit, discussing nothing much in particular, avoiding any more serious discussions. The full moon loomed low on the eastern horizon, just over the island, seeming huge in the refraction of its golden yellow rays. A warm wind stirred, swinging *Mission* around on its anchor so that the moonlight flowed under the bimini and reflected off the compass binnacle. The warm wind rose, and the moonlight bathed them in the serene comfort of Bahamian night. Even so, Joe remained edgy, looking out at the pass, half expecting the cigarette boat to show up, sneaking in as it had two months ago. He glanced at Alex's pistol hanging in its holster, glad to have it handy just in case.

"I think we ought to eat the steaks tonight," Frances said.

It had been an age since Joe had steak, and mention of it made his mouth water.

"Great," her husband agreed. "May be our last chance to use the grill."

In the sweetest voice possible, Frances asked Mary if she would help her prepare supper. Without hesitation, Mary stood up to follow her below, and with a most cheerful and pleasant expression declared she was ready to assist in any way.

Despite some ever-stiffening breeze, Alex managed to light the butane grill on the stern.

In short order, the four of them were feasting on T-bones at the oval table in the salon in as much luxury as yachting could afford. Frances offered a blessing and added a short prayer for pleasant happiness. Mary smiled and said she couldn't imagine being with nicer people.

"This is about as good as it gets," Alex observed, sawing the last morsel off his T-bone. "It may not be quite so easy tomorrow night when we're at sea."

Mary took a swallow of water, wiped her mouth with her napkin, and gave Alex a serious look. "Do people always anchor here before going back to Florida?" she asked, the first time since afternoon that she had addressed him directly.

"Sailboats usually do," Alex replied. "And it's a good stopover, too, for anybody going to the Abaco."

"Are you planning to go straight on to Charleston?" she asked.

"Undoubtedly," Alex said. "It's absolutely necessary." Joe was watching Mary, trying to determine how she felt about going or staying.

"We could see if that other boat is headed for Florida," Frances suggested, "if you want to see if they'll let you go with them."

"Oh, they already offered," Mary replied.

Alex sat up straight and frowned, glancing at Joe.

"They offered," Joe confirmed without explanation.

Alex looked worried. "To take Mary?" he asked. It sounded as if he was concerned that Joe might be included in the offer.

"Mary should go," Joe added. But when he said it, she stared at him as if she had been offended somehow, and he pondered it, a bit confused.

"Or you can stay with us," Alex said.

"How long will it take to get to Charleston from here?" Mary asked.

"Two and a half days, maybe three, depending on the weather," Alex said. "That reminds me, we'd better check the forecast again." He slid out of the bench seat, and went over to the chart table, turned on the VHF. There was a weak but intelligible signal on a weather channel. They sat silently, listening to the computer voice give the numbers. The broadcast confirmed that a tropical depression, indeed, had formed and was moving toward Puerto Rico and could turn north.

"A tropical depression?" Mary asked. "Isn't that a hurricane or something?"

Alex grimaced. "Not yet," he said. Then he shut off the radio, and stood up to go up the ladder. He paused and addressed Mary. "You let me know first thing in the morning about whether you want to leave or not. That's going to be the last chance for you to decide." He gave her a long, serious look and then turned toward the others at the table with a smile. "Everybody better get a good night's sleep."

"I think I'll sleep in the cockpit," Joe said, "just, uh, in case."

Alex nodded. "Probably not a bad idea."

A little later, Joe lay in the cockpit undisturbed except for an occasional *clank* as *Mission* tugged against her anchor. He heard Mary moving from the head to the other forward cabin and climbing into a bunk, and he wondered again about how she had seemed offended when he suggested she go on *Terajay*. He wondered if she was packing her suitcases or just getting something out of them. Would she leave them in the morning if she were given the chance? And shouldn't she, after all?

But he realized he would miss her. And it would have been interesting to see how she handled being at sea. What seemed most attractive was that she had more than just a little sense of adventure in her. Well, if she did stay with them, he'd see how she would respond if...no, when anything went wrong. There would be unexpected problems from time to time; you could count on it at sea. Why should she risk subjecting herself to that?

Chapter Six

It was a minor annoyance that kept him in semi-consciousness. Then at one point, he thought he heard something else, a deep drone off in the distance, its Doppler sound changing pitch as it passed on. He sat upright, realizing it was the roar and *throb, throb* of the cigarette boat. He had a vision of the long, sleek black hull racing across the waters of the Bahamas, out for trouble in the middle of the night—possibly even looking for them? Would those men come into the lagoon and try to repeat what they had done to him two months ago? His pulse racing, he got up from the cockpit seat and took the pistol out of its holder. If they came, even if they did have an automatic weapon, he would take them on.

But when it passed on by and the sound faded, he lay back, wondering what other unsuspecting boater they soon might be menacing. Trying to relax, he slept lightly, fitfully, listening and thus more irritated by the clank of the anchor chain, until fatigue overcame concern.

In the light of morning, Joe awoke to the sound of rustling in the galley and smelled coffee brewing, and spied Alex on his way toward the chart table. They greeted one another, and Alex tuned the radio to the weather channel. The computer voice had been replaced by a human giving an announcement about what was now a full-fledged tropical storm, located sixty miles north of Puerto Rico, now with winds in excess of forty knots, and which might become more organized and strengthen. Its projected track would take it into the Bahamas and then across northern Florida. The storm was moving northwest at nine knots. While listening, Alex searched through the charts and found a large-scale one of the Atlantic. Joe looked over his shoulder to get a visual idea of the storm track.

"Doesn't sound good for the Bahamas," he ventured.

"Nor for Florida," Alex said. "Looks to me like we've got a couple of days to get away from it," he added.

"What do you think?" Joe asked. "Should we go on to Fort Lauderdale or West Palm or somewhere?"

Alex shook his head. "Better to head north. Get on up the East Coast, since we've got a couple of days. How far did we say Charleston was? Three days? I'd much rather take my boat there than to Florida." He stood up, a sign of finality to his decision. "I think the coffee's ready."

Joe stared at Alex's back as the older man walked around to the galley. There was something more he was not telling about his reasons for going on to Charleston, Joe sensed, and he figured it had to do with the boxes in the forward locker. He decided that this was the time to find out. He followed Alex around to the galley and joined in fixing their coffee.

"Did you hear the engine sound during the night?" Joe asked. "It sounded like that damn cigarette boat from Coopers Town."

Alex looked up, startled. "No. Are you sure?"

Joe nodded. "I'm positive. What do you think they're up to?"

Alex looked away, but his concern was evident in his expression. It was time to confront the issue.

"Could it have anything to do with those boxes in the forward locker?"

Alex gave him a quick surprised glance and then looked away. "How did you know about them?"

Joe shrugged. "I awoke and saw when the men brought them on board that night." He leaned closer. "Now, look, Alex. I need to know what's going on here. What's in those boxes?"

Alex frowned, shut his eyes for a moment, and then sighed. "Money," he replied, almost whispering. "It's my money, some I had on deposit in the bank here in the Bahamas."

"You mean, in cash?"

Alex looked up at him, weighing his answer. "That's right," he went on. "I need it for a business transaction."

"Oh, for God's sake!" Joe said as he began to realize what Frances had meant that time she mentioned "insider trading."

"It's two million dollars," Alex said, "in hundred-dollar bills. I have to take it to somebody in Charleston."

"Why cash?" Joe pressed. "Isn't that illegal, to sneak in cash?"

"It's my fucking money," Alex cried. "I can do what I want with it."

Feeling anger and anxiousness, Joe thought about that. The idea of being involved at all was repugnant. And he wasn't sure about its being legal. Why hadn't he challenged Alex about the hidden boxes from the beginning instead of getting this far along? He knew why—it was his own desperate need to get to the States.

"But I didn't count on the bastards in the cigarette boat or whatever you call it," Alex continued. "I'm afraid that they may have been tipped off about the money. I never did trust that damn Bahamian banker. Otherwise, I don't know why they would have risked coming aboard this boat at Coopers Town."

"How would they know?" Joe asked, his anger shifting from Alex, mentally focusing on Long Hair and the oily-smooth companion. Studying Alex's face, he saw for the first time the lines and wrinkles of age—features of stress that would go unnoticed when Alex was in his usual carefree and jovial disposition.

"Maybe one of the men who delivered the money from the bank is in cahoots with them or something," Alex speculated. "That's all I can guess. Maybe they don't know anything, and it's just my imagination." He shook his head. "In any case, I have to go on to Charleston and hope for the best."

"And risk putting all of us all in jeopardy?" Joe was growing incensed. "Just to protect your money? When I signed on with you, I didn't agree to get involved in something illegal."

"I don't think there's anything illegal about it. So you're not abetting a crime or anything by being along."

"Well, so you say, but I'm not so sure," Joe countered. "Anyway, what about that storm that may be coming this way? For the sake of the ladies, don't you think we ought to seek shelter in the closest port?"

"That storm's too far away to predict where it's going. Heading north just puts us farther from it."

"We make six or seven knots while it moves at ten, twenty knots, maybe faster."

Alex shrugged. "It could just as well go into the Gulf, or rake up the Florida coast. I've also got the problem of no insurance until we get north of the Florida-Georgia border."

Joe considered the alternatives, if there were any. Alex believed heading on north, away from the tropical storm, was the safest course. Or was it just blind greed? Would he put them all in jeopardy, even his own loving wife, Frances?

"You can get off and go with that other boat," Alex said, "and take Mary with you." He looked up, pleading with his eyes. "But I told you I need you aboard," he added.

Joe met his gaze, and they exchanged a long look. Joe started to shake his head.

"If you stick with me," Alex said evenly, "and we make it to Charleston okay, I'll give you a hundred thousand dollars."

Joe was shocked to silence.

"I'm serious," Alex said. "It means that much to me."

"I have to think about all this," Joe said, wheeling around and going up the ladder. What would a hundred thousand dollars mean to him? A new boat? A new livelihood? A new life? And all he had to do now was give in, compromise his ethics, possibly abet a crime, and agree to the decision to sail north in the face of a storm?

Mad enough to chew nails, he surveyed their surroundings, noting first the deserted shoreline of the uninhabited island. Too bad all of this hadn't come clear in Coopers Town, he thought. There would have been a lot more and better alternatives. Had he known everything then, he and Mary could have told the Smiths good-bye and taken the next ferry to Marsh Harbour and...

The thought of Mary and himself going somewhere together gave him pause. Affording her his protection and care had become important somehow. Well, he had been brought up believing men were to take care of the weaker sex. And so he had a responsibility to Mary, and to Frances as well, for that matter. But not to Alex?

He peered at the sky. It looked like it was going to be a gorgeous day, not a cloud to be seen. A light breeze rippled the pretty light green lagoon. Who could have a care in the world? And yet, here was this problem about the money. And who could know where the storm would go, after all, or what was the safest course to avoid it? He took in a breath and let out a deep sigh. He had agreed to come on this trip, and his sense of professionalism dictated that he could not get out of it just because the going got rough. But he hadn't understood Alex's true nature. How could such an attractive and personable guy run around with women behind his wife's back and get involved in illegal business deals? Perhaps it was just the result of growing up as a rich kid, having everything you ever wanted. In that sense, maybe Alex was kind of a victim of circumstances in a twisted sort of way, just like everyone else.

"Damn!" he muttered, putting his hands to his eyes to shut out the world for a minute or two. When he looked out again, he knew what he had to do.

"Okay, I'll stay," Joe said, going back down below and finding Alex seated at the table, a worried look on his face. "But we have to let Mary go on the other boat…and Frances, too, if she wants."

Alex brightened up, like a punished child who's been told he now can go outside and play. "You're a prince," he said, smiling.

"But the women have to go on the other boat," Joe reiterated. "No sense in their having to be involved."

"Well, Mary can do as she likes," Alex said. "Maybe it would be best for Frances, too. But I can't imagine her being anywhere but with me." He put out his hand. "Look, Joe, I do appreciate you agreeing to stick with me on this." He grabbed Joe's hand and shook it. "What a great friend you are."

"Or what a great fool," Joe said, taking his hand back.

"I'll make my offer good, my friend," Alex said. "I promise."

Joe shook his head. "Let's just hope we come out of this okay."

Now all they had to do was tell the women what had been decided.

"Go on another boat? You have to be joking!" Frances exclaimed. "No way, José. This boat's going to Florida, not Charleston, and you with it, Alex. What have you and this Jonah cooked up anyway? There's a storm out there, dear, and we need to get to shore pronto."

"I just have to get to Charleston, Frances. Can't you understand that?"

"I don't understand anything anymore, Alex. I don't understand why you keep working when you ought to be retired. I don't know why you have to make 'deals' of all things. And now you've made one that causes us trouble. It just doesn't make any sense. And now you want us to die on this sailboat going across the ocean with a storm coming. And everybody thinks *I'm* the one off my rocker? Ha!"

In spite of her seriousness, Joe had to smile, and he was glad Mary appeared from her cabin so as to distract them from noticing his reaction. They ceased the argument to greet her and offer coffee. When she had a cup, they all sat down at the table to see what Mary had on her mind.

"I wonder if it's too late for me to decide to stay with you all," she asked.

Joe took in a deep, audible breath.

"I've been thinking," she went on, glancing at Joe. "It's not right for me to leave you before getting to Charleston. Joe would have to stand watch by himself and everything. And besides, you all just need a fourth person on board."

There was a moment of surprised pause.

"What a dear girl you are," Frances said, reaching over and patting her hand. "But we're not going to Charleston after all." She looked at her husband, "are we, Alex?"

He wiped his hand across his eyes and down his face. "Joe thinks you two ladies should go on to Florida with the other boat," he said.

Joe nodded. "I do," he said, looking at Mary. "It's the best thing."

134

"What? And let you two go on to Charleston by yourselves?" Frances exclaimed, slamming her cup down on the table hard enough to slosh coffee all over. "Don't be silly." She slid off the seat and went to the galley for paper towels. "No, we're all going to West Palm. Tomorrow morning we'll be at the dock, making plane reservations, going home, and getting away from that old storm and this insane sailing business." She sat back down, wiped up the spilled coffee, and tossed the paper towels across to the sink, punctuating her certainty.

"West Palm is probably where the storm's headed," Alex pleaded. "If we take the boat there, we'll just be leaving it right where it will be destroyed. You don't want that, do you, dear?"

"Listen, Alex," Frances said, leveling her eyes at him. "I'd a whole lot rather see this boat on the bottom of the harbor instead of on the bottom of the ocean." She glanced at Joe. "Well, tell us what you think, Joe, dear. What's your idea?"

Joe hesitated, glanced at Mary, and then looked away for a moment, considering the alternatives. "The best thing would be for you and Mary to go on to West Palm with the others," he said. "Then let Alex and me take the boat on north, out of harm's way." As he spoke, he thought it was just as foolish as it sounded. But there it was.

"I think by going to Charleston, we'll avoid the storm," Alex said.

"How do you know where it's going?" Mary asked. "They have just as many hurricanes in the Atlantic as they do in the Gulf."

"Well, not quite as many," Alex said. "Besides, it very early in the season. This thing will dissipate soon, anyway."

Joe started to challenge that, but decided there was not enough evidence one way or the other.

"But you don't know that, Alex," Frances replied. "I just want to go home!"

He sighed. "You and Mary need to get ready to go to the other boat," he said. With a kind of desperate finality, he stood up and went over to the radio to call *Terajay*.

Mary looked at Joe, giving him a long, considered stare. He looked back, trying to read her thoughts, but couldn't decipher them. She then looked at Frances a moment before turning to Alex.

"I'm going to stay with you, if it's okay," she said.

Alex paused, looked back at her, and put the radio mike down.

"Wonderful!" he said, glancing at Frances.

"Mary, you don't know everything about this," Joe said. His protective feelings for her grew very strong. "I think you should go on."

Mary gave him a very serious, but tender look. "I'm staying if you are," she said. She looked at him for a long moment and then turned to Frances. There was a silent exchange only understood by the two of them.

"Well, all right, Alex," Frances said. "You win. We fools will go to our graves with you trying to get to Charleston for some insane and ignoble reason that someone as self-centered and selfish as you can have. I don't know why I married you in the first place. People say I married you for your money. Well, I did! So there! Just one thing after the other. Lord knows, we have to go traipsing around in this old boat and have almost no time at home, and I just don't know why I didn't marry some old, dull actuary like Mary did and have a nice, quiet, dull life so I have to go into acting in order to get some excitement. I'm sorry, dear, I don't mean to be insulting, but the truth hurts sometimes, and anyway, you didn't marry some rich playboy like I did and have to pay for it all your life, and don't you smirk at me, Joe—Jonah! We wouldn't be having all this trouble if you weren't here. But anyway, here you are, and here we are, and I just don't know—"

She was interrupted by Alex, who had come over to sit by her and embrace her. "Shhh, shhh," he whispered to her. "It's okay." He reached over and gave her a kiss on the cheek. "It's all right." For an instant, she seemed to melt in his arms and be calmed. Then with a jerk, she pulled away from him, pushed past, and stood up.

"Don't you treat me that way, Alex!" she shouted, grabbing up the nearest thing, which happened to be a spoon, and throwing it at him. It struck him on the cheek and fell to the table. He tensed for a moment, then shook his head and looked away. Frances put her face in her hands and wept.

"Aw, Fran," Alex said, reaching over for her hand. But she pulled away, ran to her stateroom, and slammed the door. Mary and Joe sat in stunned silence.

"Well, now that that's settled," Alex said in a calm voice, "I guess we'd better prepare to get underway."

He and Joe looked at one another, and then at Mary. Mary's mouth was hanging open, still in surprise.

"Don't worry," Alex said. "She'll come around."

Mary stood up and began clearing the table. From his seat, Joe passed dishes to her in the galley. He wondered what was going through her mind. Why would she insist upon going on with them? He felt the need to urge her to leave, but he was still uncertain about the safest route away from there. If he was incapable of making any decisions about that, then he didn't want to influence her own judgment. He did realize that he cared, though. It occurred to him that perhaps Alex's flirtations with Mary had heightened his own attraction to her. Then he became aware of the deep-throated putting sound of a diesel engine, coming closer.

Alex squeezed by and went up the ladder. "Looks like *Terajay* is coming over to see who's going with them," he said.

Joe and Mary followed him up topside, just in time to see the thirty-five-foot sloop back its engine and drift over close to port. Frances, also attracted by the sound, came up into the cockpit, her makeup refreshed to hide any sign of her former outburst.

"Morning," Jason, this time clad in swim suit, called. "Have you heard the latest about the storm?"

"Sounds like it's heading into the lower Bahamas," Alex replied. "I expect it'll shift to the west at some point." Joe thought that sure was wishful thinking.

"Well, my plan is to go on to West Palm and duck back in an inland cove somewhere off the Intracoastal," the man said. "We should be there tomorrow morning. What about the lady who wanted to go with us? I guess you're going on to Florida now yourselves."

"Looks like everyone's going to stay on board," Alex said. "We're going on north."

"Really?" the man exclaimed. "And not just straight across to Florida?" He shook his head. "You're mighty brave."

138

Listening to the conversation, it occurred to Joe that in a thirty-five-footer, maybe the quicker trip over to the mainland would be not just the best course of action, but the only one. Even though *Mission* was more than twenty feet longer and a whole lot better equipped than that boat, going straight to Florida just might be the better thing for them to do as well. But the decision was made.

"You could go, Mary," he said, "and everybody will understand." As he stated the obvious, he could not comprehend why she was being so obstinate. Mary was regarding Joe in a way that he was not sure how to interpret.

"And go back home to what?" she said.

Joe gave her a smile and a gesture of a helpless, "I don't know," feeling that he was unqualified to advise anybody. Mary took in a deep breath, her hands gripping the railing, wringing it. The other boat was drifting away.

Alex gave Mary a silent stare and shrugged. "It's up to you," he said.

She glanced at Joe again for an instant. He met her gaze, and she nodded.

Frances reached over and embraced her. "Oh, Mary!" she said, "I'm glad to have your company. These old men act so...like *men*. I need you to...keep things balanced, or whatever." While she held the younger woman, she looked at Alex, daring him to disagree. Alex smiled and gave a thumbs-up gesture. He looked back at the man on the other boat.

"Have a good sail," he called, giving a dismissing wave.

"Good luck!" Jason waved back and shoved his engine throttle forward. The four of them watched and waved as *Terajay* turned west and headed off.

"Well, okay, then," Alex said, sounding cheery and off-handed. Giving Joe a "well, here we are" look, he cranked the engine and asked him to bring the anchor in.

Heading for the open waters behind *Terajay*, they came through the pass and were surprised to see *Blaster* a hundred yards up the shoreline, beached in the sand. The engine cover appeared to be open, and someone was leaning over it.

"Isn't that the boat from Coopers Town?" Mary asked.

"Oh, the one with those awful men?" Frances added.

"Yeah," Joe said. As they passed, the engine noise from the two sailboats made the man with the wrench in his hand turn and look.

"Looks like they've got engine problems," Alex said.

"After running around all night, they must have blown a gasket or something," Joe speculated. "Couldn't happen to a nicer bunch." He was able to make out the expression on Long Hair's face, an ugly, ominous look. "Bad luck for them, good luck for us, I think." He glanced at Mary, wondering again if she had made the right choice.

Following the other sailboat motoring out of Great Sale Lagoon and moving into the expanse of greenish-blue water, they put out the mainsail and were on the way.

"Let's follow *Terajay* a while before we turn north," Alex said, "in case the men on the cigarette boat are watching."

140

Joe nodded. "Good idea."

Mary came over and sat down beside him while the island and the cigarette boat slipped away behind them. The whole idea of where they were headed and what they were doing was somehow disgusting, enough to make him feel sick. And here was poor Mary being dragged into the whole mess more by accident than anything. And here he was not telling her the whole story about what was happening. And here they were about to sail across the ocean with a possible hurricane on its way.

"I'm so sorry," he whispered to her. Mary glanced at him and then took his hand.

"There was nothing you could do," she whispered back. "And, anyway, I'm glad to be with you."

For the first hour, they all stayed in the cockpit, both sailing and running the engine, sparing a few words of nervous conversation. Everyone took more-than-occasional glances aft, sharing Alex's concern about "the pirates," as Frances had dubbed them. They soon passed *Terajay*, but continued on west until they were certain that even the top of their sails were not visible to *Blaster*, hopefully still stranded with motor trouble on the beach at Great Sale Cay.

Then Joe fixed their position by GPS, checking it against his DR track, and plotted a course to a point west of Mantanilla Reef, which would take them to deep ocean at the northwest corner of the Bahamas Bank. They made the turn to starboard. Even though it was a good course for the wind, Alex decided they should lower the sails in order to be less visible, and motor for another hour to put a second horizon between them and the pirates. Off to port, they could see that *Terajay* was heading due west toward West End, on Grand Bahamas Island, or toward Memory Rock, where they would be able cross the channel on the shortest route to Florida.

"One last chance," Joe whispered to Mary, waving his hand at the smaller boat. She gave him a tender, but resolute look and shook her head. He sighed, feeling as if he should have ordered her to go, but realizing that he had neither the power to do that, nor the right, for that matter. He looked at Alex, thinking that, as owner and thus the one in command, Alex had the right to order the women to take the safer boat.

One thing about this man, Joe realized, he would make a decision and act upon it. Whatever else might be said about Alex, this was his strength. Joe wondered if he himself would ever regain that kind of certainty.

After the appointed hour, when *Terajay* had faded off in the haze, Joe and Alex put the main up, and Joe checked again to see that they were on course. It seemed as if a great weight had been lifted from them. Alex relinquished the wheel to him, and went below with Frances.

"You seemed so happy last night," Joe remarked to Mary.

"It was a happy time, wasn't it?"

"Is that why you decided to stay with us?"

"Well, partly that," she replied, pausing a moment, looking at him with an unasked question. "It seemed like the right thing to do."

"I hope so," Joe said. "The rest of this voyage may not be so much fun as last night." He looked off to the southwest to see that the other boats were just in sight on the horizon.

Frances appeared on the steps, coming up from below, looking for a book she had misplaced. "Are you two enjoying yourselves?" she asked, taking a seat and looking out at the clear green waters ahead, broken by a light chop of waves.

"We're quite happy," Mary replied.

Alex climbed up with a cup of coffee in hand, asking if anyone would like some of the fresh pot. Having no takers, he joined the others in the cockpit.

"We were just saying how good a time we had last night," Mary told him.

Alex smiled. He was just going to let the whole thing drop about how he made advances to her. And it seemed that she hadn't let it bother her. Being so attractive and an actress, she probably had brushed off many an advance in her career.

"A little moonlight, a little whiskey," Mary said. "It was a lovely evening."

Joe thought about how the mood of things had changed so quickly following the swim. He reached down and turned on the autopilot.

"Is happiness a state of mind or an activity?" he asked. They all looked at him curiously.

"Is what?" Frances asked.

"When people are happy, is it because they are doing happy, enjoyable things, or are they just inherently happy people?"

"Well, both, wouldn't you think?" Alex responded. "I mean, you have to create happy situations in order to have the chance to enjoy them."

"That's true," Joe said. "But it's not just what we create. I mean, like last night, we had the moonlight, the balmy breeze, steaks on the grill, the liquor. Weren't we just there to enjoy them? And then when it was over, was that the end of it?"

"No," Mary said. "I went to sleep last night thinking how pleasant it all had been. It was the best time I've had since Earnest died. No, there's something that remains from happy times, a kind of residual memory that boosts us up for the future—something we wouldn't have if we hadn't had the experience."

"So happy events more or less charge our batteries, is that it?" Joe asked. "As long as we have a charge of pleasurable, happy things in our memories, then we are in a state of happiness?"

"And so, are you saying that when the charge goes down in our happiness battery, then we're unhappy?" Alex asked.

"What is all this about?" Frances challenged. "Here we are, sailing off into the ocean with pirates, and a storm maybe coming our way, and Alex has this problem about some stock deal, and you're talking about happiness?"

Joe considered that. Yes, there were serious problems maybe as close as the horizon ahead. But the horizon to the north was a sheer dark blue line beneath an azure sky, the few puffy cumulus clouds above mere accents to the beauty of the scene.

"I've never lived a day that there weren't some kind of problems," Alex said. "You just have to deal with them as they come and enjoy life otherwise."

Joe regarded Alex as if for the first time, realizing that it was that attitude that made him such an appealing person in spite of his numerous faults.

"Oh, that's you all right, Alex, sometimes the problem-creator," Frances said, "always dragging me into some kind of trouble."

"And you always go, dear," Alex said, smiling. "And you always end up having a good time."

"That's what you think," she said, putting on a pouting expression, which melted when Alex leaned over and kissed her.

"I guess I'm just trying to get at what's true about who we are in terms of how we think and feel about it," Joe said.

"Or are you saying that how we think and feel about things is what determines who we are?" Mary asked.

"Something like that," Joe agreed. "But it also gets into the question of how events often get shaped by who we are and how we look at them."

"You know, one thing I've learned from being an actress is that whatever happens on the stage is what you create in your acting," Mary mused. "You have to create the character that you're playing, and you also have to create the atmosphere, the environment, the interaction of people and events. In order to make the world of the play real and believable to the audience, the actors have to produce it, make it, create it onstage. And that's the art of theater."

"And maybe also the art of life," Joe went on.

"Are you saying that we make up life?" Frances threw another scornful challenge at him. Joe had to smile. If anyone in the group was capable of making up one's own reality, it had to be Frances.

"Well, let's consider Mary's situation for a minute," he suggested. "Here she was in the beauty salon in Marsh Harbour, having her hair done. And suddenly, here you were, meeting her, entering into her life, convincing her to come go sailing with us and all. So now, here she is aboard the boat, headed for Charleston, maybe in the path of a storm, and a victim of the world you created for her by your insistent invitation."

"Wait a minute!" Mary said. "I'm the one who decided to come along. Don't blame Frances, for heaven's sake!"

"And Mary's had two other chances to leave us," Alex said, shaking his head. "I don't think it's fair to blame Frances."

Joe held up his open palms, looking apologetic. "Oh, well, I didn't mean to blame you, Frances." He backed off, although he believed what he had said.

"Oh, yes you did!" she replied. "Of course, all I was trying to do was something nice for both of you! You've acted so much like a has-been that I was trying to put some zip in your life."

Joe realized that he was supposed to say something about Mary being the zip, and it was kind of forcing the issue in an embarrassing way, but then he realized that, in fact, Mary was becoming the zip in his life...or could...or something.

"I'm sorry," he said. "I suppose I never should have brought it up. I do thank you, Frances, and Alex, for inviting me along. I didn't mean to sound ungrateful for all you've done and are doing." He looked at Mary then, realizing that he may have sounded like his meeting Mary was all a mistake. "I'm very glad you did come along," he told her.

She gave him one of her inscrutable looks. Alex was pondering.

"To go back to my idea about the battery," he said. "The problem with you, Joe, is that your happiness battery's been discharged for so long that it won't even take a new charge, no matter what you do. Isn't that right?"

Joe closed his eyes and nodded with a wry smile. "Maybe so," he said.

146

Frances told him off. "So shut up about all your theories about happiness and whatever. 'Cause you don't know enough about happiness to talk about it."

"That's true," he admitted, giving in, feeling put down.

Alex stood up and stretched. "Well, now that we've gotten that out of the way," he said, making his way past Frances to go stand on deck, "let's create a little happiness, shall we?"

"I'm all for that," Mary said. She smiled and gave an expansive, stage-like wave of her arm. "Isn't it a lovely day!"

Alex went over to Frances and gave her a big hug, and she kissed him on the lips. Joe decided they did know how to create their own good time. Alex then took Frances by the hand, smiling and asking if they could go take a nap together. She nodded and let herself be escorted down below. Alex shot a wink at Joe as he descended the stairs.

"Can you manage for an hour or so?" he asked. Joe nodded with a smile. Mary nodded too, settled back, and they rode along silently, just enjoying the pleasant, easy roll of the boat in the gentle waves.

"Do you think we're doing the right thing?" she asked in a soft voice so as not to be heard below. Joe peered at the hatchway to see if Alex was in earshot.

"I think so," he replied. "Sometimes, you have to make a decision and then go with it. The one thing that's certain: we can't just stay in the Bahamas."

"Why not?" she asked. "I mean, if a storm were really close, then why not just anchor the boat where we were last night and go ashore?"

"Two problems. First is that the anchor wouldn't hold the boat in high winds. Second, that island's very low. If you had a storm surge, an especially high tide, it might flood the whole island."

"Well, why not go to Florida, then?" she asked. "Can't the boat be made safe somewhere there?"

"Maybe, maybe not. Often the boats just end up in a big pile of wreckage up on the beach. In fact, there's one marina in Fort Lauderdale that has signs explaining why they will sink your unattended boat beside the dock if a hurricane's coming, so as to protect their own facilities."

"I didn't know it was so complicated," Mary said.

"Life always is," Joe replied. He mused, but did not say, that Alex's concern for the safety of his million-dollar boat had a lot to do with the decision to sail on to Charleston. Well, if he had a million-dollar boat himself, Joe thought, maybe he would feel the same way.

"But what about being out on the ocean?" Mary asked. "Isn't that the most dangerous?"

"If you're in a very bad storm," Joe recalled from his navy training, "the best place to be is at sea, where there's deep water and no rocks and shoals to run into. That's what has killed most sailors, not the water and the waves." He paused. "Provided you're in a seaworthy boat," he added. "And I suppose this one is."

We may just find out, he thought, but did not say. He noted that Mary had a serious expression, considering the idea.

"I don't know whether to be worried or not," she admitted. "Are you worried? About the storm, I mean? Or those thugs in the speedboat?"

148

He sighed and gave an offhand gesture. "Some," he said. "But, as Alex said, there's always something out there, you know. Life's always throwing something at you."

"That's true," she said, "but we don't have to ask for it, necessarily."

"I expected you to go with the other boat," Joe said. He then was surprised by the way she looked up at him, with an expression of hurt, or something, that he didn't quite understand. "I mean, well..." He searched for a way to inquire. "To use an old expression, you didn't have a dog in this hunt, exactly."

She gave him a look of deep exasperation. "I suppose you would have been happier if I had gone on that other boat."

"Oh, no," Joe stammered. "I didn't mean that at all." He was a bit taken aback. "I'm glad you stayed." He struggled to think of how to fix it. "It would have been very lonesome standing watch up here all by myself."

"Well, I'm glad you think I'm good for something," she said, and turned her head away. He could see her take a couple of angry breaths and set her lips tight.

"I'm sorry," he said. "I didn't mean to sound... unwelcoming or anything."

"You just don't...always get it, do you?" She slapped her hand against the seat cushion and then wiped her eyes with the back of her wrist. Then she took a deep breath. "I guess I'm just feeling sorry for myself," she admitted, calmer now. "I guess it's just that, until Earnest died, I never did anything without him. We took all our vacations together and had the same friends, and were always together." She pulled a tissue from her pocket and dabbed at her eyes. "All of this is so new to me. I'm just having a hard time... adjusting, I suppose."

Joe nodded. "I understand. I know how you must feel."

She looked at him with an expression that said she knew he didn't understand at all. "Forgive me," she said, in a tone of resignation. "I was forgetting myself."

She stood up, stepped out of the cockpit, and made her way on deck. Speechless, he watched her hold on to the shrouds, walk forward, and take a seat on the superstructure above the cabins. There she sat for a long time, staring off in the direction they were heading. Joe shook his head, wondering what he might have done or said that irritated her so. Women often were hard to understand; he'd learned that long ago.

It made him think about Eileen again. How was it that he and she had lost the ability to understand and communicate with one another? He considered Frances and how Alex seemed to be able to manage her. Frances's sense of caution was a good balance to Alex's desire for adventure. If she doubted the wisdom of heading off to Charleston on a course that would take them more than a hundred miles offshore with the possibility of a storm pursuing them, well, her opinion deserved a hearing. But she had stuck with Alex and would not let him and Joe take the risk of sailing north by themselves. And Mary had done the same thing. He wondered what his ex-wife, Eileen, would have done in this situation—taken the boat to Florida, he supposed. Being abandoned to undertake the vicissitudes of life alone was what he now considered to be the normal course of things. And so, regarding Mary's back as she sat on deck, he realized that she just now had grown angry with him for not appreciating the way she had stuck with them. Yes, he decided, he should appreciate it.

"I imagine you'll be finding another wife someday," Joe remembered a good friend saying to him, not long after his divorce. They were playing cards, he and some other old friends, all of whom had been married at one time or another, and now hung together for companionship and to stave off loneliness.

"I'll never marry again!" his red-haired friend, nicknamed Rowdy, had exclaimed. *"I'll never make that mistake again!"*

At the time, Joe had thought it great advice. The response of Zorba from the story *Zorba the Greek* occurred to him. When asked if he had been married, Zorba called it a catastrophe: "Am I not a man, and is a man not a fool?"

What a strange thing for me to be thinking about, he thought, bringing himself back from the reverie. He glanced down at the compass, corrected the course, and steered on in silence, watching Mary, "the guest," settle back against the mast and place her broad-brimmed pink striped hat over her eyes.

So your captivity, your "impressment" will continue, he thought, smiling, feeling a new sense of… well, liking for her, thinking that it would have been less cheery without her aboard. He stared off at the distant horizon ahead, wondering just what the next few days of being together would yield.

At lunchtime, Frances and Alex appeared, looking very refreshed, attentive to and smiling at one another and seeming to be very much in love. They brought up from below ham and cheese sandwiches on whole wheat with lettuce and tomato, with great sweet pickles and a big bag of potato chips. Alex took a Heineken, but Joe surprised himself by his lack of desire for alcohol and joined the others in a glass of Crystal Light. There were a few clouds in the sky, and the breeze was balmy. Everyone thought it was a beautiful day, and nobody mentioned the storm that seemed so far away from them. By the end of lunch, the wind had come up some and shifted to the west, making it possible to sail with both jib and main. Alex killed the engine, and they continued to make six knots.

"You two better go take a good siesta," Alex said. "We'll be back on port and starboard watches tonight."

Joe nodded. "Hasta la vista, me amigos," he said as he went below.

Mary passed down the lunch plates, came down, and helped Joe wash them and tidy up the kitchen. Whatever had ticked her off earlier, she seemed to have gotten over, he guessed. They bade one another a good rest.

"Are you comfortable in there?" he asked as they headed to their separate cabins.

"Oh, yes," she replied. "I've become rather accustomed to sleeping in a closet."

They laughed, and before he could think to be inhibited, he patted her on the back. She smiled at him as she went in the little stateroom and closed the door. Happy, Joe climbed into the V-berth and almost instantly was asleep.

He was awakened in the late afternoon by the sound of two gunshots, and he bolted from the bunk into the passageway, adrenalin pulsing in his head. The cigarette boat gang? Then he heard some loud oaths from Alex, followed by laughter. Laughter? Joe rushed topside to find Alex at the port rail, a pistol in his right hand, his left hand shielding his eyes from the setting sun. Mary followed Joe up the ladder.

"A big shark," Alex explained. "Didn't mean to give you all a start there. I can't see him, anymore. Well, damn!" He set the safety on and came back in under the bimini, shaking his head. "I may have hit him once. Damn, I hate those things."

Frances was sitting at the wheel, even though the autopilot was steering. "I hate them, too, Alex, but I wish you wouldn't always have to be shooting at them," she complained. "That gun is so loud!"

152

"Well, you didn't mind shooting back at Coopers Town, did you?" he joked.

Always careful about her appearance, Frances was especially well attired this afternoon, Joe noted, in a white blouse and green slacks. Alex surveyed the surrounding sea again for the shark. Not seeing it, he picked up the holstered pistol and went below. Frances lay back on the port bench and stared out at the horizon a minute.

"Sometimes I miss being at home so much," she said. "I could be tending my garden or something. But instead, all I do is go around on this boat with Alex, staring at the horizon."

"I imagine you have a very nice home," Mary said.

"Oh, well, it's a big old house with lots of antiques that Alex hates. But I collect them because it gives me something to do at home." She paused. "But how about you, Mary? Do you have a big mansion to keep by yourself, or what?" She made an expansive sweep of her hand as if to indicate a large estate.

"Just a modest sort of house," Mary replied, grinning at the expansive notion.

"You just come home with us to Atlanta," Frances went on. "Since we're gone all the time, our gardens are all weeds. You can have all the gardening you want... that is if that dratted storm doesn't come and blow us away. Why in the world we're always out here on the silly ocean instead of being at home taking care of things, going to luncheons and teas, and symphonies and plays, and acting like civilized people, I just don't know. Why I had to marry a man who thinks his name is Jack Tar or something, I can't imagine."

Joe realized that Frances was just a bit high. It was time for one of her "calming-down pills," he had heard Alex call them. On impulse, Frances grabbed up the bottle of Bull Frog.

"It's time you got some sun on that back and chest of yours," she declared, making for the seat beside him.

Joe cringed, but before he could say anything, she had grabbed the tail of his polo shirt and was pulling it over his head. Patiently, he allowed it.

"Now, that's better!" she exclaimed, pouring lotion into her hand, eyeing his naked upper torso. Without ceremony, she began rubbing him down, back and then chest and even stomach. Joe felt like an obedient dog being given a bath.

Noting that Mary was watching, he reddened with embarrassment. Mary noticed and smiled at him. In a moment, Alex was coming up the ladder. Joe glanced at him, noting his irritated expression when he saw what his wife was doing. Joe looked at him, pleading for assistance.

"Now look here, Frances," he said. "What are you doing to that poor fellow?" He came over and put his hand on the helm, indicating that he was taking over.

Joe gladly stepped aside and away from Frances, using it as an escape.

"Joe, how about going down to the chart table and finding the large-scale chart that shows the Atlantic from Miami to Charleston, or maybe it just shows as far north as Savannah. I'd like to check some distances."

Joe was off and down the ladder in an instant, grateful for the opportunity to flee. Frances, in an effort to show Alex she wasn't minding him, turned her attention on Mary.

154

"By the way, it's time we considered your case," she declared, rubbing the last of the lotion into her hands. "We do need to find a good match for you, dear. There must be a dozen widowers out there with a million each, just lying in wait for some pretty little thing like you." Mary laughed.

"I like that idea, except maybe you could find me one with two or three million."

"Let's don't set the bar too high," Frances quipped. "Your present opportunity is not that good."

Overhearing, Joe realized that Frances was now knocking him. His anger flared, but then he remembered her mood swing problem. How strange it was to have someone rub you down with lotion one second and then insult you in the next. But somehow her telling Mary that was a little painful because, he realized, what Mary thought of him had begun to matter quite a lot. Well, Frances was right, of course; he had little to offer a woman like Mary.

"You look so serious all of a sudden," Frances was saying to Mary. "Did I step on your toes? Or maybe Joe's?" Not waiting for a response, she peered below, almost screaming. "Get back up here, Joe."

Working to keep his temper, Joe tucked his shirt back in. Without hurrying, he found the chart and brought it topside.

Frances was at him again. Look here, you ole devil! I'm not finished with you yet."

Alex looked at his wife and put his finger to his lips like a librarian. She frowned at him, blinked, and gave a little shiver.

"Are you shushing me, dear?" Frances replied, reining herself in somewhat.

"Did you take your pill?" Alex mouthed silently. She wrinkled up her nose, but shook her head.

"Come steer," he said to Frances.

She shook her head in a contrary manner.

"Please, dear," Alex said in a sweet, soothing voice. "For me."

Frances sighed and went to take over. Alex gave her a little kiss and made his way below, winking at his companions as he passed.

Frances sighed again and sat back. "Maybe I talk too much," she muttered as an apology.

Joe felt his angry feeling melt away. "We're all a little tense, I guess," he said, giving her a gentle smile. Frances looked for an instant as if she might cry.

"That's right," Mary said. "I think we're all a bit nervous about the storm and everything."

Alex reappeared at the hatch with a glass of water and a pill, sitting beside her and offering them. She took the capsule demurely and gave him back the glass.

"Everybody knows I'm a little zany," she said, glancing at Joe. The tone in her voice, however, let him know he'd better not agree with that statement. Then she looked out ahead.

"We're approaching something in the water," she announced.

Both men looked ahead to see something glinting a flash of sunlight in the distance. They were sailing in a light chop, still in the shallows of the Bahamas, but in the slightly deeper waters of the northwest corner.

"Something floating in the water," Alex said. "Good spotting, dear."

"Well, of course," she said, "I'm not new at this, you know."

"You're a fine sailor," Alex assured her. He lifted the binoculars to his eyes. "Can't make it out, could be one of those big containers off a ship or something." He lowered the binoculars and dismissed it.

"But I'm tired of steering anyway," Frances said. Joe offered to take the helm. She very gladly relinquished it and took a seat on the port bench.

"Time for another nap, anyway, don't you think?" Alex said. "Wouldn't you like to get a little rest?" He took her hand.

"Of course," she said, rising to follow her husband. "Don't run over that thing up there, you ole devil."

"I promise," Joe replied with a grin.

"We're coming up on the northwest corner of the Bahamas," he said, changing the subject, reaching down and pointing to the spot on the chart. See these arrows over in the ocean to the west? Those arrows show the Gulf Stream currents. When we work our way over into the Stream, it should add two or three knots to our speed." Mary nodded, and he was glad to be focusing on something other than himself.

"It's good of you to take all that from Frances," Mary said, going back to the last topic.

Joe grinned. "Don't let Frances bother you," he said. "She has a condition, but she'll be okay."

"That was a rather manic episode," Mary commented. "It can be a little unnerving." She reached over and patted his hand. "I'm glad you're so unflappable."

Changing course to port in order to come close to the still-distant floating object and satisfy his curiosity, Joe gave an offhand nod. "I just try to get along," he admitted.

"I like that about you." Mary leaned back and closed her eyes, and they rode along in silence.

Joe continued to peer at the object in the water ahead. When he was a couple of hundred yards away, he began to realize that maybe it was a small boat adrift. He commented on it to Mary and suggested she take the binoculars, step out away from the dodger's windshield, and take a look.

"It's bigger than a little boat," she said. "Here, you look." She handed him the binoculars and took the helm.

He stepped out on the port side and focused on the object ahead. He could see it was not just a small boat. No, it was the bow of a much bigger boat. Then he realized it was sunk, with the bow sticking out and the stern underwater.

"It's a wreck!" he cried. Stepping back under the bimini, he took the helm back from Mary. "Better go wake Alex," he said. She made her way below while he turned to pass closer.

By the time Mary returned with Alex, the wreck was twenty to thirty yards off to port. It was a cabin cruiser, a motorized pleasure boat. Its stern was resting on the bottom, visible in the shallow green water. The bow bobbed in the waves, the superstructure half submerged, half exposed.

"Bullet holes!" Alex exclaimed. Joe spotted the torn, jagged rips, maybe as many as fifty of them, through the cabin and wheelhouse area.

"See the name?" he gasped. "It's that *Sea Splendor.*"

"Oh, Lord!" Mary wailed.

Through the waves lapping over the cabin, Joe could make out what looked like something dark. Then the dark shadow moved, came out, and sped off.

"A shark!" he cried. They watched in horror as its dorsal fin slipped across the surface and then away out of sight. Joe put the helm over to go around, forgetting the sails. The boat jibed in the light wind, and he turned back to put the wind on the bow, making the sails snap hard in a luff. Alex gave him a reproachful glance, but came over and took the throttle, stopping the engine and then backing to bring them to a halt. They all looked back at the wreck.

"Are there any people?" Mary asked, trembling.

Joe looked around, shaking his head. It was gruesome to realize that the shark had taken care of whatever the bullets had not. "We need to report this to the coast guard," he said, offering the helm to Alex. "I'll go get a fix off the GPS."

As Alex stepped up to the wheel, he put his hand on Joe to stop him. "I don't want to let anybody know we're here," he objected.

Joe gave him a resolute look. "We have to," he said. "It's the law."

Alex met his gaze for a moment, then looked down and nodded. "I guess so," he said.

Agitated by the discovery, Joe nearly tripped going over to the instrument to write down the latitude and longitude.

Frances came up the ladder and joined them in their horror. "Who could have done this?" she asked.

Joe and Mary looked at each other. "Those thugs on *Blaster*," he said.

"The cigarette boat?" Mary asked in a trembling voice.

"I told you they were pirates," Frances declared.

"Drug runners or pirates or something!" Alex exclaimed.

"We have to call for help!" Frances shouted. She all but pushed Joe down the ladder getting to the radio at the chart table below.

"Wait a minute, Fran," Alex called down to her. "We can't give out our position."

But Frances wasn't listening. She grabbed up the microphone. "Mayday, Mayday, Mayday," she said. "There's a wreck, a shipwreck. Coast Guard, are you there?"

Joe brought the paper he had written down the coordinates on and stood beside her. She was between him and the radio, and so he couldn't tactfully take the mike from her. She made a similar call again.

"Calm down, Frances," Alex called. She gave an irritated wave away at him with her hand.

"Boat calling Mayday, this is, uh, *Lucky*, over," a male voice came back over the radio.

"Oh, this is *Mission*, and we're out here, and there's a wrecked boat with bullets in it and nobody, and it's sunk, and we just don't know…"

Joe offered to take the mike, but she wouldn't let him.

"Where are you? This is *Lucky*. Come back," the radioed voice said.

Joe handed her the paper. She took it nervously, and read the coordinates incorrectly, jumbling the numbers. Just as Joe was about to correct her, the voice came back again.

"You're up near Mantanilla Reef, aren't you?"

Joe nodded to Frances. "Up near Mantanilla Reef," she repeated into the microphone.

"Just wait there," the voice said. "We'll be there soon."

Frances thanked them and put the microphone down. She grabbed Joe's hand for comfort. He gave her a little hug, wondering all the while why they hadn't raised the coast guard, too. With his other hand, he took up the mike and called.

"*Lucky*, this is *Mission*. Request you try to relay our position to the US Coast Guard, or the Bahamians, and pass along the report about the wreck, over." They waited a few moments, but there was no reply. Joe called again, but still there was no answer. Giving Frances's hand a reassuring squeeze, he went up the ladder to consult with Alex, telling him about giving the position to the other boat.

They were still within fifty yards of the wreck, which bobbed in the waves. He was replaying the radio conversation in his head when the truth struck him.

"Hot damn!" he said. They all looked at him. "Something's funny about that. First of all, Frances didn't read the latitude/longitude coordinates right, but still that guy knew we were near Mantanilla.Reef." He glanced at Mary again, noting her worried look.

Frances came back on deck. "I never heard him try to call anybody," she reported.

"You don't suppose that *Lucky* was really that *Blaster*?" Joe asked. Then he realized that the voice indeed sounded like the headman on the boat at Coopers Town.

Alex was not slow to pick up on the idea. He put the idling engine back in gear and throttled up, turning to leeward to refill the sails. "We've got to get out of here!" he said. "Get away from that wreck as soon as possible."

Frances looked at him quizzically.

"If it's that cigarette boat, we don't want them to find us," he said.

Joe agreed. "They're very fast," he pointed out.

Everyone looked behind them.

"I'll go check the radar," Joe said, descending the ladder, and went to the navigation table and set the radar from standby to radiate. He watched the sweep on the eight-mile range and saw nothing. He set it for sixteen miles and then turned up the gain. Still seeing nothing, he breathed easier and went up the ladder.

"At least they don't know which way we're going," Alex said, taking up the binoculars and scanning the horizon in all directions.

"Should we try to call the coast guard again?" Mary asked.

"Wait," Alex said. "Whatever we say to the coast guard, those guys will hear." Once again, he looked at the horizon astern.

"And they might have a direction finder on their radio, which would point to us if we transmit," Joe added, also looking astern.

"All I've ever heard the coast guard do is ask people in distress a bunch of stupid questions," Alex said.

They pondered silently. Mary brightened with an idea.

"A cell phone...oh, that's right." Her voice trailed off. They glanced at Frances, but no one dared mention why they didn't have Alex's cell phone.

"Oh, Alex, let's head for Florida right now!" Frances cried. "Let's just go home!"

Alex shook his head. "If the bad guys get here and don't find us, they'll search for us toward Florida. With four or five times more speed than we have, they could do a lot of searching." He explained that most anyone in a sailboat at their position would be en route to West Palm or Fort Pierce or Canaveral. "They'll never think to head north into the open sea."

"There's still that hurricane moving north," Joe reminded them.

"I hope it gets those sorry pirates," Frances said. "I hope they get sunk and drowned." No one needed to say that what could happen to the pirates also could happen to them. Frances sat down beside Mary, and they took one another's hand.

"I agree with you, Alex," Mary said. "I just hope they don't see us."

Joe smiled at her, appreciating her good sense. Through the plexiglass window in the top of the bimini, he looked up at the sails. They weren't very full in the light wind.

"Maybe we ought to furl the sails like we did before," he suggested, "since there isn't much wind, anyway. It would make us a little harder to see if the mast were bare."

Agreeing, Alex turned into the wind. They lowered the main and furled the genoa, and then went back on course. When it was done, Frances began to weep. Mary embraced her. Alex motioned for Joe to take the helm and then escorted his wife below, stopping to glance at the radar.

"Call me if...anything..." Alex called back to them. Mary moved back closer to Joe at the helm.

"What next?" she said with evident emotion.

Joe shook his head. "Well, between the storm to the south and now the pirates, this is getting to be more than interesting."

He saw Mary bite her lip and look aft at the horizon, apparently stifling her feelings. At almost any point on the horizon, it was easy to imagine a sleek black hull, speeding toward them.

"Here we are, passing the reef," Joe said a few minutes later, pointing to the subtle change in the color of the sea. "You can see the water turn dark blue as we drop off the Bahamas bank."

Mary sat up, and the two of them watched the fathometer's depth gauge fall. Once again, they looked astern, and then both looked ahead. Observing their passage, Joe imagined the sight of the hull beneath moving over the underwater cliff and out into the

164

great expanse of dark, deep waters of the very wide, very lonesome ocean—the great darkness, the great abyss, the great nightmare.

"So much is out there," Joe said. "So much is unknown."

Chapter Seven

Since there were just slow-rolling swells, Frances called Mary down, and the two were able to make a big pot of beef vegetable soup. Meanwhile, Alex fiddled with the radar to get it tuned up for maximum range, noting that they now were about six miles north of the bank. When dinner was ready, the ladies called them to the table. Giving a last look around, Joe set the autopilot and went below. They were all relieved when Alex told them that there was no sign of anything on the radar, but he left it radiating and sat where he could glance at it.

"Since they haven't spotted us by now, then it's pretty certain we gave 'em the slip," he reassured everyone.

"Suppose they pick us up on radar?" Frances asked.

"I don't recall seeing a radar antenna on their boat," Joe replied, "but they may have a radio direction finder. It could give them a heading toward us, but that's all."

The four of them ate supper without a lot of conversation. Frances was being extra sweet and polite, especially to Joe, whom she referred to once as her "dear friend." He smiled at the lavishness of the term, but took it as a kind of peace offering for her attack on him that afternoon. He accepted it graciously, but wondered how long it would last.

After supper, Alex went over to the chart table again and dialed up the weather on the VHF. The report placed the center of the tropical storm about a hundred miles southeast of Miami, and was expected to reach the Exumas by morning. An NOAA reconnaissance plane had reported maximum sustained winds of forty-five knots, gusts of fifty-five to sixty knots. Estimated minimum central pressure was 1001 millibars. The storm was heading to the north-northwest.

"We could still turn and go to Canaveral or Saint Augustine or somewhere, couldn't we?" Frances suggested. "Surely those pirates aren't that far north."

"There's a good chance that's about where the storm will hit Florida," Alex replied. "I think we're doing just right, heading on north."

Joe had studied the chart several times earlier in the day. He had seen that it could head right on up the Straits of Florida, thereby cutting them off from making port anywhere along the coast. He thought again how *Terajay* and any other boats leaving the Bahamas would be sailing straight to Florida. He guessed that Jason and Theresa would make it in before dawn. But Alex had made the decision to head for Charleston, and now the die was cast.

Night fell as Alex and Frances headed topside to take the first watch. Joe and Mary washed dishes, cleaned up the galley, and secured whatever was out and loose. The waves coming from astern had heightened enough to make *Mission* pitch and wallow a bit, causing them to bump hips in the narrow galley. He was glad to note that she did not appear seasick at all, and realized she had become a pretty good sailor. Through it all, however, Mary was

168

not talkative, reticent almost, Joe realized. In fact, she appeared still very much nervous and worried.

Leaving her to dry the last of the dishes and put them away, he slipped into the seat at the navigation table and took another look at the radar. After a few sweeps, he turned the gain higher for a final sweep. Then his heart stopped for a moment. To the south, he saw the faintest blip. He watched the sweep go around again, and there was nothing. He adjusted the scope and then got it again—at ten miles out. Checking their position on the chart, he calculated that the blip was around the area, more or less, where they had found the wreckage. Was it *Blaster*? Who else? As he stared at the screen, Mary came into the salon.

"See anything?" she asked, the edge of nerves in her voice.

Joe shook his head. "Naw," he lied. He stood up and stretched as if he had no care in the world. No reason at this point to make her any more frightened than she already was. "How about a nightcap?" he suggested, digging into the liquor locker.

"Fine," she said.

He found a half-full bottle of fine brandy. Steadying himself against the motion of the boat, he poured two-fingers' worth in a couple of short glasses, surreptitiously peering at the radar again. Even though they might have radar, it was located relatively low to the water while *Mission*'s radar on the high mast could "see" the cigarette boat.

Joe and Mary slid into the circular seat of the dining room table an arm's length apart, Joe positioning himself so he could still see the radar. Mary sipped at her brandy and gave a little shiver. Joe took a bigger swig.

"Warms the insides, doesn't it?" he commented. She nodded and took another sip. They sat silently, side by side, a few minutes.

"I don't know whether to be scared or not," Mary said, then turned to look at him, her knee touching his thigh in the process. He met her gaze before she glanced down at where they touched.

"You mean about the pirate boat?" he asked, conscious of the warmth of body contact.

"Yes, that, and the hurricane and…" She gazed at him again. "Everything."

Joe let out a deep breath. "Hard to know what's a real concern, isn't it?" he replied, glancing at the radar again. "I mean, we don't even know for sure that those guys on the radio were those thugs. We don't know if the storm's coming toward us or will divert in another direction." He shrugged again. "Always blind to the future, aren't we?"

"You know," Mary replied, "when Earnest was alive, we seemed to have the whole world under control." She took a big gulp of her brandy. "Then one day, without the slightest indication that anything was wrong, he just died." Her voice broke. "He was just gone…"

"I'm so sorry," Joe said, realizing that it was not only her grief, but also the tension about their present situation that had set her off. He reached over, gave her hand a gentle squeeze, and then took his hand away. "In high school, I had a very fine teacher who asked us to evaluate situations by determining whether or not we could be agents of purpose or victims of circumstance."

"And so you think of yourself as a victim of circumstance," she guessed.

170

He nodded, getting up to get the brandy bottle. "Maybe life has taught me that cynicism is what's real," he said, glancing at the radar screen on the way back to the table. The blip showed up on a sweep, a good bit to the west of where it had been initially. Whatever boat that was, it was heading toward Florida.

He walked back to the table with the bottle, staggering a bit as the boat pitched and the liquor hit him. As he refilled their glasses, Mary gave him a disapproving look.

"Are you angry with me?" he asked.

She shook her head. "Just disappointed, I suppose, about being cynical, I mean."

He shrugged apologetically. "I didn't know you cared."

"Sometimes, you can be just so irritating!" she exclaimed, energized by her feelings. Then she made a fist and punched a playful kind of push on his leg. He grabbed her hand and held it there. She turned her palm down and caressed the spot she had punched, and he caressed the back of her hand.

"I didn't mean to be," he mumbled, more conscious of her body than of his own words, more aware of his yearning for being touched once again after so long without...

"Hey, you two!" It was Frances peering down from the cockpit. "Y'all better get some rest, because we're going to be calling you to take the watch pretty soon."

Joe smiled. "Yes, ma'am," he replied.

Frances kept staring at them, until they both shrugged and slid out of the sofa, complying with her command. Joe took the glasses to the sink to wash them while Mary went forward to the head. Afterward, he went to the chart table and watched the radar make its sweep. Seeing nothing, he set its range out to twenty miles, but still there was no blip, no *Blaster* or anything else. Presumably, the cigarette boat was headed toward Florida at high speed. He called to Alex to come down to tell him what he had seen, doing so quietly so as not to alarm the women.

"It was probably them," Alex said. "Damn!"

"I think we should risk calling the coast guard again," Joe said. "If these guys hear that the coast guard knows about us and about them, they will be very reluctant to come after us."

Alex pursed his lips. "If the coast guard hears about all this, they'll start asking questions," he said. "They'll want to know why these thugs are after us. Or they'll tell us to turn and go in to Canaveral or somewhere."

"Well, we don't have to tell them everything," Joe argued. "We could keep the hidden money secret."

Alex shook his head. "I can't risk it," he insisted. "It means everything to me." He raised his eyebrows. "And don't forget about your fifty thousand dollars if we make it."

Hearing that, Joe gritted his teeth. "You said a hundred thousand," he reminded him, feeling a pang of shame about having yielded to a mercenary impulse back at Great Sale.

"Fifty, a hundred, whatever," Alex said flippantly.

"And what about Frances, and Mary?" Joe shot back. "They count too, don't they?" The two stared at one another.

"Look," Alex said, "suppose we turn toward shore, and then we got over there just as the storm begins to churn up the sea," Alex said. "Can you imagine trying to get through one of those narrow Florida passes in high waves with shoals and sand

172

bars shifting around? I'd rather take my chances at sea, in deep open water. Moving away from the storm instead heading right into its path still makes a lot more sense to me. Don't you think?"

Joe evaluated Alex's argument and had to admit that he couldn't counter with anything more reasonable. "Let's just hope for the best," Alex said. He turned and went back to join his wife topside.

Joe watched him climbing the ladder and becoming a shadow in the gloom. Despite Alex's ulterior motive for going to Charleston, his decision to head north to avoid the hurricane possibly had kept them away from *Blaster*. He took a last look at the radar to see if the cigarette boat gang, if that's who it was, was still heading west and not pursuing them. No, radar showed only the ocean out there in the darkness. They were truly at sea now.

He glanced at the radio, contemplating how easily he could just pick up the mike and transmit to the coast guard before anyone could stop him. But Alex had made a good case for not doing so. Then he noticed something that made his pulse race. The radio transmitter was set on low-power transmitting, which was for use in harbors, where only short-range sending was needed. It probably had been set that way at Great Sale Cay when they had thought about calling *Terajay*. That meant two things: In all probability, the coast guard had never heard their earlier transmission. And second, the cigarette boat must have been close by since they did hear the transmission. He started to go tell Alex, but hesitated, and decided just to keep it all to himself. He switched the power setting to full-power transmitting so it would be ready if needed. Then he called a "see you in three hours" to the Smiths topside and thought again about Mary.

Mary now was in her stateroom with the door open, lying on her back in the lower bunk, still dressed, but with her blouse unbuttoned, a mere hint of her bra showing, her breasts youthfully firm for someone her age, he noted. She had a book in hand.

"The radar's clear for twenty miles in all directions," he said to reassure her, not mentioning that the cigarette boat would not make a blip on the screen if it were more than about ten miles away.

"I'm relieved to hear that!" she replied.

He turned to go to his cabin, but she called him back.

"It's pretty warm in here," she said, sounding much more pleasant, pulling her blouse together modestly. "Could you see if you can open that vent thing for me?"

Joe stepped in and reached up to drop the screen down from the little hatch in the overhead, pushed it open, locked the keeper, and closed the screen.

"It might be cooler on this top bunk," he commented, noting the air streaming in. "If you want to make the change, I can move your suitcases to the lower bunk."

"Oh, that's too much trouble," she said. "I'm okay."

"Or maybe I should trade rooms with you," he suggested. "You might be more comfortable up forward."

There was a pause. She did not answer right away.

"I don't mind," he said. He was still standing beside the bed, his legs and lower torso beside her on the bottom bunk. He stepped back where he could see her. She looked up at him, her eyes more or less moving up his body, noting, even as she turned her gaze to his face. She smiled.

"Maybe another time," she said, shifting her gaze back to the book.

"What ya' reading?" Joe asked, noting that his pulse had quickened.

"Oh, just the Bible," she said. "I found it on the bookshelf in the salon. I thought it might be fun to find some of the passages about ocean voyages and such." She held up the page where she was for him to see. "I've just started on the book of Jonah."

"Uh-oh!" Joe replied, his voice a bit hoarse and nervous. "Watch out, now! That's not very pleasant reading when you're at sea."

"Maybe not, but if Frances is going to call you Jonah, I suppose I'd better find out what it's all about." She glanced below his waist again and then smiled up at him. "Sweet dreams," she told him.

In his rack a few minutes later, being gently pitched up and down in the waves, the gurgle of wake reverberating in the hull, Joe replayed the scene, pleased with his somewhat boyish response to her. In younger years, Joe had been a lover of life. He had considered himself something of a hedonist, who understood what it was to immerse in the good pleasures of being human. Why he was that way had come from his childhood in a somewhat wealthy family with social prominence. He was intelligent, handsome, and athletic. Good grades in school came as easily to him as sexual exploration with his childhood friends, and both seemed very natural. The idea that life was to be enjoyed was an attitude ingrained in him.

But with adolescence—that time when one learns to make who one is fit in with what society says he should be—Joe had become aware of his responsibility to become a man. He learned to play the part very well, knowing in his heart that he was still that same boy with all the same impulses and desires and fears and uncertainties. Like most every other virile male, like Atlas, he assumed the mantle of the world, became a naval officer, a teacher, then later the owner of a small business, a husband, a father, president of civic groups, a churchman, a Sunday school teacher, an upright and honest and involved citizen. But all the time, he, in part, was dissembling, keeping his boyish heart of hearts backstage. But from the time of his traumatic divorce to the present, Joe's interest in a sexual relationship had been dormant, as if he was stunned to unfeeling, his emotions comatose. It had affected even his ability to formulate any plans for the future and to act on them. That had as much to do as anything with his ending up here on *Mission* with the Smiths, now embroiled in Alex's smuggling, as if having no plans led inexorably to disaster.

In this condition of failure-by-default, however, he had now come across this Mary, who was awakening him to affectionate feelings once again. He was discovering that he liked being with her, seeing her, talking to her, caring about her. And moreover, like the light breeze coming off the darkened sea into the vent above him, desire swept into his mind as he contemplated the form of her breasts, the way he had seen them, covered by the silky bra between the lapels of her open blouse. *"Maybe another time,"* she had said. The world and all its possibilities lay before him. But could he allow himself to emerge from his emotional cocoon? Was it safe to allow himself to have feelings for someone again? Or would it bring on another heartbreak?

And so, lying there in the bow of *Mission* with Mary in the adjoining cabin, he considered that maybe it was indeed safe. Trying to take courage in this decision, he drifted off in his reverie, allowing his imagination to conjure what someday might be.

Chapter Eight

After resuming watch with Joe in the wee hours of the night, Mary, much awake, took a seat at the wheel first. While there were a few puffs of cumulus clouds to the south, the moon peered over the horizon, reflecting its shaft of yellow gold to the east in the rippling sea. First rubbing his eyes and getting adjusted to the light of his red-lensed flashlight, Joe read the latitude and longitude from the GPS and plotted their position. Mary asked where they were. Joe, somewhat groggy from the lack of enough sleep, switched on the flashlight and pointed to the fix he had plotted on the chart, explaining that they were about fifty miles east of the coast of Florida, with Cape Canaveral being the closest point of land. Then the two of them rode along in silence for a while, Joe contemplating the gloom of the ocean and the cloudy sky and shifting his gaze to contemplate her form sitting at the wheel, lighted by the tiny red glow from the instrument lights.

"A penny for your thoughts," Mary ventured.

"Oh, well, uh," Joe stammered. "I was thinking about how we, you and I, I mean, didn't know each other a few days ago, and now we're spending all our time together." His voice trailed off, reluctant in his lack of confidence.

"Yes, I know," she said, hesitating a moment. "After being so close to my husband for so long, I've been so alone ever since. But I guess I've already told you that."

"I know," he said.

"Was your divorce like that?" she asked.

"Sort of," he replied, "except that there are hard feelings as well as sad ones. Death of one partner or the other is better," he added, and then realized it was a thoughtless thing to say. "Oh, well, I didn't mean to…"

"I guess I understand," she said. "My older brother went through a very painful divorce. He took to alcohol and drank himself to a stroke at an early age." She shook her head. "I had the gift of a truly loving relationship with Earnest, at least. And so maybe his death was better."

They fell silent, going along in the darkness for a while, the boat pitching rhythmically in the smooth, dark, rolling ocean.

"At least I didn't play around on my wife," he said.

"Like Alex might, you mean?" Mary said. "He seems to have a way… You noticed that at Great Sale?"

"I didn't want to jump to conclusions," Joe said, knowing full well he had suspected Alex of "exploring the possibilities" with Mary.

"Well, don't worry," she said. "The very idea of a married man acting like that disgusts me. Especially since he's so likable in other ways." She shook her head. "Poor Frances."

"Maybe it's no wonder she flies off the handle occasionally," he agreed. "You remember that thing about the cell phone? When she threw it overboard?"

"The phone rang? And Frances threw it overboard?" Mary recalled. "Yes, what was that all about?"

As much as Joe wanted to explain, he felt it unwise to tote any tales about Alex. "I never did know exactly," he said, deciding a little white lie wasn't too bad. "I thought it was something private between husband and wife, so I didn't inquire."

"You're probably wise," she agreed.

"Nothing is permanent," he muttered.

Mary nodded. "It's funny how, until Earnest died so suddenly, I had come almost to believe he and I could never be separated."

Joe understood. "At one time, I thought the same thing about Eileen and me."

"Maybe you and she will get back together," Mary suggested. "It happens, you know."

Joe shook his head. "Not in this case," he said. "Too many bridges burned…"

"I see," she said with an upbeat that he noticed, and then paused. "I know you're lonely," she added.

He thought to make some lie of denial, but just shrugged and made a gesture of resignation. Then they regarded one another in the darkened cockpit of the sailboat, rolling easily, the splash of the wake at the bow the only sound. Yielding to a strong impulse, he set the autopilot and moved around beside her and took her hand. In the darkness, they stood silent and motionless for a few moments, until Mary reached up and caressed his cheek. Then they embraced and held one another, their breathing felt one to the other.

"I know you're lonely, too," Joe found himself saying. "I wish I could help…take away your pain."

She held him even more tightly. "I never thought…" she whispered. "I never thought I'd feel…" She fell silent.

"I know," he said. "I understand."

They clung to one another for a while, staggering a little as the boat rolled. Catching their balance, they moved their feet, and laughed. It became a little waltz, and they changed their embrace to one of dancing, moving in rhythm to the roll, in the harmony of the waves over the dark, deep ocean.

Then someone turned on the VHF radio below and tuned it to one of the weather channels. Self-consciously, Joe and Mary parted. She moved away and sat down behind the helm, and Joe moved forward on the bench, where he could hear the radio, the distant broadcast signal weak and hissing. Alex was at the chart desk, listening.

The storm was now a category one hurricane, passing over Nassau, heading north, winds in excess of seventy miles per hour.

"Is that bad?" Mary asked, in a tone that sounded like she already knew it was.

"Not good," Joe said, moving his legs to let Alex climb up into the cockpit.

"Buenos noches," Alex said, forcing a cheery voice. He peered out the dodger's windshield at the sea.

180

"Well, it's calm enough here," Joe said. "Just a few light swells."

"Makes for great sleeping," Alex replied. "You two better go get a little rest. I'll take it for a few hours." He took over the helm from Mary, saying, "Thanks, sweetie."

"I'm ready for a little rest," Mary admitted. She glanced at Joe, her smile just visible in the red instrument light, and started on below. In the dark salon, she met Frances, and Joe heard Frances ask if she heard correctly about the storm being over Nassau.

"Oh, Lord," Frances said. She came on up, gave a cursory greeting to Joe, and started in on Alex. "So now what do we do? *Now* do we go over to Florida and go ashore like sensible people?"

Alex waved the idea away. "If we did that, we'd be heading perpendicular to the storm rather than away from it. It surely would catch up with us then."

"Lord, help me from this crazy husband of mine."

"Hush, Frannie," Alex said. "Look out here. Did you ever see such a beautiful night on the ocean? Look! The moon's out!" He pointed to the bright shaft of moonlight glistening on the dark water.

Giving Mary time to finish with the bathroom below, Joe remained to watch a few more minutes as the glow grew brighter than it had been when he and Mary had been topside. So he thought he'd go point it out to her before she fell asleep.

Wishing the Smiths a happy sail, Joe climbed down the ladder in the darkness. Finding the door to Mary's cabin closed, he decided he was too late to mention the moon. He went into the head, took care of his needs, brushed his teeth, and washed his face. When he came out, he stepped into his forward V-berth cabin, and as he did so, realized to his surprise, and then excitement, that the darkened form of Mary in a night gown sat at the end of his bed.

"Oh," he whispered. "I guess… you wanted to trade cabins…" He began backing out the door.

"Shhh," she whispered, beckoning with her hand for him to come in.

He gulped and, with his hands trembling, shut the door behind him. She reached out and took his hand. He sat beside her, and they embraced. Then he kissed her. Their lips met, and they held it for a long time. It was not sensual so much as it was tender. They held one another for a long time, rocking with the motion of the waves, *Mission*'s engine thrusting them through the dark ocean. After a while, Mary spoke.

"Let's get in bed," she whispered. "But just to hold each other, I mean." She stared at him in the darkness.

"Sure," he whispered, and felt her pull away, climbing up into the V-berth.

Hesitating a second, Joe slipped off his shirt, Bermuda shorts, and thought about his underwear, but kept it on, and climbed in beside her.

"Let's just embrace," she whispered. "Just be close, all right?"

He nodded, touching her. She rolled over in his arms.

"I have to do this slowly," she whispered. "Oh, Joe! I don't believe we could be…" Her voice trailed off.

"I know," he said softly. "I know."

She patted him, and they held their embrace, the waves' pitching motion rocking them gently until she was sleeping. In a daze of emotions, he sighed a few quiet breaths, feeling relief and affection and happiness and sadness all together until he, too, drifted off to sleep. In the moonlight before dawn, *Mission* continued heading onward, away from the approaching storm, carrying them north across the Atlantic.

Chapter Nine

When Joe awoke, the sunlight was streaming in, and he realized someone was knocking at the doorway.

Frances was standing at the door, peering in and saying, "Oh, my goodness! Mary? I just...well, well."

Joe opened one eye and looked over his head to see Frances, hands on her hips, standing there, looking for all the world like his seventh-grade homeroom teacher.

"Well, I guess it was bound to happen," she said. Then it occurred to him that she was talking about the still-sleeping Mary, lying beside him. He tried a smile on Frances, but she didn't return it.

"Well, it's your turn to take the watch," she proclaimed, as if dictating his punishment for being such a naughty boy. She turned on her heel and marched up the ladder to tell Alex what she'd discovered.

Trying not to awaken Mary, he slipped out of the bunk and pulled on his Bermuda shorts. What a wonderful thing to have spent the last few hours with her! They had only touched in embrace, not sexually at all, and how perfect that had been. They were not ready to go any further; he'd known that, he no more than she, because each of them was still putting to rest their past lives and loves. He kissed his fingers and then laid them ever so gently on her shoulder.

And what was it Frances said when she awakened him? Oh, yes, some kind of scolding as if he and Mary were schoolchildren. The memory flashed through his mind of the time in childhood when he and his next-door neighbor Betty, both eight, were "showing" and Betty's mother walked in on them. So what was that all about with Frances? Why, the whole affair, the meeting up with Mary, the inviting her along, all of it was Frances's doing. What in heaven's name did she expect? Then he realized how silly he was being, reacting to Frances that way. Consider the source, he told himself, as he went into the head to wash up. In fact, they all should be so happy, just as he was happy! Heading into the galley, he poured himself a cup of coffee, noting through the vent in the overhead that Alex had them under sail again. He bounced up the ladder to greet the day.

"Well, good morning there, my boy!" Alex called from behind the helm. He still had on a black sweatshirt that had warded off the nighttime chill. There being just the slightest breath of wind, the sails were furled, and they were running the engine. His eyes were a bit bleary, and the dark stubble of his beard had begun to show. His amused expression showed that Frances had just given him the news.

"Good morning!" Joe smiled back. "Sorry to have overslept."

Frances, bundled up in a padded pink jacket, was brushing her hair, looking away as if Joe, the miscreant, wasn't to be spoken to.

"How are you?" Alex asked. "Everything okay? I mean, well, I know everything must be okay." He laughed, finding the humor in his own words. Joe smiled back. But Frances drew herself up from the seat.

"Men!" she grumbled, disappearing down the hatch. Joe had shrunk back out of her way and turned to watch her go.

"I, uh… well, I'm not sure what to say," he muttered.

"You shocked her a little bit, that's all," Alex said, grinning, once his wife was out of earshot. "Every now and then, Frances gets on this Victorian kind of kick, like people aren't supposed to be human or something." He chuckled. "Congratulations, is all I can say."

If Alex hadn't made that chuckle sound lurid, perhaps Joe would not have grown angry. It was one thing for Frances to jump to conclusions, but Alex was different. The tone of his "congratulations" made Joe's relationship with Mary sound sordid. Having learned that Alex had girlfriends, Joe didn't like the point of view Alex was taking. He turned away, gritted his teeth, and tried to find some way to express his feelings.

"My relationship with her is more meaningful than that," he said, not able to restrain his anger.

Alex raised his eyebrows, somewhat taken aback.

"I see," he said. "Well, I didn't mean anything by it. You will have to agree, though, that it's all rather sudden."

Joe cooled a bit and nodded. "I suppose so."

"Boats have a way of bringing things out," Alex replied, "making them happen." He smiled. "And everybody knows everything that goes on, unfortunately." He gathered up his jacket that he had shed as the sun came up and offered the wheel to Joe. "And don't let Frances get to you," he added. "I think you've seen enough by now to know how to take what she says with a grain of salt."

With Joe taking the helm, they exchanged knowing looks, and Alex went below. The image of Mary beside him in the bed came to him as he stared off at the sunlit waters to the east. Out here in this vast nothing but ocean was some new thing in his life, a mirage much like a shimmering, steamy haze, growing and taking shape.

Alex came climbing back up from below, bringing with him the heavy-duty fishing rod with a big silver spoon and yellow duster on it.

"I'm sorry about all that *stuff* from Frances," he apologized again. "She likes to be in control of things, I guess you've noticed, but she's better now." He tugged on the line just above the reel, setting the drag for the proper tension. "She *will* get off on tangents," he explained. "I think it's her moral attitude, you know? Having her own notion of how things are supposed to be, well, it sort of warps her picture of reality."

Joe nodded, thinking about the notion of "warped reality." Did Joe himself have an accurate conception of what had happened between him and Mary? Was it all just the phenomenon of "the boat" that Alex had been talking about?

"Well, let's try some fishing," Alex said, making his way aft, where they put out the line and placed the rod in its holder.

Joe peered aft, watching the shiny lure break the surface, cutting a sharp little wake in a wave. It dove under, giving off an eerie silver-blue luminescence, a pretended meal for an unsuspecting fish, one more fiction in this world of "the boat."

Then it broke the surface again as a wave lifted it up, and flew a few feet before diving in again.

"Maybe you need to let it out farther," Joe suggested.

Alex nodded and flipped the pawl on the reel, letting another ten yards out. Then he set the lever, checked the tension on the drag again, crossed his fingers in a gesture for luck, and came back through the cockpit.

"Guess I'd better check the weather again," he muttered, "no more sign of that *Blaster* boat, at least."

"Well, there's something I didn't tell you," Joe said. "After supper last night, when we were about eight miles beyond the Bahamas bank, I saw on the radar what may have been the cigarette boat. It appeared to track in toward the coast."

Alex looked up. "You should have told me."

"I didn't say anything because I didn't want to alarm the girls."

"Those *Blaster* guys have to know about my money," Alex said. "That crooked island banker must have tipped them off. Damn, I'd like to strangle him."

Joe raised his eyebrows. "Surely they've given up by now. The storm's probably driven them into port somewhere in Florida."

Alex stared out to sea. "Two million dollars is a lot of money to those bastards," he said. "Hell, it is to me, too. We'd better keep a sharp eye."

Watching Alex climb down the ladder into the salon, Joe considered the possibilities. Finding *Mission*, out at sea more than a hundred miles off the coast, would be very difficult. Of course, if the men somehow knew that the money had to be delivered to Charleston, it wouldn't be too difficult to plot their course from the Bahamas. He took a panoramic look around the vacant horizon, which bright sunlight sharply defined as a knife's edge. No real reason for concern, he decided. Then he noticed Mary passing by below. He looked at her, feeling excited. She glanced up, and their eyes met before she moved out of view into the galley. Her expression in that quick look was sober, self-conscious, uncertain, and not very open and warm. Was she in doubt about him? Or had Frances's reaction embarrassed her? He couldn't get over the idea that she had slept with him, and perhaps she could not either. It somehow seemed like he might have dreamed it.

Then he heard the sound of the radio in the salon. Alex was tuning to a weather channel again. Joe couldn't hear all of the forecast, but he made out that the storm was now more intense." A sinking feeling hit the pit of his stomach.

"Oh Lord," he heard Frances say. "It's coming this way!"

The radio mumble went on for a few minutes and then was turned off. Frances and Alex climbed into the cockpit.

"The storm's headed into the Straits of Florida," Alex reported. The three of them looked astern. All that was visible were cumulus buildups to the south, typical for that time of year. Joe made a mental calculation.

"We're about a hundred miles north of the Bahamas," he said. "And since we got into the Gulf Stream, we've been moving at ten knots." He paused. "Most hurricanes move slower than that, don't they?"

Alex nodded, moving over to make room for Mary, who was coming up. She and Joe exchanged another glance, her expression inscrutable.

"They said it was moving in a northerly direction at six knots," Alex went on. "We might get some of the outer bands of rain, but we're still way ahead of it." He leaned over to the helm, reached the throttle, and increased power a bit. The engine's whine became arduous, and slowly their speed through the water came up a knot. "I don't like to run my engine at that high an RPM," he said, "but I guess this is a special situation."

He slipped past Frances and prepared the outhaul for letting out the mainsail, a fruitless effort to get more speed, Joe guessed, as he helped set the jib as well. The sails billowed some in the light breeze, but with little effect. Frances reached out for Alex's hand and pulled him down beside her. He sat, and she hung on to his shoulder, a kinder, gentler person once again.

Mary came topside, giving Joe a more civil glance, and sat across from Frances. The two women looked at one another soberly.

"If we have to go through a storm," Joe said, thinking of a way to offer encouragement. "I can't think of a better-built, better-equipped, finer sailboat than *Mission*. We're very fortunate to be aboard her."

Alex picked up on the ploy. "There have been few times aboard this boat that I can remember everything working and in such top condition. Marvin gave her a good reconditioning. She's ready for anything."

"Well, I'm not," Frances said. She held Alex even more tightly. "Can't we go to Saint Augustine or Jacksonville or somewhere along there?"

Alex shook his head. "Same as before," he said. "We're what, Joe, over a hundred miles off the coast?"

"I can go check."

But Alex waved him off. "No need. If the storm's going north, then we need to go north and stay ahead of it. Don't worry, we'll make it."

His wife sighed. "Don't worry," she said. It sounded like a parody.

After a brief period of everyone sitting silently, pondering, Frances decided it was time to fix some breakfast for them. Mary said it was her turn, and Joe volunteered to help. Giving him a shrug, she proceeded below to the galley and began getting out bacon and eggs from the refrigerator. Joe attempted a few words of conversation with Mary, but felt rebuffed by her appearing to be focused on the task at hand. It was not that she was impolite, just reticent. They were moving into uncertain territory, he decided, in this relationship that was brewing. He recalled her distant expression as she had sat on the bow while they were anchored at Great Sale Cay, thinking about her dead husband, she had told him. Mary was not over her grief, Joe realized, and gave up discussion, deciding it was better to just leave her alone as much as possible.

He passed the breakfast up to Frances, who had pulled up the leaves of the varnished teak table in the cockpit. The two went topside, and they all enjoyed a pleasant meal. Afterward, it was his and Mary's turn to take the watch. Frances went below, asking Alex to pass down the plates. He bid them a pleasant day and went to join his wife in their siesta. Mary stared out at the sea before them, and it was ten minutes before either spoke again.

"If you'd like a nap," Joe offered, "I don't mind taking the watch by myself."

She turned and gave him another inscrutable kind of look.

"I don't mind," he added. "I know you may be tired from…"—his last words trailed off—"last night."

192

She continued to look at him, that serious, inscrutable expression hinting at a question. "I'd just as soon be up here," she said.

"Glad to have your company," Joe muttered, warmed but still unsure. He wanted to embrace her, but somehow he didn't dare, as if to try to do so would shatter their tenuous, uncertain relationship.

I'm already screwing things up, he thought, staring at her back. *I don't think I can stand getting involved again.*

He set the autopilot, got up, and walked out on the port side and peered aft. Giant thunderheads glinted white in the sunlight way beyond the southern horizon, undergirded by a layer of purplish blue. Fighting off a twinge of dread, he made his way aft to check the fishing line, using it as a way to put some more distance between himself and Mary. He thought about apologizing or something, but he wasn't sure what for.

What the hell? You're already involved, you dummy.

The fishing lure must have seaweed on it, he noted, and busied himself cranking in the line. The rod snapped back as the lure broke the surface and skipped along before diving down again. Reeling the lure up, he pulled the Sargasso weed off, checked the connection to the swivel, released the pawl with his thumb on the reel, and let the line back out. When the lure had disappeared into the sea about thirty yards aft, he set the pawl, checked the drag for proper tension, and placed the rod back in its holder. When he turned around, he saw that Mary was watching him. He looked back aft and pointed.

"That squall is going to catch up with us pretty soon," he called to her, taking a last look astern before returning to the cockpit. She was still standing at the starboard side, facing aft, hanging on to a mast stay, her other hand shielding her eyes, staring at the clouds behind them. Joe stepped up to the GPS and changed its screen so he could read their speed over the ground. They were making eight knots, not getting as much push from the Gulf Stream as before, and the almost-becalmed wind provided no help to the engine.

Returning to the helm, a silhouetted black object to the east caught his eye. Peering out at the sea, he saw a movement, focused on it, and realized it was a large dorsal fin.

"Look, Mary!" he said, pointing.

She turned to see. "What is it?"

"A porpoise, maybe, or an orca even?" Joe reached for the binoculars, put them to his eyes, and turned the focal knob.

The fin disappeared and then reappeared in the waves. It was about fifty yards off, moving along parallel to their course. The fin didn't undulate up and down, but just stayed above the surface.

"A shark," he said. "That's the way sharks swim, just under the surface. It's not an air-breather like the mammals. So it's not going up and down."

"It's so big!" Mary said. "Don't you think?"

Joe passed her the binoculars. "Yeah. More than six feet, at least."

"There's a hole in its dorsal fin," Mary noted. "Like...a bullet hole, maybe?"

"Can I see?"

She handed him the binoculars. The shark submerged behind a wave, but came up again. Joe saw a neat round hole in its fin. The sight of it made his flesh crawl.

"Could it be the same one that Alex shot at yesterday?"

"Surely not," he answered, lying. A slight gust of cooler than usual wind blew across, coming under the bimini. Joe shivered. "Surely not."

A muffled, distant roll of thunder came from closer astern. He looked up, becoming conscious of the sun being more obscured by dark cloud, the sea looking more gray than blue.

"It's gone," Mary said, scanning the area for any sign of the shark.

"He's still out there somewhere," Joe said. He could imagine the creature passing in the dark waters beneath the boat, moving along with them, unseen but ever present, waiting.

Mary stepped back into the cockpit, sat down, crossed her arms, and shivered. "That's awful! It makes you think of that boat, that *Sea Splendor*," she cried, and gave another shiver.

Joe reached over the helm and touched her arm. "That shark can't bother us," he said. "Don't worry."

She took his hand and held it. "It's still terrible." She looked up at him, her blue eyes very serious. "Do you care anything about me?" she asked.

Joe froze, as if time had stopped. He stood at the edge of a precipice. Then he was moving over to her. He embraced her and kissed her cheek.

"Of course," he replied. "I want to see you…get through all of this."

She glanced up at him, her expression turning to a mixture of exasperation and wry humor. "Oh," she said, releasing herself from the embrace. "That's your commitment, is it? Well, thank you."

For a long time, they rode silently together, the only sounds being the dull roar of the laboring engine and the parting wake of the calm, still sea. Occasionally there was a deep rumble from the distant thunderclouds astern.

Mary spoke up. "I'd like to steer a while."

Joe nodded and watched her move around the helm and take a seat. With an attitude of decisive purpose, she steered the boat with the wind in the sails, keeping a careful watch on their heading, as if taking control of it was an important therapy to her. Joe enjoyed just watching her, watching the way the wind blew little blonde tresses of her hair so that she would have to take her slender, cream-skinned hand and brush the strands away from her face. From time to time, she would meet his gaze and smile and then turn her attention back to the helm or just gaze off at the sparkling sea and the waves.

After twelve, Alex and Frances came on deck, bringing sandwiches.

"Wind's no better." Alex noted the soft sails and then looked back at the cumulus buildups to the south. "Typical summer afternoon." He peered around the bimini to view the sails and tightened the jib sheet with the electric winch. "We'll have to take the jib in before long."

"We're likely to get a thunderstorm later," Joe said, "if it follows the usual pattern. So we'll have to reef them before then."

196

Alex watched as the sails drooped in a lull. "Let's go ahead and take 'em in," he said. They busied themselves with the sheet and furling line of the big genoa jib. Then they loosed the halyard, and electrically rolled the mainsail on the boom.

"I just never can get over how easy it is to handle the sails on this boat!" Joe exclaimed.

"Beats hanging over the boom trying to fold the main and lash it down, doesn't it?" Alex agreed.

They heard a closer, more distinct thunderclap from astern. All three of them looked aft for a few silent moments, but no one dared comment.

"Better take a little rest," Alex suggested. "I'll take it for a while."

"I'll get our book and read you a chapter," Frances told him.

"Why don't you take a fix and plot our position before you go?" Alex said.

Joe nodded and went to the GPS to take a reading. Mary went below. After getting the latitude and longitude, he noted the time and went down to the chart table. Mary came out of the head, glanced one of her inscrutable looks at him, and went into her own cabin. Sighing, Joe busied himself at the chart. His position plot showed they were falling behind from their dead-reckoning track, not the best of news with a hurricane behind them. Perhaps Alex's having increased rpms on the engine would help. He thought about listening to the weather again, but decided that there was nothing new to hear anyway. Besides, every time they heard a report, everyone's blood pressure went up a notch.

He had two things to raise his blood pressure, Joe realized—not just the approaching storm, but also Mary, and the prospect of more and greater expressions of their love. He looked around at the forward passageway. The door to her stateroom was open. His pulse quickened as he went forward and peered in. There she lay, clothed and already asleep. It was hard for him to believe that this new, dear person had come into his life. Was it fantasy? He had had no idea that life could present such a wonderful thing for him. For no telling how long, he stood there, regarding her, loving her, wanting her, and swearing to himself to protect her and keep her safe.

After a three-hour, uninterrupted nap, Joe went topside to find the three of them there. He greeted them, but concentrated his attention astern. No sign of the shark, he noted, just the fishing lure trolling along. One giant thunderhead to the south was bearing down on them, its dark blue base becoming indistinguishable from the horizon. The wind died and then came up in agitated spurts. Lightning shot across the clouds and sometimes came down in jagged forks, striking in the sea not far away. Rumbling thunder followed within seconds, coming so close.

"What happens if lightning strikes the boat?" Mary wanted to know.

"They say you're shielded by the mast from being electrocuted," Joe replied. "But I don't know. I've heard of people being knocked unconscious. It's pretty rare, though."

The wind swept toward them, leaving the look of gray chill bumps on the sea as *Mission* listed to starboard when the wind hit broadside. The rain followed, first in a few drops and then a sheet of water that blinded their view. Mary scrambled away from the rain pouring in from the windward side, but stayed at the helm, holding course.

In ten minutes, the rain slackened. In fifteen, it had stopped.

"Just a storm in an outer band of the hurricane," Joe commented. The problem was, he thought, if the outer bands whirling off the center were catching up, then maybe the eye was gaining on them too.

In twenty minutes, the sun burst forth low in the west, producing great reddish streaks on the water. Joe took a towel and wiped off the seats where the wind had blown rain under the bimini top. Frances went below to see how things had weathered down there.

A series of sporadic clicking sounds came from the stern. Joe looked back to see the fishing rod bending and quivering.

"Fish on!" he yelled, and worked his way to the stern. He lifted the rod from its holder, began reeling, and realized he had a good fish. "Mary! Slow the engine to idle, and come catch this fish!"

"I'm steering," she called back.

"Well, set the autopilot, and come on!" Joe fought the fish for a few minutes until she was standing beside him. "Here," he said, passing the rod over. "Keep the rod tip up, and wind in when you feel the fish ease up. Don't rush it, but don't give him any slack either."

She took the rod, and Joe could see she knew something about catching fish.

"Wow!" she exclaimed. "I've never felt anything this big!"

At the cut of the engine, Alex had headed topside. "There's a gaff in the hatch by the butane tank," he called.

Never taking his eye off the struggle, Joe opened the hatch and pulled out the gaff. Mary had her feet spread wide apart for stability, but the rolling of the boat made it difficult to keep balance. Joe put his right hand on the rail and his left hand in the back of her pants, grasping the waist to steady her, aware that it was the first time he had touched her this way.

"Thanks," she said, cranking away. "That helps." It took about ten minutes more before the fish was exhausted and surfacing close enough to see. It was a dolphin, a mahi mahi—the fish, not the mammal—its blue and yellow colors brilliant under water. The fish saw the boat and sounded. The reel squealed as line peeled off.

"Let it run," Joe said. "Don't try to fight him while he's sounding. Just be ready to crank when he stops."

She nodded, perspiration now beading on her face. Soon she was winding in again. Once more they could see the fish, four feet in length. Mary worked him in close to the stern. Joe leaned over the rail, got the gaff in the fish's gills, and pulled him up with a mighty tug. The fish flopped on deck and was free of the gaff. Joe fell on it, tackling it almost, lying on top of it to keep it from flopping overboard.

Laughing, Alex called to Frances to bring up the vodka. He had to tell her twice before she understood and hurried up with the bottle. Alex took it from her, went aft, and poured some in the fish's gills. It calmed and died. It was a beautiful mahi mahi.

"Twenty-five pounds if it's an ounce," Alex said.

Mary was ecstatic. "Earnest will never believe this!" she blurted. Then she grimaced, glancing at Joe, realizing she had mentioned her lost husband. Joe caught it, understanding that Earnest was still on her mind.

Alex changed the subject. "Okay, Mary," he said, "now you get to clean it." At her expression, the two men had to laugh.

200

An hour later, after Joe, not Mary, had gutted and filleted the fish, they were having a feast of the freshest, tastiest dolphin baked in butter that was ever served anywhere. They were all in the salon around the dinner table, enjoying it together. Frances was civil; the sea was calm. Except for the excessive noise of the engine running at high rpm, the atmosphere in the salon was quite pleasant.

Alex told a fish story about how once he and his son caught a boat load of king mackerel off of Panama City. Mary said that once she went fly-fishing with Earnest in Montana, a river near Missoula, one of the prettiest places she had ever seen. Frances said she didn't like to fish and was glad Alex made her go only once.

"I ended up paddling the boat along the bank while he casted," she said. "All I got was a backache."

"But you ate the bream when we fried 'em, sure enough," Alex reminded her.

"You must have done some fishing in your lifetime," Mary asked Joe. "I could tell by the way you coached me on bringing in the dolphin."

"Part of a captain's job," he said.

Chapter Ten

Early the next morning, Alex checked the weather again. The storm was still moving slowly north, but so were they, and there seemed to be no immediate concern. It seemed they would reach Charleston in time, and the storm would either turn out to sea or at least go ashore south of them.

Just as Joe was about to take the watch, the diesel engine developed the valve clicking that Marvin Mann had warned about. He consulted with Alex, and they shut it down. Joe went below to put more of Marvin's additive into the oil. When they started it up again, the clicking was just as bad. There was no reason for the clicking to have started again that they could find, except that they had been running it very hard.

"I should have put more additive in sooner," Alex moaned in disbelief. "That's the best kind of engine money can buy!"

"Why does the clicking matter?" Frances asked. "It's not bothering me."

"It's not the noise," Alex groaned. "If it throws a rod, that will kill the engine, and then where will we be?"

They had been motoring, but with the sails out, so that the boat had slowed to five knots in the light wind when they stopped the engine, even though they were getting some push from the Gulf Stream. The boat had an auxiliary diesel generator, which, after a couple of hours, Alex started up and then ran for half an hour at a time to charge the batteries. As midmorning approached, however, the wind eased to an even more gentle breeze. With full main and jib, they could make no more than four knots, sometimes three. Joe checked the oil in the engine and added a quart. Alex restarted the engine and increased rpm until the clicking got bad.

"We'd better not run over sixteen hundred rpm's," Alex declared, pulling the throttle back, and left Frances at the wheel, going below. He and Joe listened to weather on the VHF, which was not receiving well at 150 miles offshore. From the Florida Straits, the hurricane was tracking north.

"Of course, as the storm gets closer, the winds will increase," Alex said, "and that will speed us up."

"But when the waves build, it will slow us down," Joe countered. They listened to the repeated forecast again, recorded its latitude and longitude, and then plotted the eye of the storm on the chart.

"Maybe it will turn out to sea," Alex said. "Most of them do make a turn to the northeast."

Joe looked at the position of the eye. "But if it doesn't, we could end up in the northeast quadrangle of the storm," he noted. "That's the worse place to be."

"Well, it could do a hell of a lot of things," Alex said with irritation. "Who knows?"

"I'm setting the autopilot," Frances called, and came down to join them.

"You've gotten us into this, Alex dear." Frances said "dear" with less than a sweet tone. "So now it's time to call for help."

"What? You mean a Mayday? We're sailing along in calm seas. Nobody would pay the slightest bit of attention."

"I mean, call the coast guard. They've got sense enough to know we're in danger, even if you don't. Tell them to send a helicopter. You got so much money, you could pay for it out of petty cash. Hell, with what you got in your checking account, you could buy the damn helicopter."

"Listen," he turned on her to say. "First of all, we couldn't reach them on the VHF if we wanted to. We're too far out. The coast guard didn't even answer us at the wreck."

"But the *Blaster* people did," Joe pointed out, considering telling that the radio had been set on short range before, but deciding not to say anything.

Alex grimaced.

"They must have been pretty close to us then," Joe said.

Alex reacted by getting angry. He pointed to the empty cell phone charger on the navigation table. "Well, we could have made a private call on the cell phone, but *somebody* threw the goddamn thing in the drink!"

"And somebody couldn't stay away from that bitch, Bea Johnson, could *he*?" she shot back.

Joe looked away, embarrassed. Alex changed his emotions like a chameleon changing colors.

"Now, Frances," he said in his smooth, soothing tone, "you know you always jump to conclusions."

"I don't know anything!" she said, tearing up. "You are so mean!"

Alex took her hand and pulled her toward him. "Everything will be all right, Franny," he said. "Don't worry."

"How can you say not to worry?" she exclaimed, pulling away. "Here we are with a hurricane coming this way, and you won't even try the radio!"

"I don't think it will reach that far, even on full-power setting," he repeated.

"Have you tried? No!" She charged down to the radio, tuned it to channel sixteen, and picked up the mike.

"What are you going to say?" Alex asked. "Wait! Just try for a radio check, okay? If you get somebody, then we can discuss our situation."

She glanced at him an instant, then spoke into the microphone. "Radio check, Mayday!" she called, compromising with him.

"Don't say "Mayday!" Alex shouted.

Despite the circumstances, Joe had to grin. She tried "radio check" over and over, and finally there was a reply.

"*Mission*, this is, uh, *Sailfish*, over."

Frances jumped at the voice. "Oh, hello, who are you? Where are you? Did you know there's a hurricane coming? We're sailing north, and my husband is crazy to have us out here, but anyway, we—"

Joe reached over and turned the radio off.

"What are you doing, you crazy Jonah?" Frances shouted at him. "I was talking to—"

"You were talking to *Blaster*," Joe interrupted. "I would swear it's that same voice as before."

"It's not possible," Alex said. "They can't be anywhere near here."

"You wouldn't think so," Joe agreed. "But somehow...Well, I saw a contact on the radar near Mantanilla Reef when we were about ten miles north of it. They were heading in to shore."

Alex looked very worried.

"Maybe they went in to some port in Florida and gassed up, and then came back out looking for us."

"That's crazy," Alex scoffed.

"I don't know," Joe said. "People will do a lot of crazy things for two million dollars."

"What's he talking about?" Frances asked, looking at her husband.

"Just an expression, I guess," Alex said. "Anyway, stay off the radio, for Christ's sake. Just in case."

She looked up at the single sideband unit that was mounted up near the radar screen.

"What about this thing?" she demanded. "Isn't it supposed to have a better range?" She flicked the on switch, her glare defying her husband. It came on and showed the number 2182 in the dial. She tried her "Radio check, Mayday" into its microphone, but nothing discernable happened.

"Doesn't this work either?" Her voice was full of consternation.

He shook his head. "I doubt it." In order to avoid further recrimination, he charged up the ladder to take the helm.

Joe went over to help Frances be sure the switch on the panel of the single-sideband was on. Still it didn't respond.

"Damn!" Frances shouted. "Why doesn't he keep this stuff up?"

It occurred to Joe that she could have been keeping up with some of the stuff herself, but he didn't say a word.

"And what about that thing?" she said, going over to the yellow box with an antenna that was mounted in an emergency release bracket. "That's supposed to be for rescue."

"That's the EPIRB," Joe said, "an emergency positioning radio beacon. You use that when you abandon ship."

"Well, that's what I'm wanting to do, damn it," Frances said, and laughed.

Mary came out of her cabin, looking refreshed from four-hour's sleep, and walked over to see what they were doing. Joe gave her hand a squeeze, and Frances greeted her with a small tirade.

"Look at this, Mary. This is ridiculous, isn't it? Here we are in the middle of the damn ocean, with a hurricane bearing down on us, and I'm running around trying to find out about all these gadgets that I've wanted to throw overboard because they mess up the decor. Just look. Who wants that ugly yellow box next to the blue settee?"

They had a good laugh together.

"Okay, Joseph," Frances said, turning her attention to him. "You get us through this predicament, and I'll give you a million dollars."

He raised his eyebrows. "You will?" he asked facetiously.

"Well, I'll make Alex give you a million, anyway," she replied. "He has all the money, and all I have is the time." She laughed again, going topside to join her husband.

After fixing sandwiches of leftover mahi mahi for everyone, Joe and Mary took the watch. Mary assumed the helm while Joe lay on the cockpit seat to nap. Awake but with his eyes closed, he thought about the cash stowed in the forward locker, conscious of the fact that Mary still did not know about it. Apparently, Frances did not, either. He had been wrong in not telling Mary about it from the beginning. Perhaps then she would have decided to leave them at Coopers Town. But instead, she now was as deep into this whole mess as he was. But he hadn't known her at that time, and at that point had felt more mercenary allegiance to the Smiths than to her. He hadn't cared much about her at that point, but now that he knew her better, it was different. He looked up at her, thinking how he hadn't been entirely forthcoming. She noted his expression and looked quizzical.

"I'm so sorry," he said.

"For what, Joe? If you're apologizing for my being here, don't forget that I decided to come along myself."

"I haven't told you everything," he said in a very low voice. "Alex is smuggling two million bucks back into the States. It's his money, but smuggling is still illegal. And maybe he's going to do insider trading or something."

Mary looked shocked. "And that money's on board now?" she asked. "Cash?"

He nodded. "It's up in the forward locker in a couple of boxes. And he's supposed to deliver it to Charleston by a certain time. That's why he's been so insistent about heading north instead of going to Florida."

Mary leaned back and shut her eyes, thinking a moment. Then she opened them with a start, looking at Joe. "And that's why that *Blaster* boat is looking for us?"

Joe pursed his lips. "I think so."

"Damn," she said.

"I should have told you this a long time ago," he said. "Well, I didn't know it all at once in the beginning. I learned about it in bits and pieces along the way."

She raised her eyebrows. "But you're in on it now?"

He rubbed his hands over his eyes. "In a way, I suppose," he admitted, as much to himself as to her. "Back at Great Sale, I should have insisted that we go to West Palm on *Terajay*. Maybe I should have forced Alex somehow…" He paused, feeling like such a louse, now too ashamed to tell her about the $100,000 that Alex had promised him.

"I'm not sure how you could have insisted," she said. "It's his boat, and so he sort of rules." She paused. "Do you think Frances knows?"

"I don't think so. Not about the money being on board and all that. Anyway, she was asleep when they brought the boxes on board."

"Too bad," Mary said. "She might have been able to get him to abandon the idea."

Joe sighed. "I don't know. All I know is that I went along with it, and now look what a fix I've let you get in." He lowered his head. "I'm so sorry."

"You were just being loyal to your employer, I guess," Mary said. "It's one of your good qualities that I admire so much." She paused. "In this case, I guess it's also one of your weaknesses."

Joe chuckled. "I guess so," he said. Then he gritted his teeth. "All I know now is that somehow I'm going to get us out of this. I don't know how"— he took her hand— "but I am."

"I believe in you," she said.

The statement, meant to be a compliment, stabbed him deep within.

"Oh, Mary," he said, slapping his hand against his forehead. "Oh God, what have I let you get into?"

"Next you'll take the blame for the hurricane, too, I guess," she said.

Chapter Eleven

During his off-watch sleep that night, after Alex had returned on deck complaining of a headache but insisting on taking over, Joe awoke and noticed that the seas were picking up. He was being rolled about some in the V-berth. On one occasion, he heard distant thunder. *Better to sleep on,* he told himself, *while you can.* He turned over on his side and spread his legs to help him keep from falling out.

He was awakened once more by the sound of Mary going into the head. Joe made out the time on his luminous chronometer and realized they had another hour or so until time to take the watch. *Oh, no*, he thought, *she must be seasick.* But in a moment, he heard her come out of the head and walk aft toward the companionway. Joe rolled over again, expecting that Mary would wear herself out before they were even due to go on watch and would end up asleep on one of the cockpit benches, leaving him to stand it by himself.

When Joe did awaken and go topside, however, he found Mary at the helm, with Alex asleep on a bench, and Frances was asleep in her cabin.

"I decided to come on up," Mary said. "I thought they needed to sleep."

Alex awoke at the sound of voices and sat up in the gloom. "Hello, ole man," he said in a raspy voice. "This lady run us aground yet?"

Joe smiled. "Not a shoal in sight."

In the dim red light of the compass binnacle, Joe could see Mary grinning, too. It occurred to him that she was becoming a pretty darn good shipmate, after all, and seemed to be most comfortable at the helm. Joe peered at the speed log and noted that they were making four knots in light wind, not enough to escape the storm if it was heading their way.

Alex went below and turned on the radio, which sounded faint topside. Then his silhouette appeared, coming up the ladder.

"I believe we're going to get a little weather," he said. "But maybe the eye will miss us by fifty miles or so."

No one replied, and the three of them contemplated the possibilities in silence. Joe began to try to anticipate problems.

"I'm worried about the dinghy," he said. "If we start taking water over the bow, it could get loose. No telling what it would take with it."

"I guess we can tow it," Alex said. "We'll probably lose it, but you're right about taking water over the bow." He started down the ladder. "We'd better wait for daylight before fooling with it, though. I'll help you put it over the side in the morning."

During the next four hours, Mary and Joe took turns at the helm. They also had to watch the way the wind shifted, being sure that it didn't back the sails. The wind was coming from the southeast, gusting on occasion, but nothing serious yet. *The more it pushes us north, the better,* Joe surmised. At one time, he thought he saw the fin of the big shark moving along a few yards to port,

214

but in the night gloom, he couldn't be sure. He imagined the vast darkness of the deep, deep sea and fought back his dread of the hellish unknown chasm below them.

At two, he plotted a GPS fix and determined that they now were sixty miles off the coast of Jacksonville, and they would be crossing sea lanes, so it was necessary to watch for ships, though they had seen none so far. He put the radar in radiate and checked for contacts within the sixteen-mile range, finding nothing. Once more the idea crossed his mind that *Blaster* could be out there. Had they given up by now? Surely, no one would venture so far out at sea in such a boat with a storm coming, no matter how fast it was. Still, when there's millions to be had, men will do desperate things.

Three in the morning came, and yet Alex and Frances didn't come up for their watch. The sky had been clear and starry all night, but now clouds were gathering to the south, and faint flashes of lightning created glimmers in the gloom. Saying she wasn't sleepy, Mary encouraged Joe to nap on the bench while she kept watch. He lay back and closed his eyes and was out very soon.

He awakened to a rumble of thunder, just as Alex and Frances were coming up the companionway. Mary was still at the helm. The wind was freshening, gusting from time to time, slapping at the sails. He sat up and greeted everyone. It was an abbreviated kind of reply he got from the Smiths, who were more concerned with what they saw behind them.

"I just looked at the radar," Alex said. "There's a boat or a ship coming toward us from the west. It's moving pretty fast." The two men exchanged worried glances.

"How far out?"

"About eight miles, at last look," Alex said. "I'd better keep an eye on it." He was interrupted by a flash that lit up the sky, followed by a peal of thunder.

"There's a squall line coming up from the south," Joe said. A gust hit the jib hard, making a whip-cracking sound. "We'd better reef up a bit."

Frances asked if anyone wanted coffee, but Alex took her below, showed her the blip on the radar, and told her to sit down and watch it. Then, when he came up, Mary turned into the wind while he and Joe reefed the sails in halfway. When Mary came back to course, the main's boom swung hard over in a gust, banging with a thundering metallic clank.

"Damn, another jibe!" Alex said.

"Oh, was that my fault?" Mary asked. "I'm so sorry."

Alex waved a dismissal. "With the wind gusting around this way, it could happen to anybody," he said. "If we had an engine with any power, I'd furl the main entirely." Alex peered down the hatchway. "Frances, where did you go?" he called, not finding her at the radar.

"I'm fixing coffee," she said.

"I told you to watch that contact on the radar."

"Okay, okay," she said, and went back to the navigation table.

Looking off to the west, Joe saw nothing but the faint horizon, which was very much obscured by both darkness and rain.

"Let's see about that dinghy," Alex said.

216

Finally! Joe thought. It wouldn't do any good to point out the fact that dealing with the dinghy was a little late in coming. Now that they might get in high seas, seawater might wash over the bow and under the dinghy, breaking it loose.

Alex reached over and flipped on the deck lights that shone down from the mast. It startled Joe.

"Is that a good idea? Lighting us up that way?" he asked. "Suppose that contact on the radar is the cigarette boat."

"Surely not," Alex said, but reached down and turned off the deck lights anyway. They peered off to the west, but saw nothing.

"I guess we'd better put on life jackets," Alex said. He went below and brought up one for himself and one for Joe. Joe asked if there was a safety line that they could rig down the length of the deck, but Alex said he hadn't seen that line in years. It was something they should have found and rigged before they ever got to sea. So now they simply put on the jackets and decided they were ready.

"Be careful out there," Mary pleaded.

Joe patted her hand and nodded, following Alex on deck. Rain pelted them as they moved forward, hanging on to the mast stays. The waves had picked up enough to make standing difficult.

"Frances says that that boat on radar is getting closer," Mary called.

Joe peered off to port, but saw nothing. "Just keep an eye out," he answered, turning his face away from the blowing rain.

"Be careful," she called again.

Hanging on to whatever he could find, he made his way forward. The waves were growing higher. Alex had unshackled a spare halyard from the mast and identified its winch position. He took the crank handle Joe had brought and fitted it into the winding hole. Having to hold on with one hand, Joe managed to take the end of the halyard forward and fastened it to the pad eye in the bow of the inflatable rubber dinghy.

"You'll have to untie the lashings," Alex called above a now-whistling wind.

Joe knelt down and began to untie the lashing line, and took it across the upside-down boat and pulled it out of the pad eye in the deck. He had it almost undone when they heard the sound of a high-speed engine off to port. It was that familiar and dreaded *throb, throb, throb,* but muffled by the wind. As he stood up to look, a bright searchlight glared across the water, sweeping around, searching.

"What the hell?" Alex said, grabbing the mast to steady himself.

The light swept back again, fixing on *Mission*, momentarily blinding the two of them. The boat raced toward them and charged past. As it went by, its light swept away long enough for Joe to see that it was *Blaster*.

"It's them!" he shouted to Alex.

The cigarette boat swung around, rolling and pitching madly, paralleling their course about thirty yards away.

"We're coming aboard," the man at the wheel shouted.

Alex and Joe dropped what they were doing and struggled to get back into the cockpit. *Blaster* inched closer, the two boats pitching wildly.

218

"Stay where you are," the pirate yelled. "Do as I say, and nobody'll get hurt."

Then two pistol shots came from behind him. Joe jerked his head around to see Frances, pistol in hand, shooting.

Ducking as bullets passed over his head, the boat driver gunned the engine, and the cigarette boat leapt forward, charging off in escape. It ran a hundred yards out and began a turn. Rushing back to the cockpit behind Alex, Joe saw the speedboat roll dangerously as it turned parallel to the waves.

"Frances, what the hell?" Alex yelled at his wife.

"Scared them off before," she said, still holding the pistol.

With a guttural roar of its engine, the speedboat made a circling turn and came charging at them again in the gloom. Just as it lunged past their bow, a staccato of gunshots came at them, appearing like sparks from the muzzle. *Plang, plang!* Bullets hit hardware on the sailboat's deck, and Joe dove into the cockpit, crashing into Alex. Both women screamed as the speedboat roared on past.

"Oh God!" Frances screamed, and dropped the pistol in shock.

Mary grabbed Joe, letting go of the wheel, and *Mission* slewed to the left, listing way over.

Joe saw that the speedboat was making another circle to the left, struggling in the high waves to come around. The shallow draft hull tossed about, being thrown off the crest of the waves. Its guttural engine roared in spurts as the propeller raced, cavitating in the foamy seas.

Frances recovered enough to reach down and pick up the pistol again. Alex dug into the cockpit table and came out with a flare gun. He loaded it and slid out to the gunwale, where he might get a chance to fire at them. Joe realized it was a pitiful response to a machine gun. They watched in terror as *Blaster*, a hundred yards off, came lunging back toward *Mission*. Joe looked for something, anything, just some defense.

"Mary, let me at the wheel," he shouted, pushing her toward the deck. "Get down, get down!" He spun the helm to the right, and *Mission* lumbered, heeling over and wallowing, turning parallel to the high waves. Joe steadied up in the trough of a wave, and the next one carried the sailboat up and crashing down, rolling way over to starboard.

"What are you doing?" Alex shouted. "You're going to—"

He was interrupted by *Mission*'s next deep roll to starboard, the gunwale dipping deep into the sea, water rushing into the cockpit. Grabbing Mary and holding on, Joe glanced back to see the speedboat astern, roaring back upon them, and the machine gun fired a burst again. Bullets whammed against the hull below. The cigarette boat charged into the trough of a huge wave, careening up on its side, its bow digging into the sea. The next wave broke over the speedboat, and it rolled, dipping its gunwale, its engines making a terrific whine.

For a moment, that seemed to stop time, the black hull teetered on its side. Then it capsized with a great "*whoomph*" and spume of spray. And then there was only the sound of the wind and rain.

Joe tugged on the wheel and turned *Mission* to the left, putting her bow at an angle to the waves. Everyone looked up to see the dark bottom of the cigarette boat tossing about in the waves, fading into the gloom astern. Mary was hanging on to Joe, heaving in sobs. Joe's pulse was racing so that he felt nauseous.

220

Frances was still crying. For a full minute, no one moved, frozen in shock.

"We have to look for survivors," Joe said, struggling to find his voice. "And see if—"

"To hell with that," Alex said. "First off, how would we get back around to them with no engine? What? Tack back in this wind?"

A great thump on the bow stopped him in mid-sentence. The sailboat pitched across a great wave, and there was another bang at the bow. The mainsail made a great popping sound as it jerked against the preventer. Then, Joe remembered the dinghy.

"The dinghy's still untied," Joe said. "It's just sitting loose up there." There was another great thump, and they all peered out through the windshield trying to see through the now-solid wall of rain.

"Nothing we can do about it right now," Alex said. "We'll just have to wait it out."

The next wave rolled them to starboard, and the two men were knocked off-balance, falling down on the benches. Joe hung on to the wheel and struggled to stand up to steer.

"They shot at us," Frances cried. "I didn't think they would shoot back."

Mary came out of her shock enough to comfort Frances, taking her hand. Then she stood up and clung to Joe as he steered. Everyone was breathing heavily, shocked and drained. Joe felt a tremendous shiver run through his body and shook his head hard, trying to shake it off and concentrate on steering. Alex took the pistol from Frances's limp hand and stowed it, along with the flare gun, in the cockpit table. Still standing beside Joe, clinging to him, Mary kept glancing back astern, peering into the darkness.

"Shouldn't we try to… do something?" Mary said, continuing to look aft.

"Hell no!" Alex said.

"I didn't see anybody come up after they flipped, did you?" Joe asked. "Still, we've got to go look." He turned to the left, knowing they would run into a trough again. "Everybody hang on."

"You're crazy," Alex shouted. "Turn back on course." His voice was smothered by the banging of the dinghy against the mast. "That thing might come loose and fly in here."

Joe could see he was right. He turned back into the oncoming waves. "We can't risk it," he agreed.

Mary looked at Joe just as the boat pitched downward and the dinghy banged on the deck.

"It's too dangerous for us to search," he said. "We'll have to try to call the coast guard."

"I'll do it," Frances said, heading for the hatchway.

"No coast guard," Alex said.

"Look, Alex," Joe said. "We have both a legal and a moral obligation to report what happened."

"Forget 'em, the bastards," Alex replied. "The coast guard will just screw things up."

"We don't have to tell them anything but just that we witnessed a terrible accident at sea," Joe argued. "We say what happened, give the position, and then say that we're too much in distress ourselves to render assistance."

"Just like by the book, huh, Captain," Alex said.

"Damn straight," Joe said. "By the book." He saw that Mary and Frances were staring at Alex with reproach. Joe glared at him and pointed to the wheel.

Alex hesitated and then moved over to take it. "Okay. Just don't mention the shooting or where we're headed or anything."

Without a word, Joe went to the GPS, read their latitude and longitude, and went below to the radio with Frances following. He made sure it was set on high power and tuned to channel sixteen.

"Mayday, Mayday, Mayday," he called. "Sailing vessel *Mission* calling U. S. Coast Guard in the vicinity of the Georgia coast."

With the VHF transmitting on full power, there was an almost immediate reply. He reported simply that they had seen a black-hulled motorboat capsize in heavy seas and read off the position. After a read-back to verify the accuracy of the report, the radioman began a barrage of questions. Joe answered by saying that *Mission* was on a northerly course, had four souls on board, and was laboring and threatened too much by heavy seas to assist in any search for survivors. He didn't want to say that they were in need of assistance themselves because that was what he'd agreed to with Alex. The dinghy clunked hard on deck above him, which gave him an excuse to say he was needed on deck, sign off, and thereby avoid responding to all the questions. Storing the mike in its bracket, he made his way topside to join the others.

Joe could see tears on Mary's cheeks, but they were the only sign of her being daunted. In a momentary stillness of the wind, something hard pelted the bimini above them, and the deck began to rattle.

"Is that hail?" Mary asked.

They saw that small balls of ice were striking the deck outside. In a few moments, they quit falling as suddenly as they had begun. Then a sound, like the rumbling approach of a freight train, surrounded them.

"A water spout! Look!" Joe cried.

Coming at them through the sheets of rain was a tornadic wind that had lifted a shaft of water from the sea. It struck the bow, slewing *Mission* to the right like some toy boat. Tons of water poured down the forward deck, lifting the dinghy up and throwing it with great violence against the dodger windshield. Canvas and plastic ripped with a scream, and the metal rods supporting the bimini top bent down like so much spaghetti. They were knocked off their feet and came up in a mass of torn canvas. The dinghy was lying on top, its hard bottom cradled in the bent, torn bimini. In the next instant, in a great gust of wind, it was carried overboard and gone. Then the water spout was gone, too.

"Oh, damn!" Alex cursed, getting up and spitting blood. A supporting rod had hit him in the mouth. He shoved the remains of the canvas away from the helm so he could steer.

Something else was banging hard against the mast, but they couldn't see what it was. Hard rain pelted them. In such warm weather, no one had thought about donning foul-weather gear, but now there was a deep chill in the air. In a slight daze, Joe sat on the bench and realized he had been whacked in the head by the dinghy or something. He tried to shake off the pain and looked around for the water spout. If it still existed, he couldn't see it in the dim twilight, nor could he see any sign of the capsized cigarette boat that would have been a couple of miles away by that time.

224

At the sound of the crash, Frances had struggled back up the ladder. She cried in horror at the sight and then went to see about her husband's mouth injury. While she attended him, the banging on the mast continued, striking every time the boat rolled.

Joe looked up at Mary. "You okay?" he asked.

She nodded, wiping the back of her hand across her eyes and steering on. Joe gave her a thumbs-up and peered up at the darkened mast.

"I think that's the radar dome banging around," he said.

Alex looked up and put his hand above his eyes. Rain obscuring his vision, Joe peered forward and saw in silhouette the big metal dome dangling from the mast, swinging like a pendulum, menacingly close.

"I hope it doesn't come down on us," Alex said. He put his hand to his swollen lip to check for blood, and wiped his wet sleeve across it.

Even with just a postage-stamp-sized main up, the wind carried them along at a good pace. The radar dome swung into the mast again with a great clang. Joe considered what would happen if it broke loose while swinging above the cockpit. If it hit someone on the head, it would be fatal. But to go out on deck now was to risk being swept overboard. He glanced at Mary sitting the most forward, in the most vulnerable seat. He gritted his teeth and checked to see that his life jacket was still fastened.

"I need to go secure that radar dome," he said.

Alex gave him a respectful look, understanding the risk. "Okay, but be careful," he said. He reached over to the steering console to turn on the deck lights.

Joe went out on the port side and made his way forward, hanging on to lifelines, his head now aching like holy hell. It was not as easy to move around there since he couldn't trust a handhold on the remaining bimini supports. Climbing up the superstructure, he grabbed the mast, just as the radar dome banged into it again. It was hanging down by its connecting cable, about at the height of Joe's head, a round white metal box, weighing at least fifty pounds.

Lightning struck close by, with a massive thunderclap. With another roll of the boat, the dome swung toward him, and he ducked. It slammed against the mast again, and he shuddered, knowing that one blow would knock him out for sure, maybe kill him. He imagined being knocked overboard, waking up in the waves, watching the dark hulk of the boat moving away in the night.

Timing his moves to the rhythmic swings and bangs, he loosened one of the spare halyards from a cleat. Just as he was reaching up to grab the dome, a wave rolled them to port, swinging it outboard. Losing his balance in the next roll, he grabbed for a handhold, missed, and found himself thrown atop the lifelines. As the boat rolled, he felt himself hanging over the side, the frothy waves rushing by near his face. The wire lifeline felt like the lash of a whip across his chest despite the life jacket, and his right knee was in pain. His feet had come off the deck, but he was wedged against the superstructure, most of his body hanging over the side, above the turbulent sea. Then a wave rolled them back upright again. The wind whistled in the shrouds and stays above. He got himself upright, grabbed a stay, and staggered up, his right knee hurt and almost giving way.

Climbing back up to the mast, watching for his chance, he lunged at the mast, reaching around it with both hands and grabbing the radar dome on the other side. The boat pitched, and his nose banged into the mast hard enough to make him see stars.

226

Clinging on to the dome with his left hand, he worked his right hand down to find the loose halyard. Spending more time hanging on than tying, the rain pelting him the face, Joe managed to pass the halyard around the outer ring on the dome and secured it to the mast. Then, realizing his nose was bleeding, he dragged himself to the cockpit. Mary reached out a hand to help him when he got close.

"Oh, your nose. I saw when you hit it," she said.

"Did you see me nearly go over the side?" he asked, wiping his wet sleeve across his mouth and looking at the blood.

"I was praying for you so much, Joe," she said. Joe nodded and sank down on the bench beside her, his arm around her waist.

"I thought we'd lost you there for a second," Alex said, regarding his nose. "You all right?"

Joe nodded. His nose had quit bleeding, though his whole head was throbbing.

There was a faint chopping noise in the distance. A few miles astern, where the cigarette boat had capsized, they could see an airborne searchlight scanning the ocean.

"A search-and-rescue helicopter," Joe said. "That was a pretty fast response, considering the weather."

"They'll never find that black hull in this," Alex said.

"Shouldn't we call them on the radio?" Frances asked. Under ordinary conditions, she'd have been galloping toward the radio, but in their extreme circumstances, she was quiet.

"Frances and I need to go below to secure things," Alex said to Joe, "if you two can manage."

Joe nodded, and Mary stood up to take the helm.

"We'll send up some rain gear," Alex added before closing the hatch behind him.

Joe looked up at Mary. Her wet blouse clung to her body. A mat of blonde hair dripped rainwater down her forehead, which she kept wiping away. Another bolt of lightning struck nearby, and Mary cried out in surprise and ducked her head a little when the peal of thunder rumbled over them. But to him, she seemed to be magnificent.

"Want me to take it a while?" Joe asked. He stood up, but his knee gave way, and he fell back down.

"I'm okay," she said. "You'd better lie down and put your head back to keep your nose from bleeding again."

Joe nodded, watching her steering for all she was worth. In the sky behind her, he saw that the spotlight was heading west, and told Mary.

"Are they already giving up?" she asked.

Joe shook his head. "Looks like the helo's reached its bingo fuel and is going home. They may send another one if the weather breaks."

"I wish I could feel sorry for those men," Mary said, "as bad as they were."

"We're just damned lucky that the storm got 'em." Joe laughed. "I never thought I'd be calling myself lucky to be in a storm."

"Are we in the hurricane, do you think?" she asked.

Joe blinked, wishing he could say this was the worse. "We're just on the edge," he replied, "in some outer bands on the northeastern side, which is the worst side to be on. Maybe the center won't get any closer," he added, "but who knows."

"What's this yellow light?" she asked, pointing to a small indicator on the steering console. Joe looked over.

"That shows the bilge pump is running," he said.

"I never noticed it before," Mary said, "at least not being on all the time like this."

The hatch was pushed open from below. Alex appeared in a yellow foul weather jacket, with a safety harness around him. His lower lip was still swollen, but not bleeding.

"You two go below and get some dry clothes on," he said. "I can handle it a while." Mary gladly relinquished the helm.

"The bilge pump light has been on a long time," Joe reported.

"I'm not surprised," Alex said, "considering how much water has come into the cockpit."

Mary helped Joe stand up and move to the ladder. The descent was painful for him. Every roll of the boat sent shock waves of pain through his knee. He gritted his teeth and succeeded in letting out only one groan. It was pleasant to be out of the wind and rain at least.

"I made some coffee," Frances said, hanging on with one hand and offering the cup to Joe with the other. He took it from her, and it sloshed some on one of the Oriental throw rugs.

"Sorry."

"It's not important," she said, pouring Mary a cup, too. A day ago, Frances would have made a to-do about cleaning up the spot, but concerns were a bit different now.

"Is the weather easing up any?"

"Not that I can tell," Joe said. A crash of thunder punctuated his statement. She shivered.

"How did we ever get into this fix?" she moaned. "When we get home, I'm telling Alex I'm finished with this blue water sailing business. He can have it." She peered out of the hatch. "Oh, he's out there all alone!" she cried. She thrust her arms into a foul weather jacket, pulled the hood up, and headed topside.

Mary had gone forward and was now pulling off her wet clothes in the passageway. Nude and shivering, she grabbed a towel and worked her way into the head. Joe limped past to his cabin, shut the door, and struggled out of his clothes, taking pains not to pull against his knee. The thought of a hot shower occurred to him, but then he remembered that they had shut down the hot water heater after the engine quit. Drying off as best he could, hanging on with one hand to steady himself in the rolling boat, he started to take some dry clothes out of his bag. He wrapped the towel around his middle, went into the salon, and got out the bottle of scotch. Back in his room, he sat on the edge of the bunk, opened the bottle, took a big swig, coughed, and took another. It burned down his throat in a most pleasant sort of way. In a few moments, it began to warm him a bit and provide a buzz. He heard Mary slide the head door open, out into the passageway.

"Mary," he called, "you need some of this."

"What?" she said. Then she opened the door a crack and peered around it.

"Here." Joe held out the bottle. "Drink some of this; it'll warm you up."

She stared at the bottle of Chivas, still shivering.

"My gosh, your lips are purple," he observed.

She glanced at him and then back at the bottle. The door swung open to where he could see she was holding a towel in front of her. She pulled it closer.

"This is an emergency, damn it!" Joe said, waving the bottle at her.

The boat pitched in a wave, causing her to stagger a bit to keep balance, and the towel fell below her breasts. For an instant, she shivered again and fumbled with pulling it up, and Joe could not help but look at her. With a little shrug and a grin, she held the towel with her right hand and took the bottle with her left, steadied herself against the rolling of the boat, put the mouth of the bottle to her purplish-blue lips, and took a swallow. Joe watched as her body contorted in a violent shiver, reacting to the alcohol. Seeing her so cold and vulnerable, he had the sudden urge to hold and protect her. He stood up and pulled her toward him. His towel began to slip off his waist. He took it and put it around her neck and shoulders, lifting it up to her hair, drying. She let him pull her head closer, let her towel go, and he kissed her lips. She shivered again and then leaned into him, sharing his warmth. Their bodies lurched together as the boat rolled. Then Joe staggered backward to a sitting position on the bunk. Mary glanced down. His excitement was obvious. Half embarrassed by his erection, Joe reached up and turned off the light.

"Let's get under the covers," she whispered, still shivering in the dampness.

The two of them climbed up into the bunk, and Joe pulled the sheet and blanket over them. They lay side by side for a good while, their bodies touching, warming. Thunder reverberated through the hull, and the wind howled in gusts as the boat sliced into the sea. Mary held Joe even more tightly.

"Are we going to die in this?" she asked in a hoarse whisper.

Joe wrapped his arms around her. He hadn't realized she was that frightened.

"Not if I can help it," he said, struggling to sound confident. There was no way to tell, but he guessed that the worst was still to come.

His words seemed to help, however, and he felt her relax a little, and her shivering subsided. After a few more minutes of silence, she leaned toward him and kissed him. He met her lips and held her, so attracted, so desiring of her. It was wonderful to feel poor, sweet, lovely Mary beside him. Then in silence, she pushed him on his back, inching over him in the darkness, kissing his chest and straddling his waist. Then the pitching of *Mission* in the waves pronounced their natural rhythms, consummating their love—the climax an exquisite moment of unbelievable reality.

"You are so wonderful," he whispered.

A gigantic boom that impacted his ears and chest shook the hull of the boat, coming with a great blue flash that seemed to light up the passageway for an instant.

"Gosh! What happened?" Mary asked, spinning around and looking aft.

Joe snapped on the light. He wasn't sure, but he smelled something like burnt toast, or ozone or something. After swinging himself out of the bunk, he went into the passageway where he could feel heat from the mast. Then he heard Frances give a little scream. She was coming down the ladder into the salon and had a view of both of their nude bodies. Joe backed up into the bathroom and stuck his head out of the door.

"I think lightning must have hit the mast," Alex shouted down from the cockpit. "Somebody come take the wheel." Frances scrambled up the ladder to take the helm. Alex hurried down below.

Joe ducked back into the forward stateroom, threw on some pants and his foul weather jacket, and started out of his cabin.

"You okay?" he asked Mary, who had gone into the middle stateroom.

"I think so," she replied. Her hands were trembling, however, as she was rummaging around, trying to find some dry clothes.

Alex was in the salon, feeling the cover on the mast that projected through the salon into the hull below. "It's warm," he commented. "You wouldn't believe it. Lightning struck, and the whole mast was lit up in a blue flame kind of thing!"

"Horrors!" Mary said, emerging from the stateroom, zipping up a damp pair of long pants.

"Did it blow out any electrical stuff?" Joe asked.

"I don't know," Alex said. "I need to check." He knelt down, trying to hold on with one hand as he began releasing the recessed ring handles in the floorboards. He glanced up at Joe. "Better go help Frances. Mary, I need you to help me with this." Joe zipped his jacket up and headed topside.

"Here," Frances said, motioning for Joe to take over. As he took the helm from her, lightning lit up her face just enough for him to see that she was sorely shaken. She went below and closed the hatch behind her.

The shock of events, with the accompanying rush of adrenalin, left Joe feeling sick, and the roll of the boat didn't help. He could tell that the rain had let up a little, and the lightning and thunder seemed to be moving away. He tried to blank out everything but managing the sailboat. It was not possible to steer a steady course, he discovered. All he could do was to keep the boat headed more or less north and not let it get parallel to the waves in a trough. Speed was not a consideration at this point; just keeping enough forward movement to have steerageway was the best to hope for. He glanced down at the helm console, ruing the fact that the tachometer, which had read so steadily 1400 rpms before the engine died a day ago, was now reading zero. The indicator light on the console was constantly on and had been since he took the helm. That was not good. He went over to the hatch and opened it a crack.

"Alex," he called, "you better check the bilges." Then he hurried back to the helm.

In a moment, Alex stuck his head up out of the hatch. "Is the light still on?"

"Seems to be staying on all the time," Joe replied.

Alex closed his eyes hard for a moment, then went below again. Soon Joe could see through the glass-topped hatchway that Alex and Mary had finished removing the deck plates beside the mast. Joe continued on, and the rain and wind slackened a bit. The tiny yellow light was still on, however.

In a few minutes, Alex stuck his head up again. "We must have a hole in the hull," he reported. "Water's coming in pretty fast."

Joe was amazed. "A hole? How could that be?"

Alex shook his head. "A bullet hole, maybe, from when those bastards shot at us. Or maybe from the lightning strike."

"I never heard of such a thing!" Joe said. "I thought the mast was grounded."

"I have," Alex said. "All that electrical energy that comes in on the mast has to get out somewhere. It could have made a hole in the fiberglass hull. Water's coming in as fast, or maybe even faster, than the pump can take out."

"Can we patch it somehow?" Joe asked. *Surely,* he thought, *there's some kind of patching material on board.*

"I don't think so. I can't where it is," Alex said. "You're welcome to come look and see if you have any ideas, but I can't see how we can get to it to put any kind of patch on it." He shook his head.

"Have you tried the radio again?"

"Won't work, won't even receive the weather anymore," Alex said. "The lightning must have taken it out."

"Oh, Lord," Mary exclaimed. "Don't you have a portable radio?"

"Yeah, but it wouldn't transmit more than a few miles," Joe explained. "We can receive with it, but we can't call anyone."

Alex glanced at Mary and pointed to the manual bilge pump located under the cockpit bench. "Mary, I need to give you a job."

She slid forward, and Alex showed her how to work on the manual bilge pump that was worked by a lever in the cockpit.

"Pace yourself, now," Joe cautioned. "If you go too fast, you won't last." Mary began to move the lever back and forth.

"But if you go too slow," Alex added, "it won't do any good."

Joe slipped by them and went to peer down in the hole below the salon floor plates. He couldn't see anything much but water, with a rippling above where the water was coming in. As the boat rolled, the rising water sloshed back and forth, splashing a few drops up into the salon. Under the sole plates were the eight batteries that provided what electricity they had to run the bilge pump. They could run the generator, but it, too, depended on connecting through the batteries. If they went, all power would be gone. Joe felt a pit grow in his stomach. He could feel the wind increasing, blowing so hard it was vibrating the stays and the mast.

Oh Lord God... He found himself praying, looking at Mary hunched down, pumping away. As he returned to the helm, he felt so weak and helpless. Who could know anything? All he did know was that they were now in real trouble.

Chapter Twelve

Joe and Mary rode along in the dark violence of a storm-tossed ocean, each performing their tasks while fighting for a perch to keep from getting banged and bruised against the interminably rolling and pitching boat. With the bimini gone, the wind whipped them furiously when it gusted, and salt spray stung their faces. Wiping a wet arm across his eyes, which stung from the salt, he wondered if she was as grateful as he that they had made love in bed. Joe had so much he wanted to say to Mary, and yet he had nothing to say—the event having been complete in itself. Now a different reality was upon them, supplanting the last, making the former seem like a dream.

Alex stuck his head up from below from time to time, shouting above the wind to report on the level of the water and the futility of his efforts to plug the holes, and mercilessly urging Mary to pump harder. Joe felt a sudden urge to knock Alex back down the ladder. Who the hell was he to urge them on? Wasn't his money the reason that the gangsters had attacked them and why they had not gone safely ashore in Florida? But no, Joe realized, they had to do their jobs, working together for mutual survival. But where the hell was Frances? He had not seen her for some time, and supposed that she was in her cabin resting. He hoped she was resting. Knowing her volatile, if not violent, personality, he wondered what effect all these events were having upon her. Looking at Mary's back pumping away, he wondered, whenever Frances did appear, what kind of confrontation she would create over having seen them naked in the same darkened room. What a strange thing for her to be concerned about at this point.

While he fought the wheel in an effort to keep them from getting trapped in a deadly trough between the high waves, all Joe's thoughts were about Mary, the realization that the new life they might have together was being challenged by the storm and the sea. All these ideas washed about in his head, rolling and sloshing around, like *Mission* in the heavy waves.

After what seemed like an eternity, the wind calmed a bit, and nautical twilight brought a glow to the east, the gloom giving way to eerie light, making more visible the giant swells like dancing gray mountains, one after the other, coming at them relentlessly from astern. Taking them on doggedly, one by one, Joe fought each like an adversary, keeping the bow from slewing them into a trough as each wave pushed past like rude commuters in a subway. He now could see Mary more clearly, still pumping away, looking forlornly tired. His feelings for her poured out.

"Mary" he said hoarsely, breaking their silence, "I'm so sorry... You didn't have to be in all this."

Mary did not look up at him, but slowed her pumping. "For what? You mean my being here?" she said, breathless with exertion and fatigue. "I thought we'd already been over that."

"I let you come along," He spoke louder against a gust of biting wind. "I should have warned you."

He realized as he said it that it was nonsense to be talking about it again. What could he have done to keep her from coming on the voyage? The fact that he would be paid the $100,000 made him a mercenary, but she was merely a volunteer. Her being with them was the greatest thing that could have happened to him, and the worst for her. Originally invited just for a one-day pleasure

238

sail, here was Mary, now bent to the bilge pump, toiling to help them survive.

"Let me pump a while," he offered, realizing that she might not be capable of steering in the storm, which would put them all in further jeopardy.

Mary gave it two more strokes and then thankfully released the handle and moved away, stretching and rubbing her right arm. While she came aft to the helm on the starboard side, Joe moved forward on the port, helping her strap on the harness while trying to watch the helm, and giving her a crash course in keeping the boat from capsizing. Oh, how he wished he could protect her from all this. Reminding Mary to try to keep *Mission* running with the waves, Joe discovered that, while each stroke of the pump handle was not difficult, the prospect of having to do this for hours was daunting—not simply pumping, but at the same time having to brace himself against the rolling and pitching of the boat.

"If you change hands about every two minutes, it's easier," Mary said, sounding calm, managing the helm very well.

Joe nodded and tried the technique. How long would they have to maintain this? Would the sea get any worse?

At dawn, the sea appeared as an angry foaming gray. Even though the sails were already reefed to postage stamps, they brought it all down, tying off the main and furling the jib fully. The wind gauge showed forty knots, with gusts to seventy. Joe and Mary exchanged places again, and she resumed the arduous pumping. Joe put on the safety harness and secured it to the pad eye in the deck at the helm. They were running with the waves, which had swelled to at least ten feet in height.

Looking aft, Joe could not see over the next oncoming wave. A swell would lift the stern, shoot the boat slewing forward, and then drop it in the succeeding trough. Then the next wave repeated the cycle. All Joe could do was steer to keep from getting broadside. But with no power, it wasn't easy. Along with the tiny triangle of mainsail exposed, the mast and booms offered added sail area, which afforded just enough steerageway to keep the boat under control. He considered heaving to, a process of setting a back-winded sail against the rudder to hold position. But it was impossible to manage the sails in this high wind after the mast had been damaged.

Rain pelted them, hard enough to sting Joe's back through the material of the foul-weather jacket. He looked down at Mary, who was working away at the pump. Joe kept feeling so sad for her, remembering how Mary was not aboard by choice, but only a victim of circumstances. They already had experienced fifteen-foot swells. Suppose the storm produced gigantic waves?

Oh Lord God, he prayed once more, *please help us.*

Here he was, praying, despite his doubts that God would care. What kind of god was he to put them through all this? Look at poor Mary, he thought. She didn't deserve any of this. At that moment, Alex thrust the hatch open from below and peered out.

"How is it down below?" Joe called to him.

Alex shook his head. "No better," he replied, catching himself as a wave struck the stern, thrusting the boat forward ruthlessly. After the wave passed, Alex gave Mary a mean look. "You got to pump harder," he shouted at her.

"I'm pumping as hard as I can," she shouted back, her voice breaking in a sob, but she kept going.

"Well, you'd better," Alex said, starting back down the ladder.

"Alex!" Joe shouted, his frustration exploding into anger.

240

Mary looked up, startled.

"Alex, come back up here!" Joe yelled.

"What?" Alex said, poking his head up again.

"We've got to activate the EPIRB," Joe demanded. "And call for help on the radio. It's time, now."

Alex surveyed the sea, his eyes showing desperation. "We have to go on," he said. "We have to make it to Charleston."

Joe gripped the wheel and shook it in anger. "We can't make it to Charleston, damn it. The boat might sink before we ever get close. Can't you see that?"

Their eyes met in silence. Joe had spoken of sinking—the unthinkable thought was before them.

"We have to go on," Alex mumbled, breaking his stare and looking blankly out at the sea. "No EPIRB."

"Mary, come take the wheel," Joe commanded. He lunged past her and put his fist up to Alex's face. "Give it up!" he said through gritted teeth. "You can't get to Charleston; you can't deliver the goddamn money. All you can do is call for help. Now, get the fucking EPIRB and activate it."

"Calm down, ole boy," Alex replied. "Don't forget I'm paying a hundred thou if we make it."

At that, Joe blew up. The realization that Mary's safety was in jeopardy all because he had agreed to take money from Alex brought up all his frustration. Startled by Joe's anger, Alex shrank back down the ladder.

"You can't order me—" Joe lunged at him and got him around the neck, leaning down in the hatch. Before Mary had the helm, the boat rolled heavily. Joe lost his balance and fell down the ladder on top of the older man, toppling both of them into the ankle-deep water. Seeing them sprawled on the wet deck, Frances screamed and backed away. Joe's head had hit the ladder, and he was reeling from the fall.

Alex shut his eyes in pain. "My back," he groaned.

Seeing the man hurt, Joe's anger melted, and he helped Alex sit up.

"Get away from my husband," Frances shouted, and kneeled down beside Alex to help him. "Monster!"

"I'm sorry," Joe apologized, but still took the EPIRB out of its holder on the mast. "I didn't mean to hurt him."

As he climbed into the cockpit with the device, Mary gave him a startled look. "What happened?"

"I fell on Alex," Joe said, ashamed of his fit of temper. Noting below that Frances was helping Alex back toward their stateroom, he started to activate the EPIRB, but hesitated, thinking it would be best to try again to convince Alex that they had to. Then he found a safe place to put it and began to work the bilge pump again.

"Why doesn't Alex want you to turn that EPIRB thing on?" Mary asked. "I don't get it."

"He's still trying to deliver the money to Charleston," Joe said.

"Doesn't he know we have to get help?" she said. "Aren't our lives worth more than his money?"

"He's obsessed with it, I think. He's lost his perspective or whatever."

"Please come steer," Mary said, still fighting to hold a safe heading.

Joe worked his way aft and took over. "The coast guard knows we're out here somewhere north of where the cigarette boat went down," he said, giving her a comforting hug. She returned his embrace and then worked her way up to the pump handle. Joe looked out to the west, seeing even more squalls on the horizon. The worst of it was raking up the Florida-Georgia shoreline. Mary was regarding the western horizon as well.

"Even if the coast guard knew where we are," she said, "how could anybody come through all that storm to get to us?"

Joe tried to sound positive. "They have lots of ways," he said, realizing that he couldn't imagine even the first. Besides, they could be very busy helping people along the Florida coast."

After thirty minutes, he worried that they hadn't seen or heard either Alex or Frances, and he wondered if he should go see about them. Mary suggested they change jobs again, and they were about to do so when he saw that Frances was coming up the companionway with something in her hand. As she came closer, he could see a fury in her eyes. Then he realized, in a panic, that she had Alex's pistol.

"You hurt Alex," she cried. "You must be the devil." Holding on with just one hand, she swayed as the boat rolled, causing the gun to wave wildly in the other. She caught her balance and came on up.

"I was just trying to make him activate the EPIRB," Joe tried to explain. "I didn't mean to fall on him." He had the impulse to bolt away, to duck down, but there was nothing to do but stand there at the helm, continuing to hold on and steer. Mary jumped back away from the pump and shrank back against the bench.

"Oh yes you did! I'm going to send you to hell, you Jonah," she yelled. Regaining her balance, she aimed the gun, but got knocked off-balance again by the seas.

"I'm sorry, Frances, but you're mistaken," Joe pleaded. He didn't move, but just stood there, realizing that there was nothing he could do.

Mary stood up in front of her, blocking her view of Joe at the helm.

"Get out of the way, Mary, you poor, dear, dear girl! We have to destroy the Jonah. This is our only hope." She tried to push past her, but Mary stood her ground.

"Please don't do this," she said.

"He's a devil, Mary!" she cried. "A Jonah! Don't you see? We wouldn't be in this fix if he weren't with us!" She tried to point the pistol around her.

"He's a good man," Mary said. "He was just trying to help us."

Frances glared at Joe, then looked back at Mary, appearing both angry and dazed with confusion.

"Do you know that Alex has a lot of money on this boat?" Mary went on. "He's trying to deliver it to somebody in Charleston, and that's why he's wanted to make us keep going."

Frances frowned. "What money?"

244

Mary pointed toward the bow. "See, you don't know, but Joe knows, and he told me. Alex has millions of dollars to buy stock with—about the insider trading or something. And Joe's been doing everything he can to protect us, while Alex kept pushing us to go north and not go to Florida."

The boat rolled in a wave and unsteadied Frances. She reached out her right hand and caught herself, appearing to have forgotten the pistol momentarily. Mary put her hand on top of Frances's and held the gun against the bulkhead.

"Joe's been a good, loyal friend, Frances," she said. "Aren't you making Joe the scape goat for everything?"

Frances paused and glanced at Mary.

"You know you really wouldn't want to hurt him."

Frances let out a sob and sank into Mary's arms, allowing her to gain a grip on the pistol.

"God loves you, Frances," Mary said in a quiet voice that sounded stronger than any tone that Joe had ever heard from her.

"But we're being killed by this storm," Frances cried. "Oh Mary."

"God loves you so much. We'll be safe," Mary said. "God loves you, and we love you." Her hand moved ever so gently down her arm and took hold of the pistol. Frances hesitantly released her grip.

Without turning or moving, Mary swung her arm out and flung the pistol over the side, into the angry sea. Frances collapsed onto the bench in tears. Also in tears, Mary sat down beside her and held her like a baby. Joe collapsed back onto the helmsman's seat behind him and let out a deep breath.

Alex appeared at the ladder, struggling to come up, looking to be in some pain. Noting the EPIRB was now in the cockpit, he gave Joe a reproachful look, and then realized it wasn't yet activated.

"What is it, Frances?" he asked, seeing that she was crying.

"She needs you," Mary said, still holding Frances, but motioning for him to please come take her place.

Alex came over, and Mary moved away, Frances's hand extending toward her as she went. He sat beside Frances, and she grabbed him and sobbed against his shoulder. Alex looked at Joe for explanation. Joe looked at Mary, seeing her ever more strong and capable.

"We're just…all tense," Mary said to Alex, her voice shaking, even so. "All the strain of what's happening got to her, I think, that's all." Frances glanced up at Joe with teary eyes, still confused and dazed.

"I didn't mean to hurt Alex," he apologized. "I slipped on the ladder and fell, that's all."

"We're all just human," Mary said. Joe looked at her when she said that. Mary returned the gaze. "We're all just human," she repeated to Joe.

"Oh, Alex," Frances bawled, "I can't take it anymore. Here we are in this terrible storm, and Mary says it's all because of some money you've got, and you've been chasing that Bea around, and Joe's told Mary all this and not me, and he's some kind of bad luck person, and I'm so sick and tired. I just want to shoot Joe, and I want to shoot you. I've wanted to shoot you, Alex. I've wanted to shoot you for a long time. And now Mary has thrown the gun away, and so we're all going to die, and I don't know anything. And everybody's so bad, and God's punishing us, and I just want

246

to go home!" Her words broke into sobs. Alex held her even tighter.

"I know, I know," he said, holding on to her and caressing.

"You've been so mean to me, Alex," she wailed. "You've been so mean!" Her body convulsed.

"I've always loved you, Fran," Alex confessed. "I don't know why some things...just happen. But I love you."

"We all love you, Frances," Mary said.

Joe tried to find something to say. "I was just trying to do what I thought was best," he said, as kindly as he could. *What strange things happen when humans are put in stress,* he realized. With the sea boiling all around them, it was like a million laughing demons encircling them in the dim light of the green-gray dawn, an audience to their suffering.

"We have to get along," Mary said, struggling to keep her voice steady. "We have to keep on working together—all of us."

Frances looked at her and nodded, sobbing silently.

Shutting it all out of his mind, Joe steered on, knowing that, as *Mission* ran down each wave, the boat was laboring even more. In a few minutes, Frances had regained her senses and enough composure to stop crying. Alex took her gently by the arm and helped her down the ladder.

"It's such a mess down here," she said. "Oh, Alex, what's happening? Are we sinking?"

In a short while, Joe could hear Frances calling "Mayday" again, over and over on the handheld radio. He thought about trying to give her some latitude/longitude coordinates of their position. Of course, there was no sound of any replies. Their only hope seemed to be the EPIRB.

Alex struggled back up to the cockpit and flopped down on the starboard bench, staring out at the storms to the west.

"Alex," Joe said, "I'm really sorry about… what happened. I hope your back is okay."

The older man continued to stare out at the sea and didn't reply. They went on in silence a while, listening to Frances's pleas in the handheld, coming up muffled from below.

"How can you stand to hear your own wife trying to call for help, Alex," Joe said, pointing at the EPIRB, "and not even activate the one hope of rescue that we've got?"

They stared at one another for a few moments.

"Shit, I don't know," Alex said. "Go on. Fire off the goddamn thing."

Joe picked it up and pulled the arming lever. The indicator light on the EPIRB flickered once and quit. Joe tried again, then inspected the device and saw a blackened area near its antenna. He put it to his nose and whiffed.

"It smells like burned metal," he said, tossing the thing to Alex and then attending to the wheel. "Damn! Do you suppose its battery got cooked when the lightning struck?"

Alex shrugged. "It was attached to the mast."

"You mean it won't work?" Mary asked.

Joe shook his head and laid it down.

"Well, that's that," Alex said.

"Is that all it means to you?" Mary shouted at him. "Our only hope?"

"We'll get out of this, Mary," Alex said. "You'll see."

Joe stared at him. It was just incredible. "How can you be so sure?" he said, shaking his head.

Mary laughed at Alex. "You've had it your way for so long in your life, you're...why, you're like a spoiled child. Do you know that?"

Alex adjusted his position, easing the pain in his back. "Money'll do that to you," he said. "Yeah, I get my way." He looked at Joe. "And since I'm paying you so much money for this trip, you're going to help me get my way, aren't you?"

Joe didn't answer. He didn't know what he'd do when the time came.

"Yes, we'll make it okay," Alex said. "And I'll find a way to slip my cash past the coast guard and the customs and whoever else is in my way."

"For God's sake, Alex," Joe said. "Forget the damn money!"

The older man laughed. "Easy for you to say. You never had any."

"I'm so glad," Mary said. "At least Joe hasn't lost his good sense about it."

"Look, Alex. Aren't we sinking?" Joe asked. "How could anything else matter?"

Alex stared at the forward locker where his boxes of money still lay. "Time we figured out how to survive without help," he said. Then he let out a deep sigh and put down the defunct EPIRB.

"I wonder if the pirate gang had one of those things," Mary asked. "It may have activated when they capsized."

"People like that don't carry EPIRBs," Alex scoffed. "They don't think that far ahead."

"It wouldn't have mattered anyway," Joe said. "In that storm at night, chances of that helo finding anyone off that boat would have been one in a thousand."

Alex shrugged and struggled to stand up. "I'd better go see about Frances." As he started below, he peered down and cursed. "Aw, shit!" he said. "Flooding's worse." He looked back at Mary. "Better pump for all you're worth!"

"I am, damn it!"

"Hell! I know it," Alex said, more gently, giving her a quick pat on the arm. "Just do what you can. I'll come back and take over in just a few minutes."

Suppressing her emotions, Mary doubled her efforts. It was painful to Joe just to watch.

"We could change jobs again," he called to her, "but this steering's no picnic either."

Mary looked up, her golden hair falling in wet clumps across her forehead and down into her eyes. "Anything to do something else for a while," she pleaded.

Joe nodded. Mary got up and stumbled over next to him, and he took off the safety harness and helped her into it. In the

250

disruption, the steering was forgotten for the moment. Why and how the sea chose that moment to send a huge rogue wave at them, Joe never knew. But *Mission* was slewed abeam the waves in a trough just as the giant wave arrived, cresting and breaking over. In an instant, they were rolled sharply to port so that the port gunwale was underwater. The crest of the wave washed over the deck, bringing a torrent of seawater raking across and into the cockpit. Mary and Joe slammed into one another and went down in a wall of water. The boat hung on its side for an eternity before righting again. Mary, saved by the harness, scrambled up and got to the wheel, attempting to regain steering. When Joe managed to pull himself up, he looked aft to see that much was gone from the stern—the dinghy's outboard motor that had been clamped to the rail, the life rings, and several other objects. When he turned around, he saw Alex, sopping wet, struggling up the ladder again.

"What the hell happened?" he yelled, looking at Mary as if she had committed a crime.

"We got hit by a really big one—a gigantic wave," Joe called back. "It's my fault. I lost control for just a second."

Alex waved off the explanation with despair. "Well, we've now got water on the batteries," he said. "I better try to start the generator."

After a few feeble cranks, the generator started, but quit after about five minutes. Alex cursed, realizing that water now was in the diesel fuel tanks.

"That'll about do it, I guess," he said with deep resignation.

He helped Frances climb up into the cockpit. She was wet and crying. Joe, still somewhat in shock, pointed to the torn-open life raft box. Alex saw it and his face melted in fearful recognition.

"I don't believe it," he said.

They could only sink down on the seats and fear what was next. Mary was faithfully at the helm, steering as best she could. Alex hugged Frances up to himself and patted her head to calm her down. Joe found himself staring out at the pulsing sea. Once he thought he saw the dorsal fin of a big shark, just like the first one they had seen. He started to yell out to them to look, but stifled the impulse, withholding from them one more cause for gnawing dread. He blinked and rubbed his eyes and looked again, but he couldn't spot it anymore.

Oh God! Joe thought. *What now?*

Chapter Thirteen

In a couple more hours, the rain quit and the wind began to subside. The waves dropped to less than five feet and became a confused chop. After being pushed ahead all night by following seas, *Mission* drifted to a stop.

"The main part of the storm still seems to be along the coast," Joe said, pointing at the distant clouds to the west. "It may be too rough for them to get any search-and-rescue planes in the air yet." He did believe the storm was passing on to the north, but they still would have choppy seas for some time yet. "If we could just find where the leak is," he ventured. "It seems like we could do something to stop it."

Alex looked at him with a grimace of frustration, having searched for it for hours.

"I could swim down and look at the bottom of the boat," Mary said. "I guess I could."

Joe took in a gasp of breath.

"I mean, I'm a good swimmer," she went on, warming to the idea. "If I could see it, maybe we could plug it up or something."

"It would be too hard," Alex said. "The waves would throw you around and, well..." He didn't finish the thought.

"And there are sharks out there," Frances said. She then shivered at the thought. Nobody needed to say that when the boat sank, the sharks would be there then.

Joe thought of the shark he had seen earlier, coming up from the dark depths, teeth bared. Of all the things he feared the most, this was the worst. It was more than just danger; it was his phobia. And perhaps it was Mary's as well. He closed his eyes. *Such a coward, I am.*

Gritting his teeth, he spoke. "I can go," he said, mustering his will. "I'd just as soon do that as sit here." He pulled away from Mary and stood up, taking the initiative away from her.

Alex shrugged. "We've got some wedges and plugs and stuff," he said. "I guess you could always try."

"Joe, you're exhausted," Mary said, standing up. "Let me go. I'll use my energy trying to find the hole, and you can save yours for doing the job of plugging it up."

Joe studied her expression and saw she meant it. He nodded, thinking what good sense that made.

She looked aft. "Can we put down that little ladder that we used at Great Sale Cay?"

Joe followed her to the stern and looked at the ladder. It was intact in its stowed place in the railing. He looked at Mary. "Are you sure you want to do this?"

"We have to, don't we?" she replied.

Joe took a deep breath, let it out, and lowered the ladder. "Let me get a line to put around you," he said, but Alex already was opening the lazaretto and getting one out.

"You have to take off your life jacket," Joe said.

Mary nodded, slipping it and her shoes off. She hesitated and then took off everything else as well, except her underwear. Helping to tie the line around her waist, Joe gave her a hug for good luck and paid out the line as she went down the ladder. At the bottom, she hesitated a second before letting herself down into the frothing water.

"Go down the starboard side first," he called, realizing it would put her in the lee of the hull. She obeyed and made her first dive. Joe let out the line, peering over the side to try to see her. The thirty seconds she was under seemed like an hour. Finally, she came up, letting out a big breath.

"Can you see okay?" Alex called to her. He and Frances both were at the lifelines, watching her.

"Good enough, I guess," she called back in a breathy voice. Then she went down again, this time for longer. Joe let the line out more as she swam forward along the hull. It took five dives to get to the bow. Each time she came up, it took a little longer to get her breath and go again.

"Don't let the waves bang you into the hull."

She rested a full two minutes before diving down again. At about amidships, on her eighth dive, she popped up to the surface.

"I've found it," she gasped, just as a wave banged her against the hull. She pushed off with her hands and took in deep breaths. Then she went down again and stayed for close to a minute. Joe was about to decide to pull her up with the rope when she came up again, close to the stern. Without a word, she made her way to the ladder and just hung on to it for a few moments. Then she struggled on up. Joe helped her climb on deck and back to the cockpit, where she collapsed on the bench, her lips blue and trembling. Frances had brought up a blanket and wrapped it around her.

"Oh, Mary, it must have been awful," she cried. "You brave, dear girl."

"It was scary at first," Mary admitted. "But I got used to it after a while."

Joe wondered if, when it was his turn, he would get over his own fears.

"There are four holes," she said. "They must be bullet holes from when those guys shot at us. They're not so big"— she indicated with her fingers— "but I guess it doesn't take much to let in water." Alex showed her the plugging materials he already had assembled. She looked through them and selected some wine corks. "These look about right."

Alex grinned. "I knew I should save all these corks," he laughed. "They came out of some pretty good vintage wines, too."

Joe picked up one and inspected it. "You really think this will work?"

Alex shrugged. "I haven't got any other ideas. Do you?"

So with that, Joe stripped, stuffed the corks in his underwear to hold them, and then looked up self-consciously. Without comment, they all moved to the stern, where he was tied into the rope and sent down the ladder. Knowing that he couldn't allow himself to pause or he might balk, Joe jumped off at the last step and shivered as he hit the water. Mary hadn't told him how cold it was. He guessed she didn't want to make him any more nervous about it than he already was. Swimming along the port side, pushing off as each wave came, he got to the spot Mary had indicated.

256

"Lord, help me," he prayed and dove under. Trying to concentrate on the hull, he avoided having to see the vast expanse of deep, dark water below him. By the time he located the first hole, he was out of breath, realizing that fear and nervousness were taking his air. He tried to stuff one of the corks in, but it wouldn't fit. He surfaced and breathed.

"How about it?" Alex called from above.

Joe shook his head. "I've got to have a knife to shape the ends," he said. "And maybe a hammer, or something." He made his way back to the stern and went up the ladder.

On deck, Alex brought the tools and sharpened the end of the corks. "Damn things nearly crumble when you cut," he said.

Frances brought a large ladies' pocketbook with a shoulder strap on it and suggested he put the tools and corks in it instead of in his now-soggy underwear. He put everything inside it and zipped it up. With a sigh, he went back down and slipped into the water.

The first cork, with its sharpened end, he got in the hole and pushed it with his hand to tighten it. Trying to hit it with the hammer was not a good idea, he found, because the hammer didn't hit very well underwater. But it worked as a pusher at least. His breath was more than gone when he made it to the surface. The next hole was more irregular and left a small leak beside the cork, but it seemed to hold. Just as he came back to the surface, a wave banged his head against the hull and made him see stars. He dropped the bag, but caught its strap before it slithered down below him. His strength was ebbing, he could tell, and the cold was beginning to penetrate. As he treaded water at the surface, trying to catch his breath, he wondered if he'd have the stamina to finish.

It took longer to find the third hole. It was farther up the hull than he had expected. Fumbling with the cork, he let it go, and it popped up to the surface. Frantically, he went after it and caught it before it could drift away out of sight. That mistake cost him some vital energy and left him breathing hard. Going back down, he got the damned thing in the hole and shoved it home. As he fought back to the surface and tried to breathe, a wave hit him in the face. He sputtered, getting some water in his lungs, and coughed violently.

"Joe, are you okay?" Mary yelled from the deck.

He coughed again and waved his hand without looking up. There was one more to go, if he could just get his breath again. Another several minutes passed until he was able to make the last dive. His lungs were not fully clear of the seawater when he went down, so he had less air. By the time he found the hole and got the plug in it, he was beginning to sense a dark dizziness. He shoved one last time and kicked upward, thinking his lungs would burst. When he broke the surface, a wave washed hard against him, and his head struck the hull. All went black, and he lost his understanding of where he was. The sea was chilling him now, closing about him in a comfortable sort of way. He saw only water, and sound became just a dull, fizzy buzz. He was so tired. How easy it would be just to slip away and let everything end, all the pain, all the worry.

Out of the blue gloom, a dark shadow loomed. Less conscious of his absence of breath, maybe becoming less conscious altogether, Joe sensed the dark shadow growing larger, more dynamic, filling his vision. Closer it swam, until he could tell it was the great shark, a greenish gleam in its eye. It came right at him, its head a death mask, a skull with gleaming eyes and teeth, coming closer, preparing to claim Joe once and for all as its own.

Lord God, help me! he cried out within himself. He realized he had the hammer in his hand. As the beast swam toward him, he drew back his arm to make some pitiful effort to lash out at the shark. The shark was at him, teeth bared. Joe struck, and the

258

hammer hit its nose. The shadowy hulk of the shark shot right on by, its leathery skin rubbing him as it passed. With a desperate kick, Joe's head came up on the surface for an instant, and he gasped a new breath before going under again. Vaguely he had heard Mary calling. He knew the shark would come back for him. Would it rip away his leg? His genitals? Take his insides? He knew so little about anything. There was so much unknown. How arrogant he'd been in all his cynicism. The rope around his chest jerked, abrading his torso painfully. *Oh, Mary! Why did you come so late in life? I want to be with you! I want to live!*

Again there was a painful tug at his chest and under his arms. The lifeline was being pulled on. He felt himself dragged along the side of the hull. Something grabbed at his head, moving down to his neck, under his chin. Then it pulled up. His eyes rose above the water, and he was conscious of an arm pulling him up. His head came back up into the world of air and light.

"Come on, Joe!" It was Mary, hanging on the ladder, clinging to him. "Please, Joe!" she pleaded. "Come on! Come on!"

He gazed up at her and saw frantic concern in his true love's eyes. With that, all Joe's desire, the craving for life returned, rushing into his exhausted body. Fumbling, grabbing the side of the ladder, he pulled up with all his might. Mary grabbed under his arms and tugged. He managed to get up the steps. Frances flopped over the lifeline beside Mary and took Joe's other arm. Then with all his remaining strength, he pulled up to get a knee on board. With a mutual groan, they rolled him in, and he lay there on deck, exhausted.

"Are you all right?" Mary asked him.

He coughed and nodded. "Just give me a minute," he whispered, out of breath as well.

There had been times on this voyage that he had believed he would die, but this had been his first time to feel the sensation of death. It had been there in the sea that morning. When he had hit his head, gone under, and blacked out, had he felt that dying would be all right? His hopes for life with Mary had seemed so vague then. Dream and reality had merged in the darkness of death—the great all right. Yet, now he was alive, and so the going on would continue, and dreams would take a back seat once more.

When he came to, he realized that Alex was working the pump. Joe pulled himself up to standing, feeling at first a throb in his head, then his vision cleared. He scanned the ocean, looking for any sign of the shark. He'd tear that beast apart if he had the chance. Sparked by the encounter with the shark, Joe's frustration and anger and adrenaline welled up inside. His urge to live, to beat these enemies of nature came back stronger than ever.

Throughout the rest of the morning, they all took turns, in silence, giving all their energies to pumping the water out. By afternoon, with the seas running no more than two feet high, the cabin had merely a few inches of water sloshing across its deck. Between turns at the pump, Frances and Mary managed to make some tuna sandwiches, and even found some tepid beer.

Joe dug out the chart book, which was soaked but readable. Based upon the last fix from the GPS, he calculated that the wind and waves and the Gulf Stream had pushed them farther north.

"We may be drifting toward the Carolina coast," he announced. "Maybe even toward Charleston."

"Wouldn't that be ironic," Mary commented.

Alex bit his lip when he heard that.

Looking up at the mast, Joe studied it for a while. "You know, I think we just might be able to get the mainsail up."

260

"Yes, maybe so," Alex agreed, looking hopeful. "I have a way to manually crank the furler. Why don't we try it?"

"Those wine corks seem to make good plugs while we're just drifting," Joe said. "I don't know what will happen to them if we were to start moving through the water. But what the hell?"

"We can take it slow and easy," Alex said. "I don't see that we've got much to lose."

So Alex rummaged around below and found the strange cranking apparatus for the furler. With Alex at the mast cranking, and Joe manning the halyard, they got the mainsail up half way. *Mission* began slowly to come around and respond to the helm.

Using what little light of the sun he could see through the clouds to guide him, Joe took up a course to the northwest, and the boat sailed at about three knots. All four of them cheered. They crowded into the cockpit and pretended to dance and whoop and holler and release an awful lot of tension and worry. They knew they were not safe by any means, but at least they had done something to save themselves.

261

Chapter Fourteen

Landfall! In the afternoon they could make out the coastline of South Carolina to the west, a thin line reflecting beams of sunlight coming through the clouds. The sea had calmed to three-foot rollers that rocked the wounded sailboat, lumbering ever closer to Charleston.

"Oh, Joe," Mary cried. "That means we're going to make it, doesn't it? We're going to survive after all?"

He gave her a huge hug. "I believe it," he said. "I didn't think so yesterday, but now I believe we will."

They were interrupted by the sounds of Alex and Frances stirring about down below. They both yelled down the news about seeing land. Frances rushed up to look, and Alex followed. They, too, were ecstatic, embracing one another and then Joe and Mary.

"The Good Lord is taking care of us," Frances declared.

Alex stared at the sight of land, and a serious frown swept across his face. He and Joe glanced at one another, and Joe could see that their troubles were not over yet.

"I'll see if I can make a pot of coffee, if the propane's all right," Alex said, going below. "Frances," he called, "try your portable radio, the AM/FM. We ought to be close enough to Charleston to get some news." She followed him below. Then in a few minutes, they heard static and then a rap song.

"Ugh, I can't stand that noise," Frances yelled above the radio. "Whoever called that music?" She tuned the dial again and got a piano concerto, which she left on, turned up the volume, and sat back to listen. "Civilization," she said. "Thank goodness."

"News, Frances. *News*," her husband shouted.

Frowning at him, she got up and tuned again, this time getting headlines on the hour. The announcer was reporting on the bankrupt Greek economy and proposed bailout efforts by the European Union. Then he shifted to the subject of the storm, saying that the eye of the hurricane had moved on out to sea about thirty miles south of Cape Hatteras, North Carolina. Damage from high winds and storm surge had been reported all along the Georgia and South Carolina coastline.

The next item stunned the four of them.

"The sailboat in distress we reported on yesterday that was spotted by a coast guard search-and-rescue helicopter off the Georgia shore is believed to belong to Alexander L. Smith, the chairman of Smith-Southern Company of Atlanta, recently subpoenaed in a price-fixing lawsuit. Due to the severe weather, the coast guard had to discontinue its search for his boat yesterday, but reports its plan to resume operations this morning."

"What did they say?" Alex stumbled out into the salon clad in his undershorts. The rest of them were too shocked to notice. "Subpoenaed? Is that what he said?"

"They're talking about you, Alex," Frances said, "about us and—"

"Hush," he said. "Listen."

"The coast guard received a radio distress call from Smith's boat, *Mission,* yesterday, reporting seeing a capsized black-hulled speedboat during the storm. The search-and-rescue helicopter was dispatched, but ran short of fuel and had to return without finding the overturned craft or any of its occupants. In other news..."

Alex staggered and fell back onto the settee.

"What did he say, Alex?" Frances asked. "Price-fixing? What does that mean?"

Alex put his hand to his face and rubbed his eyes and began explaining it all to Frances.

In the cockpit, Joe realized he was off course and began steering again.

"They were talking about Alex, weren't they?" Mary asked.

"This subpoena business could lead to criminal charges or something." He whistled. "That's trouble."

"For Alex, you mean?"

"Maybe for all of us," Joe said. "If he's dodging a subpoena, there could be a warrant out for his arrest." He thought a moment. "And then there's the money."

"Now, he'll need it to pay lawyers," Mary said, watching Alex down below explaining things to Frances.

"There's still some question about how illegal it is for him to be bringing that much cash into the country," Joe said. "And at this point, he sure doesn't need to have another felony on his hands."

"But he can report that he's bringing in the money, can't he?" Mary guessed. "That ought to make it legal."

"I imagine so," Joe agreed. "It'll be interesting to see how much of it the IRS will take."

"Don't they... what? Freeze assets or something?"

"Oh gosh, maybe so. If that happens, how do I get paid?"

They watched Alex embrace Frances and say how sorry he was. Then as she sat there still in tears, he took her hand and led her aft to their stateroom.

Visibility was increasing. With the binoculars, Joe scanned the shoreline, and by comparing what he read on the navigation chart, he began to identify landmarks. Taking bearings to them, he was able to plot a rough position and then adjust their heading toward Charleston. An hour later, he sighted the old and new Cape Romaine lighthouses in the distance.

Alex, alone, appeared back on deck, now fully dressed.

"How is Frances?" Mary asked.

"Sleeping," Alex answered.

Joe showed him the chart with their position now established. Alex nodded and went back below.

"Pretty quiet, isn't he?" Joe commented.

"He's got a lot to worry about, I imagine." Mary moved over closer to Joe and whispered, "What are we going to do? Just go on and let things happen?"

266

Joe shook his head. "I guess so. I don't have a plan. About all we can do is take this boat on in, tie up at the dock, and let customs do what they will."

"I wish Earnest's brother Wade was here," Mary said. "I think I told you he works for the CIA. He'd cook up a plan."

"Well, I'm no secret agent, that's for sure," Joe said.

The salon floor was beginning to dry. Even though the boat could start leaking again at any time, there seemed to be no more flooding, so the corks must have been holding.

Alex returned topside, and Joe wanted to try putting out as much mainsail as possible in the light air in order to get on inside the harbor. But Alex insisted that they maintain their two-knot speed on account of not wanting to risk having the corks pop loose. Joe accepted that idea, as impatient as everyone was to get in. He wondered, however, if Alex was just trying to be sure that they didn't arrive before evening.

Coming into the channel on the last hour of the rising tide, the flood current added a couple of knots to their speed. The sun was setting behind distant cumulus, creating a beautiful red glow at sunset. They passed a fishing trawler headed out to sea, likely his first chance to go shrimping in several days. The men on board stared at *Mission*.

"I'll bet we do make quite a sight," Mary said, "with our bimini all broken down and that radar thing hanging off the mast."

"I wonder if they will notice the bullet holes," Alex said. "I hope not."

"Here comes Homeland Security," Joe said, pointing at a speedboat coming out of the pass toward them.

"I'm going below," Alex said. "God, I hope they won't bother us."

The boat, manned by two officers, pulled up alongside them, its blue light flashing. "Where are you coming from?" one officer called.

"Bahamas," Joe replied.

"Looks like you got the worst of the storms," the man yelled.

"It was pretty rough."

The two officers shook their heads. "Glad you made it," the first man said. "We'll let immigration know you're here," he added. "Since it's Sunday evening, they won't board you until tomorrow. Be sure to put up your quarantine flag, if you got one."

Joe nodded, waving as they sped off. So his gamble that immigration and customs had closed for the day was why Alex had wanted to wait until evening.

Alex reappeared at the companionway. "They didn't ask how many people were aboard, did they?"

"No," Joe said, "why?"

"There's a place we can anchor over close to Fort Sumter," Alex said, not replying to Joe's question. He came up and pointed out the spot on the chart. "Head about two-zero-zero from the next red buoy."

"We could make it on down to City Marina," Joe said. "If we anchored off there, they'd come out and tow us to the dock in the morning."

"Just anchor where I said, if you please," Alex said. "I have my reasons." He ducked back down the ladder and returned with the yellow quarantine flag and instructed Mary to go fly it from one of the halyards.

Joe made the turn as instructed. Alex was still virtually the captain of the boat, indictment or not. As he watched Mary climb up on deck and uncleat a halyard to raise the flag, he wondered what reason Alex would have for remaining on the outer side of the harbor, so far out from the city of Charleston. Joe had been entertaining thoughts about jumping off the boat at the marina, calling a cab, and taking Mary out to dinner at one of those great restaurants downtown, near the Battery. Of course, that was not possible, the law requiring that they remain on board until cleared by customs. It was going to be interesting, when the agents did come on board, whether or not they would conduct a search and find the money in the forward locker. And if so, would they believe that Joe, Mary, and Frances were all ignorant of its existence?

"Let me take the helm," Alex said, coming to the wheel, "while you go ready the anchor for dropping."

"Where's Frances?" Mary asked. "Is she okay?"

"Totally zonked," Alex said. "She was so shaken up and exhausted that I gave her a good dose of sedative. Don't worry, she'll sleep like a baby and be her old self in the morning."

As Joe made his way to the bow and began unhitching the anchor pins, he remembered the last time Alex gave Frances that much medicine. It was during his first night on board back at Man-O-War Cay. Alex had been up to something sneaky then, he recalled, so did that mean Alex was up to no good tonight as well?

Peering out at the darkened hulk of Fort Sumter, Joe could see that they were being carried eastward, indicating that the tide had turned to ebb. *Mission* still was moving at two or three knots, carried by the breeze in the mainsail. Joe lifted the anchor forward so that it would fall in the water as soon as he released the brake. As he did so, he frowned, realizing that the boat had not slowed any as it approached the fort.

"This water's pretty shallow in here," he called back to Alex. "Better ease the sheet on the mainsail and slow down."

Alex didn't reply. Joe looked back at the cockpit, where he could see Mary sitting idly to the side, and Alex was still at the wheel.

"Are you looking at the chart? I think you're getting in very shallow water," Joe shouted again. "Backwind the mainsail, Alex."

Then the boat lurched to a halt, throwing Joe against the lifelines.

"Holy shit, we're aground," he yelled. The keel shoved into the mud, and the boat yawed and listed slightly, hard aground. Joe picked himself up off the lifelines. "Holy shit."

"I told you it was too shallow in here." He dropped the anchor anyway and then made his way back to the cockpit.

"Well, at least we ain't gonna sink anymore," Alex laughed.

"You did that on purpose, didn't you," Joe said, livid. "What the hell?"

"Now calm down, ole boy," Alex said. "I was just making sure you'd spend the night right here and not get any bright ideas, that's all."

"Spend the night? Hell! Even at high tide tomorrow, it'll be a trick getting off, even if we can find a way to call Sea Tow out here."

"We have their card in the chart table, by the way," Alex said. Without further explanation, he climbed up to the mast to lower the main. Still livid, Joe helped furl the sail while Mary eased the halyard.

When they finished, Alex went to the bow locker and pulled out two boxes. Joe and Mary followed him out on the bow to see, dumbfounded. Alex rummaged around and found a small rubber inflatable.

"Help me pump this up," he ordered, handing Joe a foot bellows.

"What's going on?" Mary asked.

"Good night, sweetheart, well it's time to go…" Alex intoned the lyrics of an old song.

"You're planning to slip off, aren't you?" Joe said. "We risked our lives to get you here, you and Frances. And now you're just going to go ashore and disappear, and leave us holding the bag."

"You'll be all right," he said. "Keep pumping."

"Pump the damn thing yourself," Joe said, kicking the raft at him.

"Last thing," Alex said. "I never was aboard on this voyage, you got me? The story is that Frances hired you to bring her and the boat here while I stayed in the Bahamas." He stared at the two of them. "Is that understood? You won't get a penny of that fifty thousand until you've been cleared by customs and everything is clear."

"Fifty thousand? It was a hundred thousand," Joe said.

"Pushing me down the ladder and hurting my back cost you fifty," Alex said.

Joe wanted no part of it. "Tell customs yourself."

"I won't say that you weren't with us," Mary said. "It's a lie, and I just will not do it."

"Neither will I," Joe said

"I thought you were my friends," Alex said. "What's happened to all our camaraderie, pulling together and all? Don't you want to help me?"

"Some things matter more than money, Alex Smith," Mary said. "You'll pay. Eventually you'll pay."

"Fools," Alex growled. He grabbed the bowline of the inflatable and then dropped the boat in the water, tying it off to a cleat on the sailboat. "Keep quiet tonight at least."

He climbed down into the raft. The ebbing current swirled strongly, making the raft pull at its tether, banging against the hull.

"That's a powerful current," Joe said. "There must be flood waters coming down the Ashley from all the rain." He had been thinking that perhaps it was his duty to jump Alex, restrain him in some way. But then the sight of all that current running past made Joe realize that Alex wasn't really going anywhere, or at least not where he thought he was going.

"So what about the current," Alex said. "Pass me oars and then those boxes."

Joe sighed and handed down the boxes containing the two million dollars, painfully aware he likely was forfeiting that hundred thousand which was supposed to be his. But at that moment, he didn't want any of Alex's filthy money.

Alex stowed the boxes in the raft and then sat down to row. "Mary, tell Frances to take a plane home. I'll call her when I can." He paused. "Now, cast me off," he ordered. "And keep quiet. I'll be far gone by morning, so you people can keep all your glorious honesty and integrity, and I'll keep the money."

Joe undid the line from the cleat and tossed it in the boat. The current began to carry it seaward. Alex began rowing, but the current was too strong, carrying him sideways toward the main channel and out into the blackness of the night.

"Mary, go get the handheld radio," Joe said.

"Alex had it in his pocket," she replied.

In her nightgown, Frances came up the ladder, awakened by the banging of the raft against the hull. She began calling for Alex. Seeing him in the inflatable, she reeled, making her way out on deck.

"Alex!" she yelled. "What are you doing? Are you leaving me?" She cried out and put her hands to her face. Then she looked out at him again.

"I'll see you at home," he called to her. "Don't worry." But he was losing control of the boat.

"Row harder." She leaned on the lifelines, peering into the gloom.

"Current's got him," Joe said, watching helplessly as the raft went in circles while Alex tried to row in the rushing water.

"Oh no. Alex, poor Alex," Frances screamed. She stumbled back into the cockpit, threw open the table, pulled out the flare gun, aimed at the sky, and fired. With a great swoosh, the sky lit up as the glowing flare burst high above and began floating downward, casting a brilliant red glow over the water.

It was less than a minute before they heard the sound of roaring engines from the north.

"Look, a blue flashing light," Mary said, pointing.

"Coast guard, or the Homeland Security boat," Joe said.

It came zooming up beside them, slowed a moment, then sped up, heading toward Alex's inflatable boat, now already between the rock jetties on its way to the Atlantic. Soon they had a spotlight shining on the raft and its unhappy occupant.

"Well," Mary commented, "Frances said she'd always wanted to shoot him. So now I guess she's done it."

They watched as Alex was hauled aboard the security boat along with his little raft, his oars, and his money boxes. In short order, he was being delivered to their headquarters ashore for questioning.

"What do we do now?" Mary asked, taking hold of Joe's arm.

"Not much we can do," he said. "At least, we've survived. What else is there?"

Epilogue

At high tide the next morning, the coast guard dispatched a tug to pull *Mission* off the shoal and tow them to the dock. Two immigration officials and a Homeland Security agent awaited them at the pier and boarded immediately.

Joe presented them with everyone's identification and passports and his own license. The agents wanted explanations.

Frances said that she hadn't known a thing about all the money, but she was sure that Alex must have been trying to get them to Fort Sumter so that he could contribute the money to the preservation and maintenance of the Fort Sumter memorial, and that she herself was a member of the National Trust and loved Fort Sumter and would have fired on it herself if she had been there when the Yankees had it, and when Alex got out in the inflatable boat, he was just still trying to take his money to give to the fort, when the bad old current started taking him out to sea, and that was why she shot off the flare gun, and she just hoped that it hadn't caused everyone too much trouble.

The Homeland Security man wanted to know why their passports hadn't been stamped for departure from the Bahamas, and Joe couldn't keep himself from smiling. Mary tried to explain how she never could get back to her tour group and did the best job of providing a reasonable account of their circumstances. Joe tried to explain that his professional duties required that he, first and foremost, saw to the safety of the vessel and its crew under extraordinary conditions, a responsibility that overrode any other considerations.

The three of them were allowed to go ashore with their luggage and walk to a restaurant for breakfast, but warned not to leave the marina. Then the customs agents began to dismantle what was left of the insides of the boat in search of contraband, essentially wrecking whatever was left of the already storm-damaged interior.

Around ten that morning they met with the agents again, who, having found no more money, drugs, or other contraband on the boat, returned their papers to them. They gave what information they could about the fate of both *Sea Splendor* and *Blaster*. While Alex was being detained for further questioning, the three of them were free to go as long as they provided their addresses of residence, since they would be called later to make depositions.

Joe began to face the harsh realities. Without the money Alex had agreed to pay him, without a boat or a job in the current recession, he was destined to loneliness and quiet financial desperation. He believed that he had nothing to make himself the least bit attractive to Mary. She would return to her own home and her own life in Birmingham.

He went back to take one last look at *Mission*, which was to be hauled out and impounded indefinitely. He noted the torn and shredded windscreen, the radar dome hanging limply from the bullet-ridden mast, and the tattered sails. What a contrast to the beautiful sailboat he had seen in Man-O-War Cay that first day aboard.

In one way, he felt as beaten up as the boat looked. It had been the toughest sail he'd ever made. There would be no money and no thanks from Alex and Frances, no medals or accolades of any kind. But, standing there, staring at the boat, he realized, after all, that he was smiling.

A young couple on their way to their own boat came down the pier behind him and stopped to look at *Mission*.

"Wow," the girl said. "Caught in the hurricane?"

Joe nodded at them. "Well, the edge of it, anyway."

"Man, that must have been rough," the guy said. "Were you the captain?"

Joe thought a moment. The captain? No, Alex had been the captain, no doubt about that. "I was the navigator," he replied. The navigator finds the way. The captain takes control. From now on, he swore to himself, he would always be the captain.

He took the ladies to the marina office, where they phoned for airplane reservations—Frances to Atlanta and Mary to Birmingham. Joe guessed he would start by applying for work around the marina.

While waiting for Frances to find her credit card in her purse and read the numbers over the phone, Mary said, "Joe, suppose I buy two to Birmingham?"

Joe glanced at Mary as she spoke again. "I'll buy you a ticket to Birmingham. What do you think?"

It was so wonderful a prospect that he had to play it back in his head to be sure he heard her correctly. Then he took her hand, and gave her a big hug.

"Would you?" he asked.

No one ever mentioned Alex's pistol, or what it had fired at. It now lay on the sand in the bottom of the sea. Frances had simply shot at evil, after all. Only the shark remained, forever marked with a bullet hole in his fin. He was still out there, looking for the one who wounded him, lurking the deep, dark depths of a boundless ocean.

Made in the USA
Charleston, SC
22 October 2012